"The Deadly Trade explores a dark underworld right under our noses. An engrossing page-turner that never lets go."

—T.K. Thorne, award-winning author of *House of Rose*

THE DEADLY TRADE

BARBARA KYLE

THE DEADLY TRADE

BARBARA KYLE

Woodhall Press | Norwalk, CT

Woodhall Press, 81 Old Saugatuck Road, Norwalk, CT 06855
WoodhallPress.com

Cover design: Jessica Dionne
Layout artist: L.J. Mucci

Library of Congress Cataloging-in-Publication Data available
ISBN 978-1-954907-70-6 (paper: alk paper)
ISBN 978-1-954907-71-3 (electronic)

First Edition
Distributed by Independent Publishers Group
(800) 888-4741

Printed in the United States of America

ALSO BY BARBARA KYLE

The Man from Spirit Creek
The Traitor's Daughter
The Queen's Exiles
Blood Between Queens
The Queen's Gamble
The Queen's Captive
The King's Daughter
The Queen's Lady
The Experiment

Non-Fiction:

Page-Turner:
Your Path to Writing a Novel that Publishers Want and Readers Buy

This book is dedicated to
Stephen Best and Liz White,
whose advocacy gives voice
to those who cannot speak.

1

I was trying hard to think of toys to keep my mind off death.

A plush bunny or a classic teddy bear, which would a two-year-old like? I had no clue about toys. Or kids. But planning what to get my nephew Liam for his birthday eased the sorrow that had darkened my night. Darkened all of February, in truth, since my sister's death five weeks ago, and now we were grinding into an icy March.

The plush yellow bunny, I decided.

Thoughts of my sister's sweet little guy didn't help much, though, as I made my way on foot up the slope from Craigmuir's frozen river. Liam, motherless, cared for by my grieving parents since we lost Julia. Then, yesterday's sickening fire at the stable.

Such a killing winter.

Spring, I thought with a yearning heart, could not come soon enough.

I was on my way to Paul Leblanc's house with Julia's border collie, DuPre, who had come to live with me. She shivered on her leash.

Last night the temperature had plummeted during a downpour, freezing the rain, and now, at sunrise, the world was sheened in ice. It sheathed trees and phone poles and wires and made the road treacherous underfoot.

Crazy to come so early. If I'd waited an hour the sun might have thawed the crust enough to let me and DuPre get up the slope without slipping. But I couldn't lie awake any longer. With the smell of stable smoke still in my hair, I'd found sleep impossible, and Paul's anxious call just after midnight had sealed my insomnia. I needed to talk to him face-to-face.

The road curving up to the rich homes of Riverview Ridge was Saturday-morning quiet, the residents nestled under their duvets. No one out but me and DuPre, straining now at her leash.

"Take it easy, sweetie. Almost there." She was as impatient as I was to crest the hill and relax our tense muscles on the flat, but I held her back. Her four feet could slip as easily as my two.

"Natalie, come tomorrow, first thing," Paul had said, his voice low, troubled. "It's about Julia."

I couldn't imagine what he meant. My dazzling big sister, thirty-three, her fame as a cellist just flowering, had taken her own life. Paul had been one of her many fans, so I'm sure he'd been shocked to hear of her suicide, but what could he possibly have to say now? Before I could ask, he'd hung up. I'd come this morning to find out.

My boot skidded. I caught myself before I went down on my ass, but the misstep sent a skip to my heart and a tremor to my splayed legs. Black ice: that gloss on the asphalt that tricks you. Worse if you're driving, the pavement looking so clear you think you're safe. My tires skidding here could've sent me slewing right back down to the river. It was still frozen, but in March, who knew how solid? Which is why I'd parked at the foot of the hill and walked, stiff-legged on the ice, cautious as an old lady.

The road was hemmed on both sides with massive old oaks, naked except for the ice carapace that glittered as the sun rose at my back. My noisy footfalls sent a crow flapping up from a bough. Branches disturbed by its takeoff clattered, *clickety-clack*. Like teeth chattering, I thought. It was that cold. I wondered, not for the first time, why my piss-poor Scottish ancestors had immigrated here to plough the cold stony soil of southern Ontario when they might just as well have gone around to sunny Australia.

The road leveled out. DuPre and I relaxed a bit. We rounded the bend, nearing Paul's house, which rose beyond its barrier of blue spruce trees ranged like sentinels. A municipal truck lumbered out from the adjoining road and rumbled past us, spitting rock salt to thaw the ice. The pea-size granules gave me traction, which was a relief, but I knew they burned DuPre's paws, and I hated to see her in pain. She flinched but carried on, head high with that stoic canine spirit that shames us whiney humans.

"Hold on, sweetie." I tugged the leash to stop her, pulled off my mitten with my teeth, and used my fingernail to pick salt crystals off her forepaw's tender pad. Its leathery softness was warm against my chilled fingertips. The faint sun glinted off the tag on her collar. My mind flashed back to the rough nylon rope, obscene fluorescent yellow, tight around my sister's throat.

DuPre suddenly whimpered as though in distress. A cut on her paw? No, her focus wasn't there but on the evergreens screening Paul's property. She jerked forward, straining again against the leash.

"Yeah, good idea, let's wake him up."

We reached the edge of Paul's property. The brittle mat of grass crunched underfoot like fragile glass. The house was oriented sideways to the road, with a wide back deck overlooking woods that led down to the river. I was heading for the front door, but DuPre's focus was on the rear. Barking in sudden alarm, she jerked against the leash, causing my boots to slip on the grass. In the slack moment of righting myself, I loosened my grip on the leash. DuPre bounded away, barking, heading for the undergrowth behind the deck. What had she seen? A deer?

"DuPre! Come back!"

I couldn't let her take off into the woods. But I didn't want to shout again, waking Paul's neighbors. I hurried after her, hoping to snatch the trailing leash. She disappeared into the dark space beneath the deck, still barking. I followed her into the shadows cast by the wooden overhang. There was plenty of headroom. Paul was having the deck extended, and I smelled the damp fresh wood overhead. The contractor's crew would be back after the weekend. I side-stepped the rubble of hunks of sawn boards and clumped sawdust.

I reached DuPre. She was barking crazily, looking up. I followed her gaze, our breaths steaming in the cold air. At the far end of the deck, deep in the shadows, a dark shape hung, suspended. My breath snagged.

A man. Upside down. His torso like a forked branch, one leg stretched taut, his foot caught in wire from the deck, the other leg splayed. His arms hung down. Still as death.

Paul.

I bolted toward him. A spear of sunlight through the deck glinted off him.

I froze. He was completely encased in a film of ice.

2

It had all started exactly twenty-four hours earlier when I received a tip-off in an early-morning phone call. The tip would eventually lead me to Paul Leblanc, very much alive then, but the twisty path took me first to the cries of frightened baby monkeys.

I'd just come back from a dawn jog with DuPre. My phone chimed as soon as I walked in the door and let her off the leash.

"Natalie? It's Cheryl. I just landed, and I've seen something."

Cheryl Ainsworth was an Air Canada flight attendant who lived a few blocks from me and commuted to Toronto Pearson International. She told me she'd arrived from Johannesburg, South Africa, and spotted cages. Smelled them first, she said. I'd met Cheryl two years ago when she walked into my office at All Creatures Great and Small to ask about our Forever Homes program: finding homes for abandoned and abused pets. She had two problems: her deceased mother's cat and her own cat allergy. We settled the golden-eyed Persian in his new, forever home with a cheerful stock analyst, and

Cheryl became a grateful supporter of my scruffy but efficient little nonprofit group.

"Thanks, Cheryl," I said after she filled me in. "I'll check it out. Go get some sleep."

I filled DuPre's bowl with kibble and another with water, then called Trevor Wapoosh. DuPre watched me, wary about this early-morning disruption as I grabbed my backpack. I caressed her shaggy ear. "Back soon, sweetie."

I drove in fog to pick up Trevor, and an hour later, as the rising sun was trying to warm Toronto's gray sprawl, we were following a mud-spattered white cube van down the airport arrivals ramp.

"There! Don't lose him." Trevor pointed, keen as a hunting dog, at the red taillights turning right, getting fainter in the fog.

I was trying to maintain some space, not stick right on their tail. If these guys suspected they were being followed, they could speed away.

Trevor, though, was zealous as only a newbie can be. He was my greenest volunteer, just three weeks in the office. He was twenty-seven, four years younger than me, and I was pretty sure the only hot pursuits he had engaged in as a graduate epidemiology student involved hunting microbes under a microscope. But what he lacked in experience he made up for in enthusiasm. On the day he'd volunteered, offering several hours a week to help out my nonprofit, I'd given my usual spiel to quell any romantic fantasies about animal rescue adventure, telling him he'd just be doing grunt work in the office and he'd said, "No worries. I'll stuff a thousand envelopes if it keeps one bear cub or fox out of a leghold trap." I'd liked him immediately.

The paradox did cross my mind that his Ojibway people had been hunting and trapping for centuries, but I have found that people take up the work we do for very personal reasons. Today, I was glad of his commitment. I didn't know exactly what the cages in that white van held—Cheryl hadn't been close enough to see—but her description gave me a good idea. Still, because I wasn't sure, all I'd told Trevor was that we were tracking some mistreated animals.

We followed the van south on Highway 427. The city traffic was light at this hour, but the fog kept me tense at the wheel, even more so as it thickened the closer we got to Lake Ontario. The van peeled off the highway at the Brown's Line exit and entered a drab industrial warren. It pulled into the narrow parking area in front of a two-story building of cinderblock and brick with the modest sign: "Superior Sails." I slowed, watching the van turn the rear corner of the building. I parked on the quiet street, and Trevor and I got out. He was one stride ahead of me, all eagerness as we headed for the back of the building where the van had disappeared.

As we reached the corner of the building, I grabbed Trevor's elbow to stop him. I peeked around the edge. The van had backed up to a wide loading door. The vehicle's rear door had been thrown open sideways and almost touched the wall, obscuring the activity behind it. I couldn't see what was going on, but I heard thin, high-pitched screeches, like babies screaming. It turned my stomach.

"Bastards," Trevor growled.

I turned to him and pointed to an outside staircase we'd passed that led to the second floor. "Let's check that out," I said quietly.

He rushed for the staircase. His eagerness was now making me a little nervous. It might have been smarter to bring one of my more experienced people instead, but many of them weren't known for classy wardrobe choices, and if we encountered any citizens anxious about wild-eyed radicals, I thought Trevor's ironed shirt and buzz-cut good looks might allay their fears. I grabbed his arm again to slow him as we walked, and told him firmly, "After me."

"Right boss," he said with quiet glee. He followed me up the metal steps. At the top was a steel fire door. I tried the handle. Unlocked. Trevor grinned.

"Remember," I told him, "we're just observing. If we can, be ready to video."

We went in silently. The room seemed to be a manager's office: desk, computer, bookshelf, bulletin boards with schedule printouts. On the far side, a broad window half the length of the office overlooked the shop floor. We both went to the window. The view below was of a space with the feel of a warehouse, windowless and lit by fluorescent panels. Huge rolls of fabric, each one as long as a car, lined one wall. Spread out along the entire length of the floor was a vast triangle of white synthetic sailcloth.

So, I realized, Superior Sails was a sail loft. I used to race a Laser dinghy on Lake Ontario and once accompanied a yachting friend to a loft like this to check on a repair to his mainsail. Looking down now at the expanse of sailcloth, I could make out the dimple in the fabric that loosely covered the small pit beneath that held the sewing machine and operator's stool. The sunken platform could be raised so the sail remained flat as its edge passed under the machine's needle.

Three men hustled across the shop floor, carrying cages in from the van. I counted thirteen cages already stacked in the far corner, with more coming.

"Colobus monkeys?" Trevor whispered as we peered through the glass.

I nodded. "And Barbary macaques, over there. And at least five red-eared guenons." Babies. Each no bigger than my little nephew when he was born. None looked more than a few weeks old. In the wild, their mothers would have been shot to make snatching the babies easy. So heartbreaking.

I forced my thoughts to the smugglers. This place was near the lakefront. Did they plan to load the babies onto a boat and power across to the States?

The three men were swarthy, and all were young, younger than Trevor, and skinny, underfed. Faded shirts, scruffy jeans, badly cut hair. Likely hard-up immigrants. They certainly wouldn't be at the top of the smuggling chain, more like the bottom link, hungry guys glad of any gig work they could find. Even this shitty job.

They stacked more cages with a hurried, heedless clatter that left the little orphans screaming and leaping in panic. A colobus monkey gripped the cage bars, and the long white hair surrounding its little brown face trembled. The terror in its huge brown eyes pierced my heart.

"Video," I whispered to Trevor. He pulled his phone from his pocket. I pulled mine out too and raised it to start recording.

"Too far away," Trevor muttered, frustrated. "And the glass distorts."

Before I could stop him, he was opening the door that led down to the shop floor. I held my breath, eyes on the men below. Looked like they hadn't heard the door. Making too much noise themselves.

Trevor crept out to the staircase. The steps were open, with just a railing. Trevor crouched on the top step. He shot me a sly grin then lifted his phone to video the animals.

That's when one of the men, wiping sweat from his neck and throat, turned and looked up. Right at us. He went rigid and shouted something at the others, foreign words. He pointed at Trevor. Trevor froze.

Damn it.

I unslung my backpack and yanked out my wallet, re-shouldered the pack and bolted out, passing Trevor. As I ran down the stairs I raised my wallet ID and yelled, "Stop right there! Police!"

I reached the bottom step and halted. The three men gaped at me. I forced myself to walk toward them slowly, pretending the confidence of authority as I lowered the ID. My driver's license.

Insane. *What now?* Spin some line about calling into the station to report them, then collect Trevor and get the hell out? But could they even speak English? We stared at one another. My heart banged in my chest. I had no idea what to do.

They did, though. They were plain scared. I saw it in their eyes. They couldn't afford to be caught. They instantly took off, all three. Hope jumped into my throat as I watched them disappear out through the loading door. I heard the van's engine roar to life. Tires squealed. Then . . . silence.

"Wow!" Trevor ran down the steps, excited, laughing. "That was so cool!"

I wanted to smack him. This could have gone so badly. But part of me was excited too, and not just from the flush of victory. Now we could help these poor orphaned babies. Several continued to scream, more panicked than ever. I tucked my wallet and phone into my pants pockets, and Trevor and I both hurried to the cages.

"Look at this little guy," he cooed. He got down on one knee, eye to eye with a macaque. Its distinctive pink face was incredibly endearing, but its tiny fingers were balled into frightened fists.

I gazed at the rows of terrified faces, feeling sick at their distress. The cages stank. I imagined the horrors the little creatures had endured: first ripped from their mothers, then suffering the transatlantic flight from Africa with no food, no water, no light, no warmth in the frigid hold of the plane. I had almonds in my backpack, but these were babies; a nut might choke them.

First things first. I should report the smugglers to Animal Welfare Services. But I knew that after they collected the monkeys, the little creatures would almost certainly be euthanized. Could I load the cages, get them out, and safe? My Civic could only hold three or four cages, but one of my volunteers had an SUV and another had a pickup truck. They could be here in under an hour. I made the decision. Act first, answer questions later. I was about to pull out my phone.

"Hey!" a voice yelled.

I whipped around. Two men strode out of a corridor. They halted, frowning at me and Trevor. One was tall and blond, muscular, biceps bulging under his T-shirt. The other was stocky, with a shaved head and one metal earring, a crucifix.

"What the fuck?" the stocky one said, looking both puzzled and pissed. A white ridge on his cheekbone stood out, an arc of four linked scars, each the size of a fingernail paring. I knew that kind of scar. I had one on the side of my neck. Monkey bite. I'd gotten mine in Ecuador when I was taking pics of a couple of young squirrel monkeys frolicking in a ceiba tree. I'd been stupidly unaware that their mother was on a branch behind me. Her teeth smartened me up fast. I doubted this guy had gotten his bite while taking photos.

"Who the hell are you?" the bodybuilder demanded. Thick accent. Slavic? Russian?

Trevor straightened up, defiant. "We're confiscating these animals."

The guy scanned the room. Looking for our backup? The rest of our team? *Our nonexistent team*, I thought with a sharp twist in my belly.

The other guy, Scarface, seemed to come to the same conclusion. "You're confiscating fuck-all," he said. "Now get the hell out."

"Not without these animals," Trevor said.

"Maybe with your balls in your mouth, Chief."

Trevor flinched. I guessed this wasn't the first time his indigenous features roused a special viciousness in men like these. The blond bodybuilder beckoned the other guy and they both marched, grim-faced, toward us. I was closer, but they ignored me. From pure primal instinct, they both went for the male.

Trevor stood his ground but with panic in his eyes, stiff as a cornered deer. He couldn't defend himself against both.

My mouth went off before I could think. "Hey, asshole!" I yelled at Scarface.

His eyes twitched to me. I backed up in jerky steps. I saw the flash in his eyes that said: *easy prey.* He pivoted and came for me. My heel touched the edge of the sail. I kept backing up, the stiff fabric underfoot. He came faster, crossing the expanse of sailcloth. When he was an arm's length from me, I sidestepped sharply, hoping I'd gauged the spot right—the dimple in the material that covered the sewing pit.

I had. His foot sank into the pit all the way to his knee. He yelped in pain and flung his arms wide to break his fall. I felt a wild surge of satisfaction. *I brought him down.*

But Trevor was in trouble. The bodybuilder rammed one fist into his stomach, the other into his jaw. Trevor swayed, stunned at the pain. He dropped to the floor and curled up, arms shielding his face. The guy viciously kicked his side. Trevor cried out.

I threw off my backpack and dug inside for the cannister of bear spray. I charged the guy, aimed, squeezed the trigger. The yellow mist spewed over his face. He let out a scream as his hand flew to his eyes. He lurched at me, the other hand clawing, bashing the cannister out of my hand. It clattered to the floor and skidded away. Now I had nothing to defend myself. The guy groaned in pain and bent over, both hands at his eyes. He staggered, blinded. But I knew it wouldn't last.

"Bitch!" It was the other guy. He'd struggled out of the pit and was coming at us, limping, murder in his eyes.

I gripped Trevor's arm, yanked him to his feet. "Can you walk?"

He nodded, unsteady and dazed, but ready to flee.

"Then run," I said.

3

"Are you sure?" I asked as I drove. "That kick was brutal. Might've cracked a rib."

"No," Trevor said. "No hospital." He winced, pressing his bloody lip with an old sweatshirt I'd grabbed from the back seat.

"That's a bad cut. And the ER isn't far."

"I said no."

"But you're bleeding—"

"Nat." He looked at me. "Drop it."

I shut up. It was his call. I entered the on-ramp to Highway 401 and concentrated on merging with the traffic.

"I'm fine," he muttered.

But he wasn't fine. And it was my fault. I never should have brought him. Still, he seemed to have the bleeding under control. And his calling me Nat was a good sign that he'd pulled himself together. He'd picked it up from the others in the office and was using it to be like one of them. One of us. It was sweet.

Time to report this. I made a hands-free call to Ontario Animal Welfare Services, jumped through their options menu, *"If you know the extension . . ."* until I finally got an animal cruelty inspector. Voicemail. Frustrating, but no surprise. I reported the information, ended the call, then called the OPP and left the same message.

"So, what happens now?" Trevor asked. "Will they come for those creeps?"

"That's the idea."

"Good. *They* belong behind bars, not the monkeys."

"Don't hold your breath. Animal welfare won't get there before those guys split. And the police don't take animal issues seriously."

"Really? So the bad guys get away with abusing those poor animals?"

"Almost always. Those animals and others."

He slowly shook his head. "What a royal fuck-up back there." It was a hostile murmur to himself: Trevor berating Trevor.

"Look, my friend," I said, "it went sideways, yes, but it wasn't your fault. No one could have done any better."

"Than what? Leaving you in the lurch, getting the shit beat out of me, and abandoning those poor monkeys? Jeez," he groaned, "I was supposed to be there for you. Instead *you* . . ." He didn't finish. The thought seemed too galling.

Must be hard being a guy, I thought. That manliness bar—held so high, forever out of reach.

"Trevor, don't beat yourself up about this. Those guys were pros. I wasn't sure before we got there, but now I think they might be part of an organized criminal operation."

He shot me a wry look. "Importing cute, furry little monkeys?" He said it like it was his turn to set *me* straight, as though vicious gangs didn't do cute.

"Listen to me. International animal smuggling rings are run by hardened traffickers. The monkeys we saw might be just a small part of a global operation I've heard about from colleagues in the States.

The illegal trade in exotic animals is huge. Profits second only to the drug trade. Globally, worth over ten billion a year."

He frowned, disbelieving. "Seriously?"

"Baby monkeys, for example, are hot sellers. And easy to buy online. A newborn Java macaque costs about four thousand dollars. A week-old capuchin goes for seventy-five hundred. Squirrel monkeys are the most popular. A baby can fetch up to nine thousand."

"What? Who pays that kind of money?"

"Plenty do. Some want an adorable little pet. Some want a surrogate child."

"That's sick."

"It is. But there's no federal law against owning one."

He mulled it, dabbing at his cut lip. "So . . . what happens? The little guys become part of the family?"

"If only. No, they need their mothers, need their own kind. Ninety percent of them die within the first couple of years. For them, being cute is a death sentence."

He was quiet for a moment, taking it in. "And the ones who survive?" I heard the note of dread in his voice. Maybe he guessed the answer.

"They mature. Grow big. By the age of eight they start to really assert themselves. That cools their owners' affection. Some have the animals' teeth removed to keep them harmless."

Trevor shuddered.

I slowed to let a monster fourteen-wheeler cut in front of us. It leapfrogged a slowpoke old Chevy then smoothly slid back into its lane. My eyes were on the road, but I felt Trevor looking at me.

"You were something else back there with those guys," he said. "The bear spray. Man, that goon was howling like you'd poked his eyes with sticks."

"I've heard it doesn't sting too long."

"Tell that to the bears." His tone was playful. I gave him a look. He winked. "Indian lore."

I laughed. I'd never used bear spray before in my life. I got it last summer when I hiked Algonquin Park with my brother. James had insisted we take it, but the can had sat in the bottom of my backpack ever since.

"You know," Trevor said, "if this is some big crime deal, maybe you could take it to that politician. The guy who threw the party. What's his name? Verhagen. He's got some government muscle, doesn't he?"

"Some." Hank Verhagen was the rookie Member of Parliament for our district. Because of his progressive stand on animal issues, I'd supported his campaign with local radio ads and door-to-door canvassing by my volunteers, and he'd invited a bunch of us to his victory party. "But this isn't his field."

"Well, he could make it his field. From the way he was looking at you, I'd say all you need to do is ask."

A blush fired my face. Hank, attracted to me? I felt absurdly pleased. I quashed the giddy feeling. Totally unprofessional. A schoolgirl crush that had nowhere to go. He was divorced, sure, but he had a family, for heaven's sake.

"Hey," Trevor said, as if remembering. "Didn't you go in there with a backpack?"

"Into the sail loft? Yeah."

"You left it?"

"Didn't seem smart to ask the Russian hulk to pass it to me."

"Anything important in it?"

"No, just stuff." A sweater. Bottle of water. Almonds. Tampons. "What's important is in your phone. You got some decent video, right?"

"I did, yeah. I know I acted like an idiot, going to the stairs, but I did get video."

"Good work. Send it to me at the office email." I would include it in a written report to Animal Welfare Services. "And copy it to Chandra Singh."

"You got it." He pulled out his phone to send the video.

I felt a cautious tingle of excitement. I was sure what we'd seen wasn't just the hustle of some lowlife crooks, and if I was right—if we'd actually busted into a corner of a widespread smuggling operation—my little animal rights group could make headlines.

I just had to follow the trail.

4

Driving home with Trevor, I left the big-city sprawl behind. Soon, farmland stretched out on either side, where strips of dirty snow lay like soiled battlefield dressings over land stubbled with last year's cut crops. The farms gave way to new subdivisions of town houses, and we arrived back in downtown Craigmuir as the morning sun chased away the last shreds of fog and the city trooped into its workday.

The carillon of St. Timothy's rang the hour. I glanced at the copper-clad steeple rising above the shops. When I was growing up, my father had been rector there, buoying the Anglican faithful with his vibrant tenor voice in good-natured sermons. Since retiring, he still buoyed people as a motivational speaker; he'd given a TED talk that people were forever emailing him about. St. Timothy's cheerful carillon still faintly vibrated a string inside me with the reassurance that "God's in his heaven, all's right with the world," though I had long ago come to doubt the truth of either of those claims.

Thoughts of my sister pulsed like a dull pain. Had Julia's suicide killed even my father's faith? No, impossible; he was too strong. And he was heroically caring for little Liam while the boy's father was away. But my mother? In the last few days, she seemed to have lost interest in living. It actually scared me.

I dropped Trevor off at his apartment near the university, told him to go to bed—I figured he had yet to feel the full pain of his beating; tomorrow he'd ache even more—and then I headed to work.

The office of All Creatures Great and Small was a modest, squat building of whitewashed stone, a former brewery warehouse, tucked into Gordon Lane across from a coffee shop famed for its homemade cheesecake. Being vegan, I couldn't vouch for the cheesecake, but I often began the workday with my thermos filled with their fragrant Lapsang souchong.

Not today. Today I wanted to talk to our lawyer.

"Good morning." Janice Cadogan, my office manager, greeted me briskly from her desk as I came through the door. "Mrs. Stavropoulos called. Again. She insists on talking to you."

"Later," I said as I hung up my coat. The woman had been promising us a sizable bequest in her will, but only if I would guarantee that all her money would go to rehabilitate injured birds. I'd already told her, as politely as possible since we sorely needed the cash, that earmarking funds that way would be unfair to other animals we could help. "*All* Creatures," after all, was in our name.

"Well, I can't put her off forever." Janice, a retired teacher, was capable and efficient, for which I was grateful, but I could live without the scolding note that edged her voice at times, no doubt from years of hectoring rambunctious ten-year-olds.

I booted up my Mac and scrolled through emails for the one from Trevor. I downloaded his video, feeling a rush of pity again for those panicked little monkeys, and fury at the people who trafficked in such misery. The video was jerky and ended too abruptly, but it did the job. I asked Janice to send it to the animal welfare inspector to follow up on my earlier call.

"Is Chandra in yet?" I asked, flagging several emails for later.

"In the back," she answered, eyes on her screen.

I headed for a desk at the rear, a quiet spot I knew Chandra Singh preferred. She was a partner at a small law firm that specialized in environmental law, and today was one of the days she moonlighted pro bono for us.

The office was one long room dominated by a central communal table of scuffed pine planks where a couple of my volunteers were busy. I passed Victor Perry, a retired architect whose thatch of white hair circled his bald pate like a messy halo. He sat writing, head bent over a note card. My policy was that every individual who supported our work, whether with five dollars or five hundred, got a handwritten thank-you. I squeezed his shoulder as I went by. As a gentleman of British background, he didn't like displays of affection, but sometimes I couldn't help myself. "Hey, Victor."

"Nat," he acknowledged, not looking up as his fountain pen continued its tidy penmanship.

I gave a mock little salute to Nicole Rubin as she typed on her laptop, and she returned the gesture. Nicole was a veterinary student at the university. She'd come to us last year, very upset, to report a little-known practice of the vet college: terminal surgeries. After the students did spay-neuter operations on dogs as part of their training, the dogs were killed. Terrible—and completely unnecessary. I'd called the dean and told him we could find homes for the dogs. Actually, I'd said that if he didn't let me, I'd launch a public campaign to expose his barbaric policy. He was politely hostile, but he backed down. And we did find homes for every dog. Nicole had been dropping by ever since to help out at the office.

I felt a familiar swell of gratitude for these volunteers and the dozen others who came in at various times to help out with our programs. They did it for nothing. Or rather, they did it for the animals. Janice and I were the only salaried employees, modest though the salary was. Janice relied more on her teacher's pension. Me, I would have done this work even if I had to *pay* to do it.

Truth is, I felt lucky. After university I'd spent four soul-numbing years as a copywriter at a Toronto advertising agency, the last half spent struggling to make my marriage work. Three years ago, I'd left both bad situations and come back to my hometown to create All Creatures Great and Small. From a shaky start-up funded by my meager savings and the donations of a few friends, we were now on our feet—precariously, some months, but definitely standing. It felt good. Like I was doing the work I was born to do. And how many people get that chance?

But, oh, how I longed to grow All Creatures. To pay these capable people and hire more staff so we could take on really big issues—the operations that abused, maimed, or killed millions of animals in factory farming, in research facilities, in global wildlife trafficking. Those fights required a political activism and commercial messaging that cost big bucks. Sure, I was proud of the smart little network I'd created. We saved a lot of abandoned and abused pets and found them forever homes. We rescued racehorses from kill pens where they awaited slaughter after their "best before date." We raised funds to rescue animal victims of natural disasters. But there was so much more to do, and I had nowhere near the money needed to do it.

Today, though, the sail loft debacle actually gave me hope. If that smuggling outfit really was part of a larger, international operation, and if I could bust it, it would not only save countless animals' lives but would also give All Creatures enormous credibility. That would attract bigger donations. Then there'd be no stopping us.

I found Chandra poring over a spreadsheet on her laptop.

"Ms. Singh," I said.

She looked up. "Ms. Sinclair."

The deadpan exchange was our silly joke, a holdover from the strict formality of our first meeting. She'd come to offer her services, and we'd wound up going to O'Dowd's pub for Friday night vodka shots, where the formality quickly dissolved.

"Did you see Trevor's video?" I had called her on the way, left a message about the monkeys, and asked her to look into it, find out who owned Superior Sails.

"I did, indeed. You've had a busy morning." She leaned back, smoothing the knee of her impeccable navy pantsuit, and added, "Me too." She beckoned me closer. I sat on the edge of the desk as she showed me a yellow legal pad covered with a maze of notes and diagrams.

"Superior Sails is legit," she said, "but the owner has several other businesses too. And players in those businesses are involved in other businesses—corporations, conglomerates, holding companies. Following the trail is like stepping into a labyrinth. Many paths, side alleys, some dead ends. Anyway, one of the major paths"—her finger traced it on the yellow paper—"leads to a company called ERV Financial Services. Their function is listed as wealth management, but it seems to be a shell company. No details about their activities. Head office address is in Cyprus, one of the world's top money-laundering centers. And here's the thing. Listed in an executive role, a name popped up that surprised me: Paul Leblanc."

That got my attention. "Not *our* Paul Leblanc?"

"The same. I wasn't sure at first, because their prospectus uses the European style with names—P. L. Leblanc—but it lists him as CEO of Leblanc Agrisciences right here in Craigmuir." She tapped her keyboard to pull up the prospectus and turned the screen to show me.

It threw me. Paul was one of the city's leading figures. I knew him well. I boarded my horse at his country estate. I liked him. I'd met him a couple years ago when he hosted a charity fundraiser at his house and my sister, Julia, the famous cellist, had performed; Paul was a fan. My mind skidded back to those panicked little monkeys in the sail loft. I couldn't believe Paul was involved, however tangentially, in the vile trafficking of animals, and I said so to Chandra.

"The link is credible, Nat," she warned me. "It should be included in any criminal investigation."

I told her I'd keep that in mind. But I was sure there had to be some mistake. I should go and see Paul. Clear this up.

"Send me the prospectus, okay?" I said.

"Will do."

Paperwork filled the rest of the day. At five, leaving Janice to close up, I headed home. DuPre hadn't been out since morning, so her bladder would be full. I lived nearby on a crescent of grand old homes built by old-money families, though my place was far from grand; I rented the little coach house at the rear of a stone mansion owned by a wealthy widow, Ruth Carson, whose late husband had been chancellor of the university. The rent was modest, and, best of all, Mrs. Carson had become a generous supporter of All Creatures, one of our main benefactors.

"Go for it, sweetie," I told DuPre as I let her out the door into the fenced yard. "Freedom!"

She bolted out then instantly slowed and sniffed the ground to start her inspection. The yard wasn't familiar terrain for her yet. She was still a little bewildered at being away from Julia and Simon's house.

Poor Simon. He couldn't cope with the dog plus two-year-old Liam, so I'd taken DuPre. *Full circle*, I thought, watching her bound after a squirrel. She'd been just a pup when I gave her to my sister to help her through one of her bouts of depression. Julia had named her after her hero, cellist Jacqueline du Pré, whose recording of Bach's *Cello Suite Number One* she had played so often when we were kids, I could still hum it half-asleep. By the time she was twelve, Julia was playing it flawlessly herself, radiating the talent that would eventually take her to concert stages from Montreal and New York to London and Berlin. Remembering brought a sting of tears to my eyes.

My phone rang. I pulled it from my pocket. At the call display, a quiver touched my heart, a free-fall mix of eagerness and unease. *Dad. But why? Was Mom okay?*

"What's up this fine day, Natty?"

I relaxed. Despite everything, his jaunty signature greeting hadn't changed since I was a kid. Good sign.

"Watching DuPre try to catch a squirrel. You gotta love an optimist."

"That dog's lucky. Found the best home she could wish for."

No, Julia's home was, but I didn't say that. Dad and I had an unspoken agreement to refuse being trapped in the tragedy, to stay as upbeat as possible.

"Natty, I'm sorry, but I just can't get to your place this evening. We'll have to reschedule."

I was sorry to hear it. We'd planned to rehearse our duet for the upcoming memorial concert for Julia. We were both amateur string players, he on cello, me on violin. Our duet, a haunting piece by Jocelyn Morlock, would be just a small part of the larger program featuring Julia's professional colleagues, all to raise mental health awareness.

"Oh. Okay. Is it work? A new invitation?" He'd been turning down requests as a speaker since Julia's death, but maybe he'd decided it was time.

"No, not work. It's just . . . your mother. She had a bad day. I can't leave her right now."

My unease swarmed back. He wouldn't say this unless it was bad.

"Do you want me to come over? I can." Their house was in Oakdale, less than an hour away.

"No, no. You've got plenty on your plate. We're okay. I just . . . need to be here."

We picked next Wednesday to rehearse. We both said together, "I sure need it," and both laughed. I meant it, but he was just being kind; he was by far the better player. He had a spark of that musical fire that had glowed in Julia. It had been a bond between them, one I'd longed to share for as long as I could remember.

"Let's make it your place this time," I said. "Gives me a chance to see Mom."

"She'd like that."

"Okay, see you then. Give her my love."

With my evening now free, maybe I could follow up about Paul Leblanc, maybe go see him right now. I called his cell and got voicemail. I called his office.

"You just missed him, Ms. Sinclair," his assistant said. "Mister Leblanc left half an hour ago."

"Okay, thanks. I'll swing by his house." His home on Riverview Ridge wasn't far.

"Well, yes, he might be there later. Right now, though, he's gone to Mont-Joli to check on the progress of the studio."

His country estate. I could be there in twenty minutes.

On the way to my car, thinking again there was no way Paul could be mixed up with criminals, my thoughts looped back to the beating Trevor had taken from those thugs, Scarface and the Russian hulk. Then a sudden realization surfaced.

My backpack. I'd abandoned it when we'd run. I'd told Trevor there was nothing important in it, which was true, but now I remembered there was an ID tag on it. I'd attached it for that holiday flight to Ecuador a couple years ago. It had my name, address, email.

A chill prickled my back. *They can find me.*

5

I drove through quiet countryside of sprawling, white-fenced acreages. This was horse country, domains of the rich. It was a lovely drive in summer, and I admired the expansive views even now at the butt-end of winter, especially this curving stretch not far from Paul's estate. I'd driven it often to visit my horse. I boarded Val at the stable behind the house Paul's great-grandfather had built and named for his Quebec birthplace: Mont-Joli.

He'd gone to check on the studio, Paul's assistant had said. A new addition being built for his wife, I remembered. I knew Denise Leblanc was an artist, though I'd spoken to her no more than a dozen times when I went to see Val, and those exchanges were brief. With me she was aloof. I didn't take it personally, figured it was the language barrier. She was from Quebec City, and although perfectly bilingual, she seemed almost annoyed when using English. Since my French was abysmal, I always felt a bit of a fool in her company. So, not the most comfortable relationship.

Driving, I was listening to Django Reinhardt's soulful gypsy guitar, which matched the twilight mood. This was the hour the French call *entre chien et loup*—between dog and wolf—the time of blue semidarkness. Dark enough that I rounded the next curve with my lights on.

This visit shouldn't take long, I thought. I simply couldn't believe Paul was involved in trafficking wild animals. The connection Chandra had found had to be a mistake, some glitch. He was such a kind man, charging me nothing to board Val. "We already feed my daughter's horse and one of my neighbors boards his," he'd said, "so what's another?" He was considerate with the stable boy too—Matt, a teenage kid, kind of slow, from a nearby farm. You can't fake that sort of kindness. Plus there was his philanthropy. He gave generously to our hospital, the university, the Y, and a bunch more local charities. He even gave All Creatures a regular deposit of three hundred dollars a month. Altogether, a really good guy. So, I thought, I'll make this quick. Clear up the glitch, then get home and take DuPre for a long walk.

The twilight was darkening to night. Neuralgia needled a spot on my scalp, a familiar weather warning: a drop in barometric pressure. Maybe the Weather Network was right; rain was coming. Val didn't like rain, especially slippery grass, but tonight he'd be cozy inside the stable. The poor old guy had been awaiting slaughter at a kill pen in Alberta, about to become meat for Japanese diners, when we'd rescued him and trucked him here. I didn't ride him, just let him be.

I rounded the bend a few minutes from Paul's estate and noticed an odd light above the tree line. An orange glow, lurid against the darkening sky. And there was a sound: faint, high-pitched. I turned off the music, lowered the window to listen.

Sirens.

I raced down the lane of Mont-Joli. The scene ahead was chaos. The circular drive fronting the house was clogged with vehicles—fire truck, police cars, ambulance, pickup trucks. Beyond them, people were running in all directions. Orange flames roiled up from the side of the house. The new studio.

I lurched the car to a stop at the edge of the lane. The moment I jumped out, the noise was overwhelming. People yelling, flames crackling, fire hoses roaring. As I ran toward the house, the night air felt as hot as an August noon.

I scanned the faces, looking for Paul. Firefighters hauled hoses that pummeled the flames with water. A dozen people, men and women—neighbors?—stood back, crowding around the vehicles, gaping at the fire. Paramedics pulled gear from the back of the ambulance, their jackets' fluorescent stripes reflecting the blaze.

I glimpsed Paul, his face smudged and glistening with sweat. He was prowling back and forth in front of the burning studio, looking desperate, powerless to help. Dear God, was his wife inside?

I reached a paramedic beside the ambulance. "Is anyone in the house?" I had to shout above the din.

"No, ma'am. Owner says it's empty."

Thank God. Property can be restored, not lives. And it looked like the firefighters were dousing the worst of the flames. Black smoke billowed up from their cannonade of water, the fire hissing.

Then, above the hiss, above all the yelling, I heard something else. Screams.

I whipped around, looking for the source. Someone raced past me. Matt, the stable hand. He was pointing as he ran, a frantic gesture. My stomach clenched. I knew where he was heading. The screaming.

I tore after him. We rounded the corner of the house together and jerked to a stop. The stable, a stone's throw from the studio, was ablaze.

The horses. *Val.*

"Matt! Are they in there?'

"Yes!"

I whipped around and yelled at the firefighters, "Back here! The stable! *Help!*"

A couple of them turned to me. Distracted looks. One shook his head grimly. Their whole focus was on saving the house.

I twisted back to the stable. It was all wood. Behind the wall of flames, the double doors shimmered in the heat. *Closed.* I gripped Matt's arm. *What can we do?* He looked at me in anguish, tears streaming down his face. Helpless.

Again, that sickening sound. The trapped horses, screaming. And another sound: hooves thudding against wooden stalls.

I couldn't bear it. My body burst forward, desperate to crash through the stable door. Heat hit me like a fist. My arm flew up to shield my face. I staggered forward blindly. The scorched air was so parched I couldn't breathe.

A hand grabbed the back of my coat, yanked me backward. I tottered, whirled around. Paul.

I clutched his arm. "They're in there!"

He stood gaping at the blaze. Helpless.

The horses' screams razored into my brain. I unzipped my coat, about to throw it over my head against the heat and plunge forward.

"Stop!" He grabbed me again, gripping my shoulders. "It's impossible!"

I swayed on the spot. *Helpless.* The roiling flames were consuming the hundred-year-old wood with obscene speed.

"Nat, you can't do any—"

"Shut up! Listen!"

I strained to hear the horses. The screaming had stopped. The thudding had stopped. The silence was even more terrible. There was only the roar of an inferno no living thing could survive.

Something ruptured inside me. Fury shot through me, wild, primal. People talk about losing your mind. I was pure, mindless rage. I flew at Paul, fists raised to destroy him.

"Your fault!" My screech in his face ripped my throat. "Bastard! *Your fault!*"

I had lost my mind.

6

The rest was a haze.

I know many hands yanked me off Paul, pulled me away from him, away from the fire.

I know I was escorted, sobbing, toward the paramedics' van. No injuries, no burns, so I was left alone.

I know a police officer questioned me. Why was I there, right at the time of the fire?

Still in tears, I couldn't find words.

Paul was suddenly there, answering for me. My horse, he said. The officer was sympathetic. Someone called him and he went back to the firefighters.

I started for my car, my legs weak as straw.

"Nat, wait." Paul caught up to me. "You're in no shape to drive."

I pushed him away, but even my arms had gone feeble. I wandered to my car, footsteps unsteady.

"Nat, stop. You're in shock." He took my elbow, opened my car door, guided me in behind the wheel. "Sit. Don't go. Just sit! I'll be back." He took off, back to the fire.

I don't know how long I sat there. It felt like days. Horses endlessly screaming in my head. When Paul plodded back to me, exhausted, the chaos was over. They'd saved his house. No more flames. Just smoke. No more people. The last police car drove past us, leaving.

Paul leaned down at my open window. "Don't go home. Come to the house, in town. Let me make this up to you."

We stood alone in his living room.

"Want a drink?" He held up an empty glass.

I shook my head. Pass. The madness had cleared. Reality had taken its place. Val was dead. All three horses were dead. Killed by negligence. Paul's.

He poured a glass for himself, scotch from a crystal decanter, then turned to me. "You alright?"

"I'm fine." My voice was hoarse, as though clogged with smoke. Grief dulled my brain. But I could still think clearly enough to lash out at him. "Sprinklers, Paul. How many times did I tell you?"

"I know—"

"*How many times?*"

"Nat, please . . ." He sounded shattered. "I'm so, so sorry."

I could hear he was drowning in shame. I bit back my fury. Rule one of civilization: You can't abandon a drowning man.

Pity crept in at the state of him. Soot grimed the furrows of his face. His hair, thick, prematurely white, usually groomed, was a soot-caked tangle. His soot-smudged chinos and sweat-stained shirt gave off the taint of oily smoke, cloying the air, as though vagrants had recently vacated the chic furnishings.

Out of the corner of my eye, I caught a movement. I turned. We were not alone. His wife, Denise, stood at the far end of the room where open French doors led to a gleaming mahogany staircase. She stood still but looked tense. No wonder. I was about to offer her a word of sympathy, but before I could speak she took a rigid step back. I saw that her eyes were red. She'd been crying. She suddenly turned her back on us, went quickly up the stairs, stepped into a corridor, and disappeared.

"She's packing," Paul said.

I turned to him. Where could she be going, leaving him on a night like this? But he didn't seem surprised. I said nothing. Who can fathom the silent currents between a husband and wife?

He took a long swallow of scotch. Let out a troubled sigh. "Nat, your horse—"

"How did it happen?"

"The fire?"

"How did it start?'

"God knows. I went to see how the work was going at the studio. The contractor's crew had finished for the day, gone home, and I wanted to look things over myself, alone. When I drove up, I saw flames." He shook his head, weary, pained. "Maybe faulty wiring. I don't know. I was told the fire marshal is going to send an inspector tomorrow." He heaved a troubled sigh. "Nat, I couldn't believe how fast the wind carried the flames to the stable."

"A stable made completely of wood."

He looked at me steadily. "Your horse, Valiant—"

"Val."

"Yes. Val. What was he worth?"

I stared at him. *Worth?* Fury surged back. Why did people see an animal's life as no more than an entry on a balance sheet?

"Just name your figure," he said. Man of business.

Jesus, had he taken my silence as a bargaining position? Did he really see this as just a *transaction*? When all that was left of Val, of those three creatures' lives, was their scorched bones?

"Forget it," I said. I was done here. I turned to go.

He grabbed my wrist, stopping me. "I was afraid you'd say that. But I can't forget it. I won't."

"Then use the money to rebuild—with some *goddamned sprinklers*."

He took it in silence. Then: "Nat. Help me here. Please. Name your price."

"There *is* no price."

"Then I will. Thirty thousand dollars."

A phrase dormant in my mind since Sunday school sprang up: *Thirty pieces of silver.*

And just like that I succumbed to the temptation. Greedily. Thirty thousand dollars could help me save so many animals from suffering, from death.

"Thirty-five thousand," I said.

It startled him. But just for a moment. "Done," he said. Did I hear a hint of disappointment? Maybe I imagined it. Imagined I'd failed his test.

"Make the check payable to All Creatures Great and Small," I told him.

"Ah . . . of course," he said quietly as understanding dawned. The faintest smile crinkled the dirty lines by his eyes. Maybe I'd passed his test after all. "No problem. I'll have my accountant make the transfer in the morning."

I told him to have his office get the bank details from Janice.

We were done. I was exhausted. And I wanted out before I regretted my spate of greed.

I started for the foyer then stopped, turning back to him. *Business.* "What do you know about a company called ERV Financial Services?"

He frowned, distracted. "Who?"

"ERV Financial Services. A wealth management company. Head office in Cyprus."

He shook his head. "Never heard of them."

"Really? Your name is on their prospectus."

His frown deepened. Almost like anger. "What are you talking about?"

He'd said it quickly, vehemently, as only a man who was innocent could. It made me feel sure I was right: This was a false path in Chandra's labyrinth.

Then again, a man who was lying would want to put me off the scent.

A door upstairs slammed. Paul stifled a groan, closed his eyes, rubbed the back of his neck. I saw that exhaustion was finally claiming him, too. "Nat, I should go . . ."

"Sure." This was not the time to press him about the monkeys. "Later."

As I pulled out of the driveway, I saw the neighbor's porch light switch off. Yes, I thought, time for sleep. I was weary to the soul. Driving home, I heard thunder rumble in the distance. Rain coming for sure. To drench Val's charred bones.

Silence inside my house.

"DuPre?" I called, looking upstairs as I sloughed off my boots. No energy even to peel off my coat. I climbed the steps to my bedroom, my legs as heavy as mud.

I switched on the bedside lamp. There was DuPre, asleep on the threshold of the open closet. All around her was debris. Shreds of faux leather. Canvas. Rubber. What the—?

My shoes. Chewed to tatters. *All* my shoes.

DuPre raised her head, blinked, yawned, stretched to shake off sleep. Beside her a pair of shoes sat untouched, red velvet stilettos spangled with rhinestones. Julia's. I'd borrowed them last summer for a gala. Ridiculous shoes. Impossible to walk in. Only she could pull it off, as poised as a movie star. "My ruby slippers," she'd called them with a wink.

My legs gave way. I dropped to my knees. Hot tears sprang. *Julia . . . Val . . .*

DuPre cocked her head as if to ask: "What's wrong?"

I could barely see her through my tears. But I heard her pad over to me, and I caught her warm, sleepy smell. She sniffed my hair. The smoke? *The horses. . . .* I couldn't bear it, the horror of it, and I shut my eyes tight in misery. I heard DuPre's soft whine, a sound of sympathy, then felt the warm wetness of her tongue on my cheek. My eyes sprang open, it surprised me so. She had never been hostile, but I knew she was only tolerating me, waiting for Julia to come and take her home. Until this moment. She stood gently licking my face as though I were a hurt puppy in need of care.

I *was* in need. My heart swelled at the generosity of her spirit. It felt like forgiveness. Absolution for missing the signs of Julia's depression. Balm for my grief over Val. I stroked her furry neck, smiling through my tears.

Exhaustion overtook me. I stood, tugged off my coat, left it in a heap on the floor amid the wreckage of my shoes. I undressed to my underwear, turned off the lamp, and crawled into bed. DuPre jumped up on the foot of the bed. Another first. She curled up around my ankles and watched me—my guardian—until sleep claimed me.

The phone's ring startled me. My mind thrashed out of sleep. I blinked at the bedside clock. Twelve-seventeen. Rain clattered against the window, loud pellets of sleet. The horror of the fire surged back.

Then a moment of joyful madness: *Val's alive. They're calling to tell me he's alive.*

I scrambled out of bed. The phone was in my coat on the floor. I dropped to all fours to snatch it as it rang again. The displayed name glowed in the darkness.

Paul.

"Nat, listen . . . there's something else. Something . . . I need to tell you." His words were slurred. He'd had more scotch.

And Val, of course, was still dead.

"You have to come back," he blurted. He sounded so disturbed, I felt sorry for him.

"Paul, it's late. I was asleep—"

"Natalie, please—"

"No. I'm going back to bed. You should too. Tell me tomorrow."

Silence. Then, "Sure. You're right. Tomorrow. But . . . come first thing. We have to talk. It's—" I heard a shudder in his voice. "It's about Julia."

7

That's how I came to be at Paul's house seven hours later, at sunrise, in the frigid shadows beneath his back deck.

I'd parked at the foot of the hill and trudged up the road, slippery after the ice storm, DuPre beside me. Followed DuPre into that gloomy space, alerted by her frantic barking. Staggered when I saw the body.

Paul.

He hung upside down, his torso like a forked branch, one leg stretched taut from the deck wiring that snagged his ankle, the other leg splayed, his arms hanging down. His whole body encased in a film of ice.

"What is your emergency?"

I twitched at the voice. The 911 dispatcher on my phone.

"Ma'am?" she repeated. "What is your emergency?"

"Yes . . . a man . . . I think he's . . . dead. Please help!"

I answered the questions numbly. Address. *Seven Riverview Ridge*. Is the man conscious? *No*. Is he breathing? *No!*

I could hardly breathe myself, my heart thumped so painfully. More questions. My name? Was I alone? Did I feel safe staying there? Assistance was being dispatched.

I tore my eyes off Paul. I felt dizzy. My legs spongy. I was desperate to sit on something before my knees gave way, but there was nothing in this wasteland under the deck. Nothing but Paul suspended in the shadows. Darkness. Frosty air. Ice.

I forced myself to look back at him. His clothes, the same as when I'd talked to him last night, blaming him for the fire that killed Val. His face was toward me, and through the blur of ice I could see that his eyes were open, his face white, as though drained. A clump of his pale hair was dark red at the scalp. Blood?

A siren. Wailing far off, coming closer.

I stumbled out, away from the deck overhang. Out into the morning sun. I blinked at the sudden light. The shrill of the sirens got louder as I made my way shakily past the ice-crusted spruce trees that lined Paul's property and reached the road.

Vehicles converged around me like an attack. Police, ambulance, more police. People got out. A choppy chorus of car doors closing. Voices, speaking quietly. I had the insane thought: *So they won't wake the neighbors?*

A female officer approached me. "Are you Natalie Sinclair? You made the call?"

"Yes. He's there." I pointed to the deck, jabbing the air.

She beckoned two other officers. They set out through the spruces. She asked a third, "The ME here yet?"

"Yes, here," an older man said coming toward us.

The medical examiner? He was jamming on a blue toque, his medical bag slung over his shoulder as he negotiated the slippery road and followed the others to the deck.

The female officer stayed with me. "Ma'am, can you tell me what happened?"

"He must have fallen. His foot—"

A paramedic knocked my elbow as he and another brushed past me, their gurney clattering on the icy road. They disappeared behind the spruces.

"I meant how did you find him?" the woman asked.

"I was coming to see him."

"So you know who it is?"

"Yes, Paul Leblanc. This is his house."

She beckoned another officer, they exchanged some words, and that guy started up the walk to the front door.

I answered more of her questions, trying to piece it together as I spoke. When I'd left him last night he was fine. I went home. Heard the rainstorm in the night. When I came back this morning, everything was covered in ice. Paul too. He'd been drinking, must have tripped on the deck wiring and fallen. Hit his head. Been unconscious through the storm, through the night's plunge in temperature. Telling her all this, I was suddenly so cold, shivery. I stumbled over words, trying to keep my teeth from chattering.

The paramedics and medical examiner reappeared with the gurney. It clattered toward us. Paul lay on it, still frozen, his limbs stiffly extended just as I'd found him. Grotesque. Now, in the bright sunshine, the blood matting his hair glowed crimson through the ice. The medical man shot a solemn glance at the officer beside me and gave a slight shake of his head. *Dead.* As if it wasn't sickeningly obvious. Nausea roiled my stomach and threatened to shoot up my throat. If I had come right after his call last night, might I have saved him?

I turned away, bent over, vomited.

I heard the gurney rattle past us toward the ambulance.

"Ma'am? Are you okay?" the officer beside me asked.

"Yes." I spit out the last of the sour bile. "Just a minute."

I wiped my mouth with my sleeve, still shaky, ashamed, and heard the officer murmur to her colleague: "See the gash in his skull? Accident? Maybe not."

What? I turned back to her. "What do you mean?"

She quickly changed the subject to cover her lapse. "I'll have someone drive you to your car. It's down the hill, you said?" She took my elbow to lead me to the police cruiser, but I pulled back.

"No, I'm fine."

"You've had a bad shock, ma'am. And the hill's slippery. Safer if we take you."

It was an order. I was escorted to the back seat of the cruiser. As I thudded onto the seat, I watched the ambulance pull away, taking Paul. In front of me a young officer was climbing in behind the wheel. I suddenly blurted, "Stop."

DuPre. I'd forgotten all about her.

I jumped out, rushed back to the cluster of police where the female officer was now talking on her phone. "My dog," I said. "Have you seen my dog?"

They looked at me blankly.

"A small border collie. Black and white. She came here with me."

No one had seen her. I pushed past them, hurried back through the spruce trees, back to the deck. No sign of her.

"Ma'am?" the woman called after me. Then louder: "Ms. Sinclair, where are you going?"

I plunged into the shadows beneath the deck. That's where I'd last seen her, barking at Paul's body. Above me, the loop of wire that had held his foot dangled, lengthened from their act of taking him down.

I turned, scanned the edge of the woods leading down to the river. "DuPre!" I called. Called again and again. Within the woods, nothing moved.

I felt a knife of panic. Julia's dog—*my* dog—was gone.

8

The office hushed when I walked in. It surprised me to see so many volunteers here on a Saturday. One by one they slowly came toward me. In their faces I saw pity, curiosity. Had they already heard? How?

Nicole read my startled look. "It was in *Craigmuir Today*," she said. She held up her phone, the source. "Trevor saw it first, texted us all."

So the local paper had posted the news online. It tumbled piecemeal out of them, each sharing a bit of the shocking story. Paul Leblanc dead. Me finding him. The fire at his house the night before. The stable razed. The horses burned alive.

"Here, Nat, you need coffee."

"She needs *space*," Trevor said. "Back off, guys."

"Nat, come sit down."

I didn't know what to say. All these people, here. I'd come hoping to find one, maybe two at work so I could ask them to help me search for DuPre, but it looked like *everyone* was here. Nicole. Trevor. Victor.

Nathan and Ellen, who always worked together. Bahira. Amber. Heather. Annika. Keith. Raoul. All here, for *me.*

Tears welled up. To hide it, I looked down at the coffee Ellen had handed me, gratefully warming my hands around the mug. I was still dazed by the shock of finding Paul. Still couldn't believe he was dead. And then DuPre disappearing. I'd been looking for her for the last two hours, driving the streets around Riverview Ridge, window down, calling her name. I dreaded coming across her lying motionless on the verge, the victim of a hit-and-run. No sign of her. I'd called the pound. They hadn't picked her up.

"How could they just let those poor horses burn?" Nicole said. Not a question, an accusation.

"I was sick when I heard," Annika said. "Literally sick." She looked it. Her face was ashen.

It was the horses they cared about. None of them knew Paul personally.

"Firefighters are paid to save people and property," Victor said with quiet logic. "Animals too, if they can, but animals are not a priority."

"I'm sure they did their best," Keith said.

I kept a stony face. Inside, I shared Nicole's outrage. I'd begged the firefighters to turn their hoses on the stable.

"And poor Mr. Leblanc," Heather said. "Nat, how did it happen?"

"I don't know." An accident, surely. Yet I'd heard the officer question that. And I'd seen the bloody gash on Paul's skull. But if not an accident—what? "I guess the police are investigating."

The horrors of the last twelve hours left me shaky. I could barely absorb it all, let alone make sense of it. But I could not let it swamp me. I set down the coffee mug on a desk. "Look, I came here because of DuPre. I had her with me when I found . . . you know . . . but after the police arrived I couldn't see her anywhere. Maybe the sirens scared her off. I'm heading out again to search for her. Could one of you please come and help?"

Everyone wanted to, volunteering in a loud burst of enthusiasm. It forced a ragged laugh from me. "Looks like I've got a whole posse."

Annika said she could take a few people in her SUV. Keith offered to take others in his truck. Trevor could take one in his Smart car. They were all talking at once. Trevor whistled for quiet, and in the silence he briskly suggested areas we should focus on. It was good to see he'd recovered from yesterday's beating. "Thanks," I told him. He grinned. He was already grabbing his coat. So were the others. I hadn't even taken off mine.

We were heading for the door when I heard, "Nat, wait." Janice, my office manager.

I turned to see her at her desk, sitting there as though it was a normal workday. I hadn't noticed her before. She beckoned me over.

"I need to speak to you," she said with a stern frown that, before her retirement, must have sent fear through her students.

I needed to leave. DuPre might be lying hurt somewhere. "Can it wait?"

"No."

That sounded ominous. "Okay." I told the others to go, that I'd join them in a minute. Several trooped out. I reached Janice's desk. "What is it?"

She lowered her voice to an urgent whisper. A few people were still near, pulling on their coats. "The cashbox. The money's gone."

I groaned inside. If she needed more to cover daily expenses, it certainly *could* wait. "How much do you need?"

"What? No. I mean, it's been taken. Stolen. There was 412 dollars there on Thursday. It's gone. All of it."

Stolen? It made no sense. No one here would do such a thing. "Who's been in except the volunteers?"

She lowered her whisper even more, to a rasp. "That's just it. I think it might be the Syrian. He didn't come to work yesterday."

I looked over at the kitchen nook. Nabil Ahmadi had been installing new cabinets, and the work was half finished. In Damascus he'd been a master carpenter, but here, as a refugee, he was getting by with odd jobs, including replacing our sad old cabinetry. He was a good worker, quiet, kept to himself. "What makes you think it was Nabil?"

"I know he saw me putting the cashbox in my bottom drawer last week."

"Don't you lock it? The drawer?"

She looked offended. "Why would I? It's safe with *these* people."

It wasn't the first time she'd unabashedly displayed her prejudice.

"Call him," I said.

"I did. He's not answering."

I did not need this now. "Maybe somebody needed the cash for something and just forgot to tell you. I'll ask everyone later."

I met up with my volunteers outside Paul's house to search. The police were gone, and the scene was eerily normal, quiet, the sun shining. I forced away the image of Paul's body trapped in ice and concentrated on DuPre. Window down, I drove the grid Trevor had given me, calling DuPre's name. Keith and Annika each drove another grid. Trevor had marshaled his group to track through the woods behind Paul's house, and I could hear the faint chorus of them calling DuPre, like a looping echo. I kept in touch with them all by text, everyone reporting in, no sign of DuPre.

After a couple of hours the texts I got began to change: Nicole: *Nat, I'm so sorry, have to get home.* Heather*: Sorry, kids to take to hockey.* Amber*: Gotta walk the dawg.* Keith: *Promised Pam I'd make dinner.*

Of course, I texted back to each one: *'Bye. Thanks for coming.*

Finally, there was just Trevor, still tramping the woods. But after another half hour, even he texted that he had to stop. *Dumb cracked rib giving me grief.*

Go home, *Trevor*, I texted. *Please.*

The afternoon shadows were lengthening as I parked near the frozen river and got out to continue the search alone. Slushy riverside paths. Chilly ravine, still frigid with pockets of muddy snow. No trace of DuPre.

I had lost Julia's dog.

It hit me hard. So much loss these past weeks. So much death. The images sickened me. The rope biting my sister's neck. Val's screams in the flames. Paul encased in ice. How in God's name had that happened to him? And now DuPre, lying gasping in some ditch, wounded? Or worse, dead? In the welter of emotions, losing DuPre felt the most terrible because it was totally my fault. As if I had abandoned Julia, and lost her all over again.

9

Paul's mysterious death. DuPre's disappearance. The next three days brought no answers about either, just sleepless nights tormented by nightmares of Paul in the ice, Val in the flames.

I received a summons to the inquest because I was the one who'd found Paul's body, and I went and answered the coroner's questions, feeling queasy again at reliving that frigid morning. I left the courthouse, my civic duty done, hoping the five jurors would get to the bottom of what had happened.

As for DuPre, I'd had a hundred "missing dog" posters printed, and my team and I papered the city with them. Every time my phone rang, my heart leapt. *Someone's found her.* But no such call came.

The animal cruelty inspector, however, did call in response to my report about the baby monkeys. He gave me the standard line that they were pursuing the matter but had limited resources, little information to go on, the trail was now cold, blah-blah-blah. I told him what we'd discovered about the connection to ERV Financial Services, and he assured me they would investigate further. I thanked him and hung up. I wasn't holding my breath that they'd do anything about it.

But that didn't mean *I* couldn't. I couldn't bring back Paul, and I feared I might never find DuPre, but there were suffering, smuggled animals—who knew how many?—that I might be able to save. I was determined to do all I could for them.

It was a gray morning, the sun a pale disk behind clouds pregnant with snow, when I parked outside the office complex of Leblanc Agrisciences Ltd. Given Paul's wealth and reputation—his company had won prestigious awards for creating more-sustainable varieties of canola—I hadn't expected the spare, modest design of his headquarters. No waterfall wall in the lobby. No gleaming chrome. No designer lighting. Just an open-concept layout with cubicles and the quiet hum of serious people at work.

"Ms. Sinclair," his executive assistant said, rising from the desk in Paul's office. "Right on time. Please, come in."

I'd spoken to Carrie Pemberton on the phone maybe half a dozen times, and the Jamaican lilt in her voice always invoked lush images of white sand and azure surf. She beckoned me to take the chair across from her desk.

"I'm so sorry about Paul," I said as I sat down. "He was a fine man. I'm sure all of you here miss him terribly."

She nodded as she took her seat. "Thank you. We surely do." She studied me in sympathy. "And you . . . what a terrible thing . . . seeing him like that."

Our eyes locked in mute commiseration.

There were papers on her desk. I glimpsed Paul's signature on a couple, and for one powerful, covetous moment I wished he'd been able to sign that huge check he'd promised me for All Creatures. The thought made me prickle with shame.

"So, Ms. Sinclair, what can I do for you?"

Straight to the point. Good. "I'm looking for information connected to smugglers trafficking baby monkeys." I explained how we discovered the operation at a location in Toronto but were forced to leave before I could get details. "I was hoping you might shed some light."

A puzzled frown. "I know Mr. Leblanc admired the work you do, but since he's . . . no longer with us . . . I don't quite understand what it is you're looking for."

"I'm not sure myself, actually. I'm just following a trail."

She looked slightly offended. "And the trail led you here?"

"Well, to a company called ERV Financial Services. Wealth management. Paul is listed in an executive position in their prospectus. But it seems the company is a shell. If I could find out more about it, about their activities, there's a chance I could save a lot of animals' lives." I pulled out my phone. "Here, have a look." I scrolled to the document.

She held up a hand. "Wait. You're saying Mr. Leblanc is an officer of this company, this EV—"

"ERV Financial Services, yes."

I could tell it was news to her. Or maybe news that I was on the trail. She straightened, as though backing away from me.

I needed to reassure her. "Carrie, I don't for a moment suspect that Paul had anything to do with the smuggling. Please, don't think that's why I've come. But I do wonder if ERV Financial Services is engaged in some illicit activity that Paul was unaware of. Do any of these other names mean anything to you?" I turned the phone to show her the list.

She didn't even look at it. "I'm sorry. Internal business information is proprietary."

"But these names are public."

"Then you should have no trouble locating them yourself."

"I thought asking you would be quicker."

"That's really not my job. And it's a rather busy day here, so . . ."

"Is there someone else I could talk to?"

"Perhaps the police?"

"Done that. Animal issues aren't a priority for them. But they are for me."

She stood. "I understand. But I'm sorry, I can't help you." She came around the desk. "Let me show you out."

She moved so briskly, I could only follow. She escorted me to the lobby, wished me well, and, having washed her hands of me, headed back down the hall.

Zipping up my coat, frustrated at the dead end with Carrie, I passed the receptionist, whose desk was beside a wall of award plaques and photographs. Among the photos, a large oil portrait caught my eye: three men, one middle-aged and seated flanked by two who were much younger, standing. The suits and haircuts were slightly old-fashioned. I recognized Paul, though he must have been only about eighteen. "Is the older gentleman Paul's father?" I asked the receptionist.

"Yes. With both sons. Painted quite a while ago."

I knew that the senior Leblanc, deceased, had begun the family business. It struck me how the other son was the only one smiling. "Does Paul's brother work here?"

"No, but he's on the board of directors."

"What's his name?"

"Logan. Logan Leblanc."

Heading back to my car, I wondered if this hadn't been a dead-end after all. Carrie was a closed book, but Paul's brother might be more open.

I arrived at the office ready to boot up my Mac and check out Paul's brother.

"Good morning," Janice said darkly as I passed her desk. She had been frosty ever since I'd dismissed her suspicions about Nabil

Ahmadi and the missing cash. We still hadn't heard from the Syrian carpenter; he hadn't returned any of Janice's calls.

"There's someone to see you," she said, nodding toward the kitchen nook.

A man in a brown suit under his open duffle coat stood looking at the posters of whales on the wall above the coffee maker. Beside him was a young woman in belted jacket and slacks. The man turned when I approached. He looked about fifty. He seemed to make a quick assessment. "Ms. Sinclair?"

"Yes."

His smile was professional. A half-smile. "I'm Detective Rourke, Craigmuir Police." He raised his ID. "This is Constable Crocker. Is there some place we can talk?"

Startled, I thought of my report about the monkeys. Had the animal welfare inspector sent this local man? "About the trafficking?" I asked.

His smile faded as he tucked away the ID. A watchful look took its place. "No." He pulled a business card from his jacket pocket and handed it to me. "Homicide."

10

"The laceration in the victim's skull was deep. The autopsy report identified embedded splinters. The splinters match the wood being used to renovate his deck."

Detective Rourke spoke calmly, quietly, at odds with my heart thudding in my ears. I'd seen that gash in Paul's skull, the crimson blood staining the ice that enveloped him. I'd assumed he'd had some tragic accident, but homicide detectives don't come asking questions about accidents.

Paul had been murdered. It was hard to take in.

"It's called ipe." He said it like *eye-pay*. "An expensive Brazilian hardwood, like mahogany. Extremely dense, I'm told, hard as nails, literally, which makes it difficult to saw. But its density also makes it less susceptible than other woods to fire. It actually has a fire rating the same as steel and concrete. It's also exceptionally smooth. Appeals to people who like to walk their deck barefoot." His gaze flicked to my feet. My Blundstone boots. Then back to my face with the hint of a smile. "Sorry. Didn't mean to sound like a salesman for the stuff. I just find it interesting."

At the detective's words, a tiny smile twitched the young constable's lips, as though she felt his fascination with these details was an old person's thing.

"You're very thorough, Detective," I said. That had to be a good thing in his line of work, but for some reason it made me nervous. So did his steady gaze at me. He was likely a veteran cop, and if I were a criminal who was hiding something, I was sure he'd eventually find it. He and I sat on stools in the kitchen nook. Constable Crocker stood at a respectful distance to one side, notebook and pen in her hands. I could hear my volunteers carrying on with their work around the corner—footsteps, the clatter of file cabinets, voices murmuring on phones—but every now and then a face would anxiously peer around the corner for a moment, then disappear.

"A two-by-four of the ipe wood was found beneath the victim," Rourke went on. "Blood on the edge. Leblanc's blood."

"So that's how he died? Someone smashed him on the head?"

He didn't answer. I felt both foolish for my choice of words and sick at the memory. *Of course* that's how he died.

"How long had you known Mr. Leblanc?"

"About two years, I think."

"Can you be more specific? How did you meet him?"

"At a charity fundraiser he hosted at his home. A music evening. My late sister was playing. She was a well-known cellist, and when I met Paul at that party he told me he'd been a longtime fan of hers."

It was painful speaking of Julia. I thought I was over the worst of it, but there was always a jab in my heart. "Anyway, that was just before Christmas, so, yes, it was two years ago."

"Would you say you and he were friends?"

"Yes. Sure."

"Close friends?"

That phrase usually meant just one thing. Sex. I knew it was the detective's meaning. "Not close, no," I said firmly. "I got my horse that spring. I knew Paul had a beautiful country estate, so I asked to board Val at his stable and he said sure."

"Did you have any problems with him as a . . . a landlord, if that's the right word?"

I thought of the times I'd urged Paul to install sprinklers in the stable. He'd always quickly agreed, then never got around to it. The horror of the fire surged back, and with it my grief for Val. A grief that I now felt as a deep, hollow regret. Val was gone. Paul was gone. What was the point of mentioning sprinklers now? "No," I said. "No problems."

"Until his stable burned down and you lost your horse. That must have been awful. Must have strained your friendship."

That threw me. He'd obviously checked about the fire. But was he actually suggesting that I'd been upset enough to kill Paul? It would have been funny if it weren't so pathetic. "Look, Paul was a good man. I liked him. And as for my gelding and the other two horses there, Paul's stable hand always took good care of them. I had *no* problems with Paul. The fire was just a terrible tragedy."

His expression gave no clue if that answer satisfied him or not. But he gave the kind of nod that says, Let's move on. "I'd like to ask you about later that night."

I swallowed. He meant when Paul died. *Was killed.*

"Mr. Leblanc's neighbor next door reported seeing a woman arrive at Leblanc's front door about ten o'clock and leave soon after. Her description included—" He looked over at his constable. She flipped back a couple pages in her notebook then read out: "Female. Medium height. Caucasian. About thirty. Dark hair in a ponytail."

Detective Rourke looked back at me. "Was that woman you?"

His implication now was horribly clear. "You don't seriously think I killed Paul?"

His gaze remained steady. He repeated calmly, "Was that woman you?"

"Yes . . . I mean, I did visit Paul that night."

"Why?"

"He asked me to come."

"Why?"

"He wanted to offer me compensation for Val."

"Your horse that died in the fire?"

"Yes. I told him to make it a donation to my organization. And then I left."

"And did he?"

"Did he what?"

"Make a donation?"

"No, because he said he'd do it in the morning, and by then he was dead."

Something subtle shifted in his eyes. Like a door closing. Had I sounded cold, callous? That's not what I meant. Not at all what I felt.

He cocked his head in the direction of my volunteers at work around the corner. "What exactly do you do here?" he asked. He sounded like he was truly curious; his flat, professional tone gone. "Your group, I mean."

"Various issues," I said. "Finding homes for abandoned or abused pets is one. Like last week when a Doberman was thrown out of a pickup truck on Highway Six. We found him half dead, broken leg, broken jaw. Or like our office cat here, who'd been tossed in a dumpster as a kitten, left to starve." I churned the words out, though my thoughts kept sliding back to the detective's evident suspicion of me. "And we do our best to expose animal abuse wherever it happens. The roadside zoos, the animals in filthy cages, no veterinary care. The so-called canned hunts where bears are chained to a stake and guys take shots. The puppy mills where the dogs are kept constantly pregnant, never out of cages. Organized dogfights where—"

"Okay, okay, I get it," he interrupted with a note of annoyance that we had strayed so far off topic. But I noticed Constable Crocker's look of pained shock at my words about the animals. I liked her for that.

"Back to that night, when you were at Leblanc's house," the detective went on, "were you alone with him?"

"Yes. I mean, no, his wife was there. I saw her, but we didn't speak. She was going upstairs. I spoke to Paul alone."

"Besides discussing compensation for your horse, did the two of you talk about anything else?"

"Like what?"

"You were there. You tell me."

That expression—*you tell me*—a command. People say it when they think you're hiding something. "I asked him briefly about a business matter."

"Oh? You had business dealings with him?"

"No. Not personally. But I'd recently learned that he might have a financial connection to . . . an activity that troubled me."

"What kind of activity?"

"Illegal trafficking in wild animals."

I'd thought it would surprise him: the upstanding Paul Leblanc, good corporate citizen, engaged in something unsavory, illicit. But he didn't blink. Maybe in his line of work he'd seen and heard everything.

"Did you accuse him of that?"

"No, not at all. I was just following up on a lead. That's all I asked him about."

"What lead was that?"

"A company called ERV Financial Services. Head office in Cyprus. I asked if he had any dealings with them."

"And what was his response?"

"He said he'd never heard of them." I was glad to say so, to exonerate Paul. Remembering his grotesque, upside-down body, this felt like giving him back his dignity.

"And you believed him?"

"I had no reason not to."

"Even though this animal issue was important to you?"

Oh, this guy was good. Because I *was* hiding something. The baby monkeys. I still didn't believe Paul was personally involved, but there was *some* connection there, and I meant to find out what. "Look, we'd both just been through hell at the fire that night. I asked him my question. He answered. I left. That was all there was to it."

He was watching me closely. "The thing is, Ms. Sinclair, it seems that you may have been the last person to see him alive."

I gaped at him. This was insane. "What possible reason could I have to kill Paul Leblanc?"

He said nothing. He stood up and nodded to the constable, who immediately took the hint and closed her notebook. Detective Rourke gave me that professional half-smile of his. "Thank you for your time. And don't worry unduly. I only want to eliminate you from our inquiry."

That made sense. Sounded rational. So why didn't I believe a word of it?

11

It was almost six o'clock when I left the office for a visit to the home of our Member of Parliament, Hank Verhagen. I'd forced my mind on work for the last few hours, but I was still jangled by Detective Rourke's questions. As I was leaving, Trevor asked to "escort" me. Sweet, really. My interview with the cop had been private, but Trevor seemed to sense I was upset. I was—and doubly so. I wasn't looking forward to this task with Hank.

We walked, since the address I'd been given wasn't far. It was in a funky, family neighborhood at the edge of the downtown core, a onetime hippie enclave of the seventies, now gentrified. There was a hint of spring in the air, a softening, tinged with the loamy smell of wet earth. Leaving for the office this morning, I'd been so encouraged by it that I'd banished my winter parka to the back of the closet. It was still cold, though, especially now at dusk, and my fleece jacket didn't do much to keep out the chill. I regretted falling for spring's phony come-on.

Worse, I imagined DuPre lying injured in some ditch, cold, hungry, terrified. I'd been doing all I could to find her, searching the whole area around Paul's house again and again, sometimes joined by a few of my volunteers, bless them. I'd put up more "lost dog" posters all around town. Called the city pound every morning to see if she'd been brought in. But there had been no sign of her. No response, either, to my offer of a reward on the local *Animal Talk* radio show. The constant worry about DuPre kept me awake at nights and anxious at work.

And now I had the added anxiety about Paul's murder. Despite the detective's assurances, I had the chilling sense that he actually considered me a suspect. I couldn't deny the facts that seemed to guide him there: The fire that killed Val. My visit to Paul's house. And my being, as he thought, the last person to see him alive. Suspecting me was scarily logical.

But of course I *wasn't* the last one to see him alive, because I sure as hell didn't kill him. So who did? I remembered his wife had been there. And the tension between them had been clear. Why wasn't *she* a suspect?

Trevor interrupted this troublesome train of thought. "So, what's up with Mr. Verhagen?" he asked, taking my elbow to steer me clear of a jogger who huffed past us.

It brought me back to the unpleasant task ahead. "I'm picking up Monty." Over a month ago, Hank had requested a dog when one became available, and last week I'd sent Annika and Heather to deliver to his house what I thought was the perfect fit, an old sheepdog whose owner had recently died. "I got a call to come and take him back."

"Take him back? Why?"

"Apparently his claws are scratching the new hardwood floor."

"Seriously? Mr. Verhagen's that anal?"

"Not him."

"Aha. The wife."

"Ex-wife." I'd taken her call. I had never met the woman; I knew only that she was a surgeon at St. Michael's Hospital in Toronto and had kept her own name. But apparently, despite the divorce, she still had some proprietary stake in the house here. "She said Monty hasn't"—what was the idiotic word she used?—"assimilated."

"Holy hell."

Yeah. I figured there *was* a place in hell for people who thought of animals as expendable. Poor Monty. They expected us to come and take him away like the trash.

The woman who opened the door frowned at me as though I'd interrupted her in the middle of performing a heart transplant.

"Doctor Vincent?" I asked.

"And you are—?"

She looked about forty-five, maybe fifty. That surprised me. So much older than Hank. I knew from his bio that he'd just turned forty-one.

She was waiting for an answer. I was in no mood to make nice. "I'm Natalie Sinclair." I held up the leash I'd brought. "We're here to pick up the dog."

"Oh, good. That animal sheds all over the furniture. Come in."

Trevor and I stepped inside. The house pulsed with noise. Two pre-teen boys pounded down the stairs from the upper floor, raced past us, then down the hall toward the kitchen—I could see an island with stools—followed by a soft bang like a screen door. Rap music throbbed somewhere upstairs. A news anchor intoned from a TV in a far room.

There was another bang of the door. Down the hall where the boys had disappeared, Hank was coming this way, apparently from outside. He had on a sheepskin jacket, unbuttoned. Black shirt. Jeans. Flipflops, despite the chilly evening. He looked great. I'd always thought so, but I never thought he had a cold heart. Until now.

"Natalie?" His surprise at seeing me was obvious. He turned to the woman. "Thanks, Mrs. Lehman. You can finish making the salad, please."

So, not the good doctor after all. Probably the housekeeper. The woman padded off to the kitchen, and Hank said to me cheerfully, "What brings you to my door?" He shot a quick, sharp glance at Trevor. "And your friend."

"This is Trevor Wapoosh."

"Hey, Mister Verhagen," Trevor said pleasantly, extending his hand.

They shook hands. All very nice. But I was pissed, and I didn't care if Hank saw it. "We came to save your floor and your furniture."

"Pardon?"

"Monty. We'll take him and be on our way."

"What? No." He looked shocked. "You can't just take him back. He's ours now."

"Well, I guess Doctor Vincent changed her mind. She called. She doesn't want him. And if the family isn't happy with him, that's not a good situation for him to—"

"We *are*. Happy with him. He's a great dog. I love him. The kids love him."

"Your wife, not so much."

"*Ex*-wife."

Much as I like his emphasis on *ex,* I was confused. Where did this leave Monty? "So . . ."

"Look," he said, "I just got in from Ottawa. I'll settle this with Jacqui later. She left here this morning."

I was trying to figure how *ex* fit a spouse who apparently still lived in this house. My puzzlement must have showed, because he was clearly about to say more but then threw up his hands and made one of those faces that says, *It's complicated*. He nodded toward the kitchen. "I've got to get back outside. Come on, join me. We can talk there."

I needed to know about Monty, so I followed Hank through the kitchen, Trevor behind me. We passed Mrs. Lehman vigorously tossing salad greens in a wooden bowl. There was a warm scent of cinnamon and apples. A pie, maybe.

We went out the screened back door to a flagstone patio with a gas barbecue where four thick steaks sizzled on the grill. Beyond it, a long, wide lawn lay dark in the dusk, but a stretch of it was lit by shiny brass lamps on posts, and at the far end the two boys were kicking a soccer ball around despite the scattered patches of snow. "Almost done," Hank said as he picked up tongs and flipped one of the steaks. I tried to hide my distaste at the meat smell. The soccer ball bounced between me and Trevor. Trevor grabbed it and punted it back to the kids and then, as if answering an unspoken primal invitation, jogged out to join their game.

Hank shot me a quick smile as if to say, *Boys will be boys*. Before I let his charm get to me, I said, "Hank, about Monty—"

"The dog stays, Natalie," he said firmly. "In fact, I want to thank you. Monty has been the best thing for Lily."

"Who?"

"My daughter. Have a look."

He pointed with the tongs to a glassed-in porch. Monty sat beside the little girl who sat cross-legged on a couch with a big picture book on her lap. I couldn't hear through the glass, but she was obviously talking to him.

"She's got dyslexia. Has a struggle reading. But she loves reading to Monty. He'll sit with her like that for hours. She's the teacher."

The big sheepdog looked adorably attentive, even interested, at least from what I could see of his eyes behind his shaggy mop. The flinty emotions I'd come here with softened. Monty was staying, thank goodness. And this felt like a happy house. Best of all, Hank was the decent man I'd thought he was. "I'm so glad he's found a good home," I said.

He nodded, a smile in his eyes. Those lagoon-blue eyes. The close-cropped blond hair. The buff build. He could have been a poster boy for an Ivy League rowing team—or, come to think of it, a gang of white supremacists. I shuddered at the injustice of that second image, because I knew the ironic truth from his public bio. It was the fair complexion of his Jewish Dutch forebears that had saved his grandparents from a Nazi death camp.

"Are you cold?" he asked.

I was, and realized I was hugging myself. He pulled off his jacket and slung it around my shoulders.

At his touch, warm blood crept up my face. I hoped the low light hid it. I held his gaze, since looking down would be a dead giveaway.

He smiled, then turned and flipped another slab of flesh and asked over his shoulder. "Will you stay for dinner? You and your friend?"

"No. Thanks. We should be getting back."

"Sure? We have lots more in the fridge."

"We don't eat our clients."

He laughed. It was a nice laugh. He flipped the other steaks, still chuckling.

There was a cheer from one of the boys, like he'd scored a goal. Hank and I watched them carry on with their game. I'd heard they were twins, his wife's kids from her first marriage. Was the little girl both his and his wife's? Or rather, *ex*-wife. Or . . . what the heck was she anyway?

"I hope Doctor Vincent will be okay with your decision about Monty," I said, fishing shamelessly.

He looked at me; I saw that he knew what I was really asking, and my blush prickled the roots of my hair. "When we got divorced," he said, "we decided to do the shared custody thing a little unconventionally. Decided it wasn't fair to Toby and Drew and Lily to have to shuttle back and forth between us. So we kept this house just for them. Jacqui and I take turns in residence, alternating month by month. She has a place in Toronto. I have a bachelor apartment here, over on McConnell. When I'm not in Ottawa."

A bubble of happiness rose in my chest. "That's—" I almost said *so cool*, but I didn't want to gush—"very enlightened." I was glad he'd explained. Glad he'd *wanted* to.

"How about you?" he said. "Married?" He was flipping the damn steaks again, slightly turned away so that I couldn't see his face. Was this just polite conversation, or was he as ineptly unsubtle at fishing as I was?

"Once upon a time," I answered. "It didn't work out."

He nodded, eyes on the meat. "Any kids?"

I could've replied with a simple no. But there wasn't anything simple about two painful miscarriages and the consequent strain on two people when one of them longs to adopt and the other is dead set against it. My longing. His inflexibility. End of marriage. "I wasn't that lucky," I replied.

He cocked his head at me. I realized how deeply personal I'd suddenly made things, and felt self-conscious. Time to get back on a professional footing.

"Hank, have you given some thought to sponsoring the research bill?" I'd emailed him about it weeks ago. I wanted him to bring a bill to the House of Commons that would limit the use of animals in research. He'd replied that the issue appealed to him and that he would ask around, see if he could get support from his colleagues. He knew he owed me. During the election, appreciating his progressive stand on animal welfare issues, I'd had my volunteers canvass for him door-to-door, and we'd also run local radio ads. The few hundred votes we'd drummed up had given him his squeaker victory, and he knew it.

"Don't get your hopes up," he said now. "I'm just a lowly back-bencher."

"But the Prime Minister has his eye on you for his upcoming cabinet shuffle."

He laughed. "Who says?"

"The *National Post*."

He waved that away. "Natalie, I promise I'll look into it. But I need to study the issue a bit more. Get all my ducks in a row."

"Sure. I'll send you more background info tomorrow." I knew when to back off pushing an MP.

"No rush. I'm home for a bit," he said. "Came back from the Hill early for my stint with the kids. Came for Paul Leblanc's funeral tomorrow."

"Oh? You knew him?"

"Yeah, we go way back. Same class in high school. Hung out together quite a bit in those days." He shook his head, blew out a heavy sigh. "What a terrible thing."

More than he knew. I suddenly wanted to share this with him. I felt I could trust him. "I don't know if you heard—I was the one who found his body."

I saw that surprised him. "Really? How horrible."

I explained why I'd been there. The fire the day before. Losing Val. Then: "I testified at the inquest the other day. And then, this afternoon, they interrogated me."

He looked suddenly serious. "Who's they?"

"A Detective Rourke."

"Alan Rourke?"

"That's him."

He blinked. "So. Homicide." Clearly, it was news to him. "My God," he murmured, "I had no idea." Then he was quiet, absorbing it. And maybe thinking, as I had: Who would want to kill Paul?

He gave me a long, searching look. "Natalie, do you have a lawyer?"

That made me nervous. I pretended it didn't. "Do I need one?" I said like a smart-ass imitating a TV cop show.

"It's no joke."

"I know, but it's fine. Rourke said he'd just wanted to eliminate me from his inquiry."

His expression was sober, the kind of look that says: *And you believed him?* "Listen," he said, "I can recommend a couple of top defense attorneys."

His tone now scared me more than Rourke had. "Okay," I muttered, jangled all over again. "Thanks." As if I could afford a lawyer from Hank's world.

The biting smell of smoke from the barbecue made me flinch. A smell like from the stable—roasted flesh. It roiled my stomach. I had a sudden sense of how out of place I was here. Hank, with his happy home, his fridge full of steaks, his country club lawyer friends, his MP prestige. There was a gulf between his world and mine.

"I should go," I said. I handed him back his jacket. I turned and called, "Trevor, time to go." Hank seemed to have forgotten the barbecue. I nodded to it. "I think your dead animal may be burning."

12

The scents of St. Timothy's church took me back to childhood: old wood, cool stone, floor wax, candles, and cocoa. Casseroles, too, baked in the big kitchen below the sanctuary. As a kid, when I'd go down there to get water for the altar flowers, I'd hear the ladies in their Sunday dresses chattering as they worked the industrial gas stove or scrubbed pots, their yellow rubber gloves squeaking at the big stone sinks. Dad had been rector here during all my school years, and I knew a lot of the church's secret places, nooks I could sneak into to read a book—James Herriot's were my favorites—and daydream about becoming a vet.

No daydreaming now at the funeral. I was here to pay my last respects to Paul.

The organ rumbled Bach as I signed the guest book, people milling around me. I stifled the urge to pin a "missing dog" poster on the bulletin board. Still no word about DuPre. I pushed my despair about her to the back of my mind and made my way into the nave.

The pews were filling up, the babble of voices quieting to respectful whispers as people found seats. There was an undercurrent of tension in the whispers; I was sure word had gotten out that the police were investigating Paul's death as a murder.

I stayed at the back and stood watching. Paul's family were seated in the front pews. Denise, elegant in black linen. From what I could see of her face in profile, she looked composed. Dry-eyed. She was flanked by two women. The young one, blonde, had to be their daughter. I tried to imagine her in her Montreal dorm getting the call with the awful news of her father's death. I hoped she hadn't been told about the ice. The other woman, elderly, white-haired, frail, was surely Paul's mother. Other relatives, young and old, filled the rest of the family pews.

One man among the family group had turned, standing, to shake the hand of a man in the pew behind him. He had groomed silver hair, a beefy build, a stance of self-assurance in his pin-striped suit. His tanned face stood out among all the other winter-bleached faces, and I suddenly realized where I'd seen that face before, at least a younger version of it: the portrait in Paul's office. This was his brother, Logan Leblanc.

Perfect, I thought. The very man I wanted to ask about Paul and ERV Financial Services.

The organ music stopped. People hushed. The service began.

Two of Paul's friends gave Bible readings. Hank gave a eulogy that was both friendly and dignified. And yet, hearing him praise Paul as a stalwart of the community, part of me wondered, *Was he really?* My thoughts spun back to those terrified baby monkeys. Could Paul actually have been complicit in trafficking animals poached from the wild? Had his reserved assistant, Carrie, been hiding something?

Paul's brother, I noted, gave neither a reading nor a eulogy. That seemed odd for such a close relation.

Finally, it was over. The throng surged out into the chilly sunshine. I was among the first wave out and stopped on the church steps, waiting to spot Logan Leblanc exiting.

"Natalie, hold on." It was Hank, reaching me.

"That was a lovely eulogy," I said as people eddied past us.

"Well, at least it didn't put them to sleep." I was about to say that I really meant it, but he quickly went on: "Did you talk to either of the defense attorneys?"

He had emailed me two names, fine lawyers no doubt, but I'd put off contacting either. Not only could I not afford them, I still couldn't believe I needed to. "No, but I will."

"Just a precaution," he said gently.

I heard a man's low laugh a few yards away. I turned to see it was Logan Leblanc chatting with a small group of men on the sidewalk. He must have passed me while I was talking to Hank. His listeners seemed entertained by what he was saying. He had put on his overcoat, black wool with a fur collar dark like sable. Seeing fur always gave me a shudder.

Hank followed my gaze. "You know Paul's brother?" he asked.

"Not personally. Do you?" I remembered him saying he'd been in the same high school class as Paul. "Was he at school with you too?"

"Two years ahead of me and Paul. Logan didn't mix much with his kid brother's bunch. I haven't seen him in years. He's based in Toronto."

I sensed he didn't feel any affection for the guy. "Are they—*were* they—in business together?"

"I'm not sure. Logan is CEO of Gold Zone, a mining company. But I know Paul had diverse interests, so maybe."

As diverse as a wealth management company with a head office in Cyprus? I wondered. *One connected to an animal smuggling operation?* A limo pulled up beside Leblanc's group of men and they stepped away, making room for him to reach it. If I was going to ask him about ERV, I had to do it before he took off.

"Talk to you later, Hank," I said.

Paul's brother was opening the limo's front door as I reached him. "Mr. Leblanc?"

He turned. Gave me a quick once-over head to toe, the kind of inspection some men feel no shame about. "Have we met?"

"No. But I considered Paul a friend. I'm very sorry for your loss." I held out my hand. "My name's Natalie Sinclair."

He shook hands with me, slowly, almost luxuriously, his expression now tinged with interest. "I'm sorry for *your* loss, too. Your horse."

That was kind. "Thank you." Though I couldn't help wondering how he'd heard about Val. From Denise, likely. Or had he seen the fire marshal's report?

"Did you have him for long?"

"Two years. He was a rescue."

"Well then, that's two years he'd never have had if not for you."

He still held my hand, an intimacy that felt uncomfortable, vaguely creepy. I slipped my hand free and was about to get to the point when I noticed, just in time, that the limo driver was dressed in funeral black and I realized that Leblanc was about to be taken to the graveside service to bury Paul. I caught myself from barraging him with my questions. Definitely not the time or place to grill a grieving brother.

"Please accept my condolences," I said.

"Thanks." He turned back to the car's open front door and got in.

I turned, about to go, and saw Denise coming toward the limo, arm in arm with her daughter and mother-in-law. The whole family was about to be driven to the graveside. I felt awkwardly in the way, yet thought I should say something to Denise to be polite. She flicked me a frigid glance then briskly ushered the two other women into the limo's back seat. Most of the crowd on the sidewalk had dispersed. I stood alone with Paul's wife.

"Denise," I said, touching her arm. "My sincere condolences. I'm so very sorry."

She shook off my hand. "Hypocrite." Her voice was low, venomous. "How long did you know?"

I blinked at her, confused. "Know what?"

"About your whore of a sister. She was fucking Paul."

13

I drove out of Craigmuir, stung by Denise Leblanc's words. I was on my way to my parents' house to rehearse with Dad for Julia's memorial concert, but our string duet was far from my thoughts. How long had my sister been having an affair with Paul? Was that why he'd wanted to see me when he'd made that midnight call?

And who else had known about it? My God, did Simon, Julia's husband, know? Did my parents? Should I ask them?

I'd taken the county road that followed the river, hoping the scenic route would quiet the questions ricocheting in my mind. It didn't. Halfway to my parents' place, the traffic slowed to a crawl, and I saw parked police cruisers ahead and flashing detour arrows. As I turned left onto the detour route, I could see, to the right, two ambulances on the riverbank and, out on the frozen river, a scatter of ice fishing huts. Had some anglers fallen through? It happened every March, people ice fishing or skating or snowmobiling, expecting the same frozen surface they'd trusted all winter. It gave me a shiver, remembering the ice that had encased Paul.

I reached my parents' neighborhood, a bedroom community of stockbrokers, lawyers, and other commuters to Toronto's commercial towers. I parked behind their Lexus in the driveway. I had a key and let myself in. The marble-tiled foyer was quiet.

"Hello?" I called, setting down my violin case. I hung my jacket on the brass hat stand. "Anybody home?"

Dad appeared. "Shhh," he said, finger to his lips.

"What's up?" I whispered back.

He beckoned me around the corner to the living room. I followed, but I couldn't see what he meant. No one was there. No one seated at the grand piano or on the wingback easy chairs.

"Over here," Dad whispered. He crossed the room toward the wide windows that overlooked the river. The drapes were open, and he went straight to the peach silk folds. He dropped down on hands and knees and let out a roar like a cartoon lion. "I'm hungry for a snack of little boy!"

A high-pitched giggle burst from behind the drapes. I spotted bare little toes poking out underneath and had to smile. My two-year-old nephew, Liam.

Dad growled and pawed the drapes. More giggles behind. Dad swatted the fabric aside, revealing Liam crouched in a ball of thrilled expectation, his eyes bright.

Dad scooped him up and lifted him high, Liam screeching in glee. He wriggled, laughing, as Dad lowered him and buried his face in the boy's neck as though to bite him. Liam dissolved into belly laughs.

Dad set him down on his feet, and when Liam saw me he grinned. "Aunt Natty!"

I got down on my knees and opened my arms; Liam toddled over with a grin and flung his arms around my neck. I stroked the silky skin of his arms. "Hi there, sweet boy."

He pulled back and looked over my shoulder then back at me, searching deep into my eyes. "Mummy?"

It broke my heart.

Dad's too, I could tell. He closed his eyes as though in pain.

I squeezed Liam in a tight hug. "Hey, kiddo, look what I brought you." I dug in my shoulder bag and brought out a musical toy, an orange plastic fish. His birthday was in two weeks and for that I would bring the plush bunny I'd bought, but I couldn't bear to come today without a gift. This kid needed every ounce of love we could give. The fish came with a bulbous rubber drumstick, and I showed him how to thump the fish with it and rattle the fins and shake the beads inside, all of which made nifty sounds.

Dad smiled. "You always were a closet percussionist."

He sat down on the sofa, sinking into it with a sigh, and I could see the energy drain from him. The horseplay romp had taken its toll. My father's vitality had always defined him, first as a preacher and now as a motivational speaker, but Julia's death had leached the vigor from him. His wavy salt-and-pepper hair needed a trim. A dime-size spot of unshaved whiskers shadowed the corner of his jaw. His ironed shirts had given way to well-worn pullovers; his polished Oxfords to slippers. He was only sixty-four, but old age seemed to have stolen into my father's bones. I knew how profoundly he grieved. Julia had been his favorite. I'd always known it, though he'd done his best to hide it. It used to hurt when I was a kid, yet even back then I'd understood. Julia was spectacular.

And now, did I have the heart to tarnish his memory of her with my questions?

Liam happily thumped the fish drum. I stood and came to Dad and kissed his cheek. He was smiling at Liam. "Where's Mom?" I asked.

His smile faded. He nodded toward the bedroom. Started wearily to get up.

"Stay," I said. "I'll go say hello."

"If she's awake."

I opened her bedroom door quietly. The room was dark except for a wand of sunlight at the edge of the drapes. Her room had always held a wisp of her favorite perfume, Sortilège, but now there was an old-person smell: heavy, musty, sour. Mom lay on her side, curled up, turned away from me, her rose quilt pulled up to her ears. All I could see was the top of her head. I came to the beside. A single bed; Dad's room was across the hall. Her hair was mussed, and even in the dim light I could see the gray roots of the auburn hair. Before Julia died, Mom would never have let her roots show. It filled me with pity. So did the three amber plastic vials on the bedside table. What was she taking? Sleeping pills? Valium? Don't judge, I told myself. Whatever eases her pain.

I gently shoved the pills aside and set down the gift I'd brought her: a crystal bell the size of a pear. She was president of her handbell ringers' club, had been the group's mainstay for years. At least, until Julia's suicide. Dad and my brother and I had done our best to get on with life, and at first it seemed Mom had as well, but about a week ago, whatever had been holding her together had snapped.

I'd been there when it happened. We were clearing out Julia's music studio at her house. Terrible job. We'd been at it a few hours, separating the mementos we wanted to keep from stuff to be sent to Goodwill. We'd moved onto the bookcases, Mom plowing on stoically as we filled box after box with loose sheet music, bound books of music, books about music and musicians, and the little collection of china ducks. Julia loved ducks. I had left Mom alone for a few minutes as I carried a box downstairs to the living room to add to the others to be picked up, and when I came back up to the studio I saw Mom snap shut a book and stuff it into her purse. Something too treasured to give away? The glimpse I'd had of it was fleeting—a slim book with a reddish-brown leather cover—but her motionless stance struck me: a kind of suspended state. Then the doorbell rang, the Goodwill guys arriving, so I'd hurried back downstairs. Looking now at my mother, remembering, I knew that had been the moment her breakdown began. Now, every time I visited, she was in bed.

I left her asleep, closing the door softly behind me, and found Dad heading for the kitchen.

"Come on, Natty," he said, "let's have tea."

Liam padded after him, as close on his heels as a baby duck. The two of them had become inseparable. Liam's father, Simon, a clarinetist, was in California; he'd just signed a contract with the Sacramento Philharmonic Orchestra, so Liam was here until Simon got settled there. My questions about Julia's affair surged back. Had Simon known? I wanted to ask Dad if *he* had known, but I bit my tongue. Caring for Liam had been Dad's salvation in his grief. He'd always been great with us kids, fiercely protective, especially of his daughters. Watching him with Liam, it was hard to tell who was the more devoted, boy or man. Why trouble him now about Julia?

I picked up Liam in the kitchen doorway and set him on my hip. He reached around for my ponytail with curious hands. His soft little fingers brushing my neck felt lovely.

Dad was filling the electric kettle at the double sink. I looked around. The place was a mess. A pot encrusted with porridge sat in the sink atop dirty plates and cups. Unopened mail was slewed among newspapers and magazines on the granite-topped island. Beneath the island, dust balls lurked. Liam's colored wooden blocks were scattered haphazardly on the floor between the kitchen and the dining room. On the walnut dining table, beside a laundry basket overflowing with shirts and tea towels, half of a small tower of books—copies of Dad's most recent, *Hope of Ages Past* by Rafe Sinclair—had toppled.

The disorder saddened me. Mom had always been as painstaking with her housekeeping as she was with her appearance. Now Dad was virtually on his own.

"Sorry, no lemon," he said, scooping loose tea into my grandmother's china teapot. "I haven't got out yet to do the shopping." He managed a sly smile. "And I know you vegans won't take milk like the rest of us savages."

"Very funny." I was glad of his teasing. "Plain tea is fine." I set Liam down on the floor among the wooden blocks. He began stacking them, choosing all the red ones. I sat down beside him, crossed-legged like him, and handed him red pieces.

I watched Dad set things out on the granite-topped island: mugs, sugar bowl, spoons, and a glass plate of chocolate cookies. Biscuits, he called them, the Scottish term a fleck in the mosaic of our family culture. I didn't have much appetite for biscuits, not with Denise Leblanc's words dripping their poison in my head.

Your whore of a sister.

I had to find a way to ask.

"I've just come from Paul Leblanc's funeral," I said.

Dad, adjusting the mugs, had his back to me. I was relieved; it was easier than broaching this face-to-face. "I meant to ask you," he said, digging a spoon into the sugar. "What happened at the inquest?"

Last week, when Paul's death had made front-page news, I had phoned Dad to let him know I'd been summoned by the coroner to testify, and why: the fire, losing Val, going to Paul's house the next morning and finding him. "*You* found his body?" Dad had asked, shock in his voice. No, it was deeper than shock, more achingly personal. I could tell that from his next words, his voice almost hoarse. "Poor Natty. As if you haven't seen horrors enough." Julia, he meant. I was the one who'd found her, too.

When I'd called him that day about the inquest, I was hoping for comfort, for guidance. I answered his question now, hoping for the same. "The inquest found evidence of foul play. The police have opened an investigation."

Dad stiffly turned. "You mean, they think the man was murdered?"

"Yes. Awful, isn't it?" I stood up, leaving Liam stacking his blocks, and came to Dad. "And that's not all that's happened. At the funeral, Paul's widow told me . . . something disturbing. She said that Paul and Julia had been having an affair."

I saw he was struggling to absorb my statement, and I felt ashamed to be throwing dirt on Julia's memory, ashamed to have hurt him. And yet, something in his silence made me think that he wasn't actually surprised.

"Dad? Did you know about that?"

"I knew something was troubling her. Deeply. But we'd all seen it before. That demon, her depression . . ."

His gaze slid to Liam. The boy was watching us. At age two he couldn't possibly understand what we'd been talking about, but his innocent face was alert, as if he'd picked up on the tension between me and Dad. Now I was even more ashamed.

"Liam," Dad said gently. "Go get that orange fish Aunt Natty brought you, okay?"

"'Kay," Liam said, scrambling to his feet. He toddled out to the living room.

"The only reason I brought it up," I told Dad quickly, lowering my voice, "is that it makes me wonder about Denise Leblanc. I have no reason to doubt what she said. I could see her rage. So I can't help wondering . . . do you think it might have driven her to kill her husband?"

Something flickered in Dad's eyes, like a man shaken awake. "What a terrible thought," he said. "But then, I don't know anything about the woman."

"Neither do I, really." Now that I'd uttered my suspicion, it sounded half-baked, like something from a B movie: the cliché of the jealous wife. I had no facts. I knew nothing. And yet, wasn't it true that most murderers were related to the victim?

Dad went to the counter for the teapot, brought it to the island, and turned his back again as he set the teapot down.

I said, "The thing is . . ." and I realized *this* was what I wanted most to tell him. What I needed most to share. "The police came to my office the other day. A detective. He asked a lot of questions about Paul. Because I'd gone to see him the night he died . . . and because this detective thinks I was the last person to see him alive." I had to swallow to go on. "Dad, he thinks I did it."

His head snapped up. He twisted around. "What? No. No, that's ridiculous."

"Of course. But I'm afraid he's serious."

"Natalie. That's absurd. No, this cannot happen." He shook his head in appalled confusion. "Isn't there something you can tell them, some . . . what do they call it . . . alibi?"

I loved him for that. Loved him for being so concerned. For caring.

"Listen," he said, suddenly firm, "you need to get a lawyer."

Hank had said the same thing. He cared too, which meant a lot. But nothing meant more than seeing Dad's distress, because it came from love.

"Hey, don't worry," I said. "I'll be fine. I just thought you should know. This detective is only speculating. He'll soon find out there's nothing there." Liam came back, banging the fish with the fat rubber drumstick. Dad glanced at him blankly. Then back at me. He looked so upset, I was sorry I'd said anything.

"Forget it," I said. "Forget *all* of it. Let's have tea and then go practice."

I was pouring our two mugs of tea when my mother suddenly appeared in the doorway. My breath caught. Her hair was wild. Her nightgown rumpled. Her feet bare.

Her haggard eyes flicked between me and Dad.

"Julia," she said, her voice a croak. "Go home . . . don't let them hurt you . . . go—"

"Mom," I said in shock. In pity. "It's me, Natalie."

She blinked at me, looking lost. "But . . . we'll fix it . . . Julia, I promise—"

"Nora," Dad said, gently taking her arm. "Come. You should rest."

"I'll take you, Mom—"

"No," Dad said. "Stay with Liam. Sometimes he wanders."

He led Mom away. I heard them cross the living room, her bare feet shuffling on the carpet. I picked up Liam and held him close.

When Dad came back, he silently picked up his mug of tea. His hand trembled. Tears glinted in his eyes.

My heart broke all over again for my poor, broken family.

At home that evening I opened my laptop and waited for my brother-in-law to answer my FaceTime video call. Simon was a hard guy to reach. Whenever I phoned, I got voicemail. My texts got terse answers of three or four words. I knew his new job as clarinetist with the Sacramento Philharmonic was demanding, taking a lot of his time, but surely he could find a few minutes to check in.

I watched a few snowflakes drift past my dark window, looking like lost souls searching for refuge from the night. Night here, but just six o'clock in California, which I'd figured was a good time to catch Simon: too late for him to be in a rehearsal and too early to be playing a concert. I pushed away my half-eaten bean burrito. Evenings were so lonely without DuPre. I missed our evening walks. Missed her trotting beside me on my morning jog. Where was she? Would I ever find her?

"Hello, Natalie." Simon's unsmiling, neatly bearded face was suddenly before me, almost filling my screen.

"Hey, Simon. Thanks for connecting. How are you?"

"Busy."

Well, aren't we all, I wanted to shoot back, but I held my tongue. "I won't keep you. Just want to let you know that all is well with Liam. It's going to be fun to do a little party for his birthday."

"Yes. Though I don't suppose he'll really know what it's about."

"Sure he knows. Two years old and smart as heck. Anyway, next year, for his third, you can do the party there. That'll be nice. For both of you."

"Natalie, I have an appointment. Is there a reason for your call?"

He'd always been a type-A personality. Ambitious. A little obsessive. A perfectionist. And I reminded myself that this must still be so hard for him, losing Julia. That people handle grief differently. That I should be patient.

"The thing is, Simon, it's a lot for Mom and Dad, running after a two-year-old at their age. How's the house-hunting going? When do you think you'll be settled and can have Liam?"

"Hard to say. Terrible market for buyers right now."

"I see." He offered nothing more. "Well, keep us posted."

He nodded. Then looked sharply to his right and called to someone, "I'm coming." Then, to me, "I have a function to get to, Natalie. Fundraising auction."

"Okay, just one more thing. The memorial concert next week. I was thinking that when you come for that, Liam could fly back to California with you. He'll be fine in your apartment. Just arrange for babysitting or a housekeeper."

"Actually, I may not be able to make the concert. We've got the Stravinsky just three days later, *The Rite of Spring*, and it's fiendishly difficult, particularly the second half. Really, it's enough to make you dizzy with its constantly changing time signatures, so I'll be practicing the solos virtually nonstop to—"

"Simon," I blurted. I'd had enough. "Of course you're coming to the concert. You have to. It's for Julia."

He gave me the strangest look. Like a teenager glaring at a teacher who was giving him a hard time. Like no one understood how he thought, how he felt, how he suffered.

I had to admit, it was true. For Simon, but also for me, Mom, Dad, my brother. We were all enduring our own tortured solitudes.

Simon and I each took a breath, calming down, and spoke civilly again, me wishing him good luck in preparing his solos, and him saying he would do his best to attend the memorial.

I said goodbye, feeling both chastened and disturbed.

14

I stood on noisy Front Street in Toronto's downtown core and looked up at the golden tower of the Royal Bank Plaza. With its thousands of windows famously coated in a film of twenty-four karat gold, the tower was meant to impress, or maybe intimidate. It did neither for me, but it did brace me for the appointment I'd made with Logan Leblanc. The headquarters of his mining company, Gold Zone, was on the nineteenth floor.

I'd come into the city on the Greyhound bus—I hated driving in city traffic—and had lunch with my brother, James, at a sushi spot near the CIBC Wood Gundy offices, where he was a retail brokerage analyst. When I told him how shaken I'd been yesterday by Mom's pitiful state, he'd nodded sadly but said there wasn't much more we could do to help Mom and Dad as they managed their way through their grief. He was right. And I was eager to move on with work. Which was why I'd come to see Paul's brother.

I joined the suits in the elevator, my mind on the caged baby monkeys I'd seen that day in the sail loft. Though long gone to their sickening destinations, they were not forgotten—I would never forget those terrified little faces. But the smugglers' trail was getting colder every day. On the bus I'd read emails from animal rights colleagues in the States answering my queries about any connection they might have picked up between wild animal trafficking and ERV Financial Services. No one had heard of ERV. As for the sail loft, when Chandra had followed up, she'd hit a dead end: absentee owner, residence in Singapore. And when she asked the manager about the monkeys, he said he had no idea what she was talking about. As for the animal welfare inspector, I'd given up expecting him to do anything. So I was hoping Paul's brother might help me connect any of these dots.

"You pressed for the nineteenth, right?" a man said, interrupting my thoughts. He held the elevator door open for me.

"Sorry, yes. Thanks."

I stepped into a lobby half the size of an Olympic swimming pool. My first thought was that the decorator must have made a fortune. On the walls, huge panels of mirrors veined with gold reflected everything in a dizzying shimmer. Mural-size artwork shone with gold motifs: a spectacular sunrise, a glittering heap of ancient coins, a spangle of stars in a black sky. Ceiling spotlights pooled light onto a black onyx elephant table with golden tusks. A ring-shaped black marble reception desk encircled a very blonde woman about my age, though a lot prettier. A marble arch above the corridor that led to the suite of offices was etched with the words, in gold: "You Are Now Entering the Gold Zone."

The whole place, so over the top, made me think of Disneyland.

My boot heels clicked over the marble as I reached the receptionist. She swiveled in her chair to face me, looked up as though exasperated, and asked, "Yes?" Not the cheeriest welcome, I thought. Then I saw the smudged mascara and red-rimmed eyes. She'd been crying. "I'm here to see Logan Leblanc," I said, feeling sorry for whatever her personal burdens were. "He's expecting me."

She tapped her keyboard. I waited. Workmen in blue coveralls emerged from the corridor, one carrying an easy chair, a pair carrying a sofa, the furniture sheathed in clear plastic. They passed me, heading for the elevator.

"Miss Sinclair." A man's voice.

I turned to see Logan Leblanc coming toward me. He had that slow way of moving big men often have: measured, confident. He held out his hand in greeting. Remembering his overfriendly handshake at the funeral, I let my palm barely brush his then dropped it to my side.

"Thanks for seeing me," I said. "I didn't know if you'd remember me."

He gave me a smile that didn't quite reach his eyes. "I never forget a pretty face."

The cheesy line almost had me rolling my eyes. Maybe he saw, because he dropped the smile and added soberly, "And there was your horse, right? Tragic."

"Yes. Val. It was terrible." The words sounded more raw than I intended. I didn't want him to think I held Paul responsible. I was over that. "Paul was very kind. I run a small animal rights group and he offered to make a donation in memory of Val , but then he . . . you know." This was going in an awkward direction. I wasn't here about Val.

"Sorry about the commotion," Leblanc said as more workmen passed us carrying out more furniture. "We're moving."

"Oh? Leaving Toronto?"

"No, just need a bigger space." An airport? I wondered. "Although," he went on, "I'm actually not here much in the winter. Mostly at our offices in the Bahamas."

Right. His forever tan.

"Come," he said, gesturing to the corridor, "we can talk in my office. You can tell me what I can do for you."

"Thanks."

"Can I have Annemarie get you anything?" he said, glancing at the receptionist, who was watching us. "Coffee? Water?"

She had clearly heard him, but she quickly turned away. She looked almost frightened. Leblanc said to me quietly, "Sorry, she has issues. We may have to let her go."

"I'm fine," I said about the coffee, feeling uncomfortable for Annemarie.

His office boasted a wall of windows that overlooked Lake Ontario. Black slab marble desk. Gold track lighting. Black leather couch. No other furniture. The walls were bare, so any artwork had apparently been stripped and packed. Across the hall, behind a closed office door, I heard muffled shouting, two men in an angry argument. This definitely didn't feel like a happy workplace.

"So, what did you want to see me about?" Leblanc sat on the edge of his desk and gestured for me to take a seat on the couch. "Something about Paul, was it?" Folding his arms across his broad chest, he casually crossed his legs at the ankle, waiting for me to explain.

"I'm actually not sure." I didn't sit. I wanted to get to the point. "As I said, I run an animal rights group, and last week we discovered a trafficking operation, baby monkeys being smuggled." I described the sail loft location and explained the link we'd subsequently found to ERV Financial Services and the fact that his brother was listed as an executive. "So I'm trying to track this down."

"Paul?" He looked shocked. "Smuggling?"

"Don't misunderstand. I don't believe he was personally involved. But I wonder if the trafficking was going on without his knowledge—this ERV entity using him, his good reputation, as a front. I asked his assistant. She couldn't help me. Or wouldn't."

"That does sound troubling. Not sure I can shed any light, though."

"But aren't you connected to his business? You sit on the board of his company."

"Well, Paul and I didn't always see eye to eye on business. Or anything much."

It struck me how little grief he seemed to feel about Paul's death—his murder. I remembered that he hadn't given a eulogy or even a Bible reading at the funeral. It was pretty clear there was no love lost between them.

"Still, I'd like to help you if I can," he said. "Do you know anything else about this finance company? What is it—ERV? Where are they located?"

"Their head office is in Cyprus."

"Cyprus." He nodded knowingly. "Favorable business climate there."

A favorability that featured money laundering. I knew that much from Chandra. I took out my phone. "I wonder if you know any of these other names," I said, pulling up the prospectus. I handed him the phone.

He looked at the display. Shook his head. "Sorry, never heard of these guys." He gave me back the phone.

He had looked at it for maybe five seconds. It didn't seem enough time to take in more than a dozen names. It was as if his mind was spinning some calculation. Hiding something.

Two more workmen in coveralls walked in. "Sir, excuse me. We need the couch."

"Oh, Christ," Leblanc grumbled. He shot me an apologetic look. "Sorry. You can see how things are."

"It's fine," I told him. I tucked away my phone. I was done here. I was fairly sure he had lied, that he knew one or more of those names, or at least knew *something* about ERV. Maybe there were cross-business currents he didn't want to touch, colleagues he didn't want to burn. Whatever, I sensed I wasn't going to get anything out of him. "I should be going."

"Look, Miss—" Leblanc smiled. "It's Natalie, isn't it?"

"Yes."

"I meant what I said, Natalie. I'd like to help you. What you've told me sounds serious." The workmen were wrapping huge sheets of plastic around the couch and taping them, a grating, industrial sound. "How about we talk at my club? It's not far. We can have a drink. Discuss it."

I didn't want a drink. I didn't want to see his rich guys' club. "Thanks, but I have a bus to catch."

"The Greyhound terminal?"

"Yeah."

"Let me drive you."

I was trying to find a not-too-rude way to say no when he said, "That donation Paul offered you. Let me make it up to you. How much did he say he was going to give you?"

That surprised me. "That's really nice of you. But it was a lot."

"How much?"

"Thirty-five thousand."

"Fine."

He had clearly misunderstood, maybe thought I'd meant "hundred." I clarified, "No, thirty-five *thousand*."

"Yes, fine. I'll have my girl call your office for the info, and then our accounts department will make the transfer."

I was astounded. "Seriously?"

"About money?" he grinned. "Always."

It seemed insane—he barely knew me. But maybe thirty-five thousand dollars was small potatoes to the super-rich. Huge to the likes of me, though. A thrill tingled me. Thirty-five thousand dollars would save a lot of abandoned animals. "I won't say no to that. But . . . are you sure?"

"Totally. A tribute to Paul."

So he wasn't completely devoid of brotherly love. Which meant the donation, enormous though it was, kind of made sense. "Well, that's wonderful. Thank you so much."

"Great. I'll get this in the works with my people, then we'll get my car." He went to the open door and called down the hallway, "Annemarie."

I opened my shoulder bag to get a business card with my contact information. It took a couple minutes to fish out my wallet from under the work folders and the "lost dog" posters. I reached the doorway. Leblanc and the receptionist, Annemarie, were alone in the corridor. What I saw made me flinch. He had backed her against the far wall. She looked frozen. He had shoved his hand into her crotch. Shock flamed through me.

In a rush of outrage, I barged out to them. Leblanc's back was to me. "Annemarie, here's my card," I said cheerily, pretending I hadn't seen what I'd seen. Leblanc, hearing me, took a step back. I thrust my arm between them, holding out the card to the flush-faced Annemarie. "Mr. Leblanc's accountant can connect with Janice Cadogan, my office manager, for our bank details. Okay?" The poor woman blinked at me, then took the card, mumbling, "Thanks," and hurried back toward the reception lobby.

"Great, all set," Leblanc said. "Now let me take you to the bus."

I stared at him. He obviously didn't know I'd seen. I wanted to yell at the creep, not let him get away with it. Only . . . what *had* I seen? What did I know about his relationship with "his girl"? Some women liked rough play. Besides, if I said anything, I could kiss his donation goodbye. Shame nipped me at that thought. "No, it's okay . . ." I stammered. "I'll walk."

"Come on, it's cold out, you don't want to walk. And I want to hear more about the work you do."

Did he? If he was an animal lover, he couldn't be all bad. Still, this felt weird.

"You can tell me how you'll use my donation, all the good work you'll do with it," he said. "I'm all ears."

I could give him that much time. The bus terminal wasn't far. "Okay. Thanks."

His car was just a few doors down from the bank tower: a low-slung, canary yellow Porsche that would cost me three years' salary. A parking ticket was jammed under the windshield wiper. Leblanc opened the passenger door for me then went around the hood, grabbed the ticket, crumpled it, and stuffed it in his pocket.

A magazine-style brochure lay on the passenger seat. I picked it up and sank into the buttery yellow leather. Leblanc slid in behind the wheel. He nodded at the brochure in my hand as he started the engine. "Resort in Miami I'm building," he said, pulling out into the traffic. "Have a look."

It was a glossy spread: architect's drawings of a hotel tower, pool, pavilions. *Welcome to Luxury. Welcome to The Calliste.* I flipped through a few pages, trying to pry my mind off what I'd seen of him with Annemarie. He asked again about the work I did. I snapped out of it and told him about our programs that rehabilitated abandoned and abused animals; the vets who helped us, though rarely pro bono; and the "forever homes" we found for the animals.

"Sounds great. And how about this investigating you do? The animal smuggling. You involved in that much?"

"I'd like to do more. I think the baby monkey operation may be just the tip of the iceberg."

I closed the brochure on my lap. The back page was Leblanc's personal pitch to investors. His signature caught my eye. "That's interesting," I said.

He glanced at me. "Oh? You want to invest?"

As if. "No, I mean you have the same initials. You and Paul." I read it aloud: "P. Logan Leblanc."

"Yeah, I've always gone by Logan." He laughed. "You would too if your first name was Percy."

I saw the bus terminal ahead. I'd be glad to get out.

"Here we are." He pulled in behind a taxi at the curb. He looked at me, smiling. "The thirty-five thousand will be in your account tomorrow. I want to hear what results it gets you, so stay in touch."

"I will. Thanks again."

I entered the bus station feeling dirty. I had done wrong, and I knew it. I'd stayed silent about Annemarie. Too greedy for the guy's donation. No, beyond dirty—I felt a little sick. The money he offered had dazzled me, blinded me. Now I saw how wrong it was to accept money that felt polluted. I would call him from the bus, tell him to forget it.

And yet, the whole weird meeting filled me with a jangled curiosity. Who *was* this guy, anyway?

Once the bus pulled away and we started south on Bay Street, I googled "P. Logan Leblanc" on my phone and scrolled through the photos that popped up. A black-tie dinner where he lounged with other suits. A Blue Jays box seat where he sat flanked by two willowy young women who looked like twins. A Mediterranean-looking terrace where he stood smiling with his arm slung around the neck of a muscled movie star I recognized but couldn't name.

And then a picture that sent an icicle sliding up my backbone.

Leblanc stood on a parched African savanna with a triumphant grin, his boot on the neck of magnificent leopard the size of a pony. Its dead eyes were glazed. Its tongue lolled. I felt a lash of nausea. Then, two more shots of him with "big game trophies": a lioness, a tiger.

In that moment, three things clicked in my mind. Three cold facts, hard as steel:

Click. Not an animal lover, an animal killer.

Click. Not a detached CEO, a man hiding something about ERV.

Click. The initials. *P. Logan Leblanc . . . Paul L. Leblanc . . .*

Could it be? Was *this* the brother who trafficked animals? Had Logan Leblanc flown under the radar by forging Paul's name?

15

The chilling hunch I'd had on the bus, that Logan Leblanc had fraudulently used his brother's good name, spawned another hunch. As soon as I was back in Craigmuir I called Chandra. "Got a minute?" I asked.

"Just." She was at her law firm. This was not one of the days she scheduled pro bono for All Creatures Great and Small. "What's up?"

"I have two questions."

"Okay," she said warily. "I take it we're not playing Trivia."

"Far from it, my friend. So, first question. What word ends this sentence—"

"Sentence."

"Smartass. Here it is. If you want to find out if someone's a crook, follow the—"

"Money."

"Excellent. Question number two. What did Jesse James say when they asked him why he robbed banks?"

"Because that's where the money is."

"Excellent again. Banks."

"You sure we're not playing Trivia?"

"When the Superior Sails paper trail led you to ERV Financial Services, was there any indication of where ERV does their banking?"

"Hmm, I might have that info. Hold on." Papers rustled on her desk, followed by tapping on a keyboard. "Here it is. Bank of Cyprus in Strovolos, Nicosia. Also Deutsche Bank, Frankfurt."

I'd certainly heard of the second one. "Wasn't Deutsche Bank involved in a huge scandal for money laundering?"

"Big time. Journalists broke the international story in the 'Panama Papers.' The bank was unwittingly laundering billions from Russian oligarchs and drug cartels."

"So, how did that scam work?"

"Well, shell companies, typically based in the UK, made fictitious loans to each other, then defaulted on that enormous phony debt. Corrupt judges in Moldova authenticated the debt—with, by the way, billions transferred to Moldova via a bank in Latvia. Then Deutsche Bank was used to launder the money through its banking network, effectively allowing illegal Russian payments to be funneled to entities in the United States, the European Union, Asia."

"Could you check something out for me? There's a luxury resort being built in Miami called The Calliste. Is it possible to find out who's behind it? Where their money's coming from?"

"Nat, what's this about?"

I told her about my meeting with Leblanc, how weird it was that he'd offered an enormous donation, thirty-five-thousand dollars, when he barely knew me and wouldn't normally have given me the time of day. He was a loathsome "big game" hunter, for God's sake, the opposite of an animal lover. "It was like he wanted to pacify me, tame me," I said, "and I think it's because there's some connection with ERV. So, if ERV is the shell company we think it is, and they're laundering their cash through Deutsche Bank, I want to know where that money is being funneled *to*."

"Okay, but you're going to need an expert on this. You're talking about a forensic accounting investigation. That takes a specialist, and it'll cost."

I groaned inside. Another expense All Creatures couldn't afford. Damn it, I should accept Leblanc's donation after all. It gave me a cold thrill to think that his own money might expose him.

"You want me to recommend a firm?" Chandra asked.

"No." I didn't know what—if anything—Leblanc was playing at, and it left me feeling out of my depth. "Not yet."

And then, late that afternoon as I was finishing up at the office, came a sudden, glorious bolt from the blue. A call from the city pound.

"Natalie?" It was Tessa, a worker I'd often spoken to. "A dog was brought in that we think is—"

"DuPre?" I blurted it in a rush of joy. "You've found her?"

"A female border collie, black and white, about three years old, right?"

"Yes!"

"Can you come to the Dawson Street facility?"

I raced across the city, breaking the speed limit, running a light. I almost skidded as I took the corner too fast into the pound's lot.

In the lobby, the faint sounds of barking further back in the building had always filled me with sadness for the poor lost or abandoned dogs, but this time I was eagerly listening for DuPre's bark. Tessa met me, wearing blue scrubs like a nurse. "Is she alright?" I asked. "Is she hurt?"

"No, she's pretty dirty but not injured."

Thank God. "Where did you find her?" I asked as she ushered me through doors into the holding area.

"We didn't. It was a call from a gentleman who was walking his dog beside the river. He found her, all alone and looking lost, no owner around."

"I love this good Samaritan already," I said, grinning. Thank goodness for DuPre's collar, I thought. Her tag had my phone number. It didn't matter that this kind gentleman had called the pound instead of me. Nothing mattered except having DuPre back, and safe.

"Oh," I said, "there she is!"

I rushed between the rows of dogs in cages. She stood in a cage near the far end, her black nose, edged with its shag of white hair, pressed right up against the wire mesh.

But as I reached her, the truth slammed into me. A young black-and-white border collie, yes, but not DuPre. The joy drained from my heart, leaving an emptiness so heavy, I felt sick.

The pup's flanks were caked with dried mud. She wore no collar, no tag. She whined, her big brown eyes looking up at me. I crouched down, murmuring gently, "Oh, you poor thing," though the pity I felt was as much for DuPre, still lost, still out there somewhere, alone and frightened.

I pulled myself together. Thanked Tessa and the other pound workers. Asked them to continue keeping a lookout and call me, night or day, if they found her.

I went home feeling lost myself. I still clung to the hope that I would find DuPre somehow, somewhere, but the hope was a creation of sheer will and faith. I didn't dare consider the alternative.

The next morning I crossed busy McNair Street, heading for Hank Verhagen's constituency office. Snow had fallen overnight, and the slush squished underfoot as Craigmuir's downtown crowd—office workers, shoppers, university students—went about their day with the resigned understanding that spring was definitely *not* around the corner. April is the cruelest month, the poet said, but in my book it was now, March, when the daffodils of April still seemed an improbable fantasy. My night had been cruel enough, with nightmares of DuPre locked in a cage and tortured by electrical jolts wired by Logan Leblanc.

I stopped three doors away from Hank's office and checked my reflection in the display window of Galt Antiques. I pulled off the scrunchie that held my ponytail and shook my hair loose. I could never see Hank without hoping I looked okay. I wanted to push past the tangle of nerve-wracking issues in my life—the heartbreak at the pound, Paul's murder, his brother's possible scam, my family's tragedy—push them all to the back of my mind. I'd made an appointment and was coming to ask a favor.

Hank's assistant, Esther, a severely stylish woman, led me past a couple of his constituents talking to his other staffers and ushered me into his inner office. He stood talking on his phone beside a wall with a giant map of the district, and when he saw me he beckoned me in. On his desk, between folders and binders, a plastic take-out clamshell with scraps of rice and peas gave off the scent of Indian curry. His lunch, it seemed. Busy man. I knew he had to return to Ottawa soon, and was glad he'd fitted me into his schedule.

"Natalie," he said in greeting as he ended his call. Why did just hearing him say my name always give me that small shiver of pleasure? To cover, I pulled out the chair opposite his desk.

"No, don't sit," he said. He sounded concerned. Maybe preoccupied with work. "I hoped we might take a walk. I've got a few minutes before afternoon appointments, and the sun's shining."

"Sure. Sounds good."

We walked toward the river, making awkward small talk. He asked if my recent fundraising appeal to pay our on-call vets had been successful. Not too bad, I said; money's trickling in. I asked how Lily was doing with Monty. Great, he said; they're best friends. We walked in silence past St. Timothy's. We'd both been at Paul's funeral there just two days ago. Hank finally said, very seriously, "Natalie, have you called one of the lawyers I suggested?"

That's what was on his mind? "Not necessary," I assured him. "I haven't heard from Detective Rourke in days. I think I'm off his list."

He smiled, a wholehearted smile of relief. "Oh, good."

It pleased me that he cared. And yet, now that he'd mentioned the investigation, I couldn't help thinking again of Paul's wife. Was it possible that she had killed him? Was Rourke, in fact, now focusing on her? I wondered how much Hank knew about Denise Leblanc. He'd been friends with Paul, not actual buddies but old school friends, so was he also friends with Denise? And had he known about Paul's affair with Julia? But it was impossible to ask any of that.

"You like ice cream?" he said brightly. He pointed to the squat building painted a funky turquoise, a popular riverside spot called The Boathouse. "Andy has the best."

"Chilly day for ice cream."

"We'll pretend it's summer, okay?"

How could I resist?

The owner, Andy, greeted Hank with a bearhug, like a long-lost brother, and as he handed us our orders—Hank's chocolate ice cream cone and my raspberry sorbet in a paper cup with plastic spoon—a couple of older ladies having coffee waved at Hank and he nodded back with a cheery smile. I admired his easygoing sociability. I'd never been much of a people person. For a politician, of course, it was the job description, and I could see he truly enjoyed it.

The humid little room was packed with the lingering lunch crowd. No free tables. It didn't faze Hank; he suggested the patio. "So, what did you want to talk to me about?" he said as he opened the patio door for me.

"I have a favor to ask."

"Absolutely. Shoot."

There were a few snow-covered picnic tables and a half dozen red canoes, turned over like beetles, awaiting spring thaw. I went to the railing that bordered the river. A couple of mallard ducks shuffled along the ice and disappeared into rushes at the far shore. Hank came beside me, licking a splotch of ice cream off the back of his hand. We'd both stuffed our gloves in our coat pockets. The sorbet cup was cold in my hand. Tasted great, though.

"Could you arrange a meeting for me with the dean of the veterinary college at the U?" I asked.

He thought for moment as though scrolling through a mental list of contacts. "That would be Garrison Walker."

"Right."

His quick frown told me the idea didn't thrill him. "Is this about your appeal for funding? I really can't get involved in—"

"No, nothing like that. It's personal. It's about my dog, DuPre, a young border collie. She went missing the day I . . . about a week ago. I really want to find her."

"I'm sorry to hear that. But what makes you think Garry Walker can help?"

"The college uses animals for research. They used to get them from bunchers—that's the name for guys who grab lost pets. You know, the dog who burrows under the fence and wanders off. The cat who slinks out the door and chases a bird too far. These guys catch those pets and sell them to labs."

"Seriously? People's pets?" He looked shocked. "That's awful."

"It is. But not strictly illegal." The thought had come to me as I'd woken up this morning. I kicked myself for not thinking of it before, but my mind had been stuck in the rut of imagining DuPre hit by a car and lying in a ditch, or lying hurt in the woods behind Paul's house, coyotes circling in for the kill. I simply hadn't thought about bunchers. "The college doesn't buy animals that way anymore," I went on, "but Dean Walker would know of other labs that do, and that might help me track down DuPre." It was true that Walker would have connections to other labs, but asking him about them wouldn't be my only question. I'd heard that his college did still buy animals from bunchers under the radar, so there was a chance that his own facility might have DuPre.

"Sounds like a good idea," Hank said. "But why do you need me to set it up? Don't get me wrong, I'd be glad to help you find Dooley—"

"DuPre."

"Right. DuPre. But why not just call Walker's office yourself?"

"Come on, Hank. My reputation. I'm the wild-eyed radical. The crazy animal woman. He'd never take my call. But you, the MP for Craigmuir, he'll be happy to see."

He looked a little annoyed. "So you want me as a smoke screen. The Trojan horse to bring you in." He added wryly, "Forgive my mixed metaphors."

I was sure he was going to turn me down. It pissed me off. This wasn't a big ask—he could easily finesse the meeting. Besides, he wouldn't even be in the position to impress the likes of a college dean if I hadn't had my supporters get out the vote for him and put him in Parliament.

Maybe he read my frosty face. "Natalie, I know I owe you."

"But?"

"No buts." He smiled that trademark warm smile. "I'll be happy to set up a meeting."

I relaxed. We had a deal. Although I had to admit that his smile alone thawed me.

He'd finished his ice cream. I'd finished my sorbet. He took my paper cup and tossed it in the recycling bin. He looked me in the eye. "Now, you could do *me* a favor."

"Oh? Like, shut up at the meeting and let you talk?"

He laughed. "I wouldn't ask anything so impossible as you not speaking your mind. No, this is about something else. It's your time I want. And your company. Tomorrow there's an event at the art gallery, a show opening. The artist is the son of a constituent. I know it's awfully late notice, but if you're free, would you consider going with me?"

I was so surprised I almost laughed. "Me?" The word sprang from a happy flutter in my chest.

"Or not," he said carefully, as though unsure where he stood.

"No, I mean . . . yes, I'd love to."

"Okay. Good. Great. Seven o'clock?"

"Fine."

"I'll pick you up."

I gave him my address and he tapped it into his phone. I'd never been to the art gallery. And a show opening sounded glitzy. Gowns and tuxedos? I'd have to wear a nice dress. And buy some shoes.

"I should get back to the office," he said. "Meeting with the Craigmuir Business Association folks." He added with a wink, "Filthy capitalists." He tugged on his gloves. "Walk back with me?"

"No, I should get back too. Zoom meeting with my board." I did a mock eye-roll. "Crazy animal lovers."

He laughed.

"Hank, before you go, are you any closer to putting together the bill we discussed? Legislation to limit animals in research?"

"I'm still going through the material you sent. Give me a little more time."

I bit back my concern. Was he sincere about this issue, or just stalling? "Sure," I said. "And one more thing. Can you recommend a lawyer who's an expert in constitutional law? We're going to challenge Bill 156."

"The new Ontario bill? What do they call it, the Security—"

"Security from Trespass and Protecting Food Safety Act. Bullshit name. We call it the ag-gag law. It's an anti-whistleblower act intended to keep anyone from videoing what animals suffer on farms and in slaughterhouses. It's the work of the agriculture lobby. They know the public outcry those video images create, so they're dug in. We're going to need a top lawyer to take this to court."

"Well, I can have Esther send you some names."

"Thanks. Listen, Hank, fighting this is going to be a tough slog. It would be a huge boost if I had a public statement from you in support of us."

He shook his head. "Sorry, Natalie, it's provincial jurisdiction."

"It's simple humanity."

"You may be right. And I wish you well. But I can't help you there."

"Well," I said dryly, "thanks for the sorbet, anyway."

He smiled. "See you tomorrow evening."

He went back downtown. I took the winding, scenic route. It ran through Riverside Park, where a few lunchtime walkers were out. I stepped onto the covered bridge that spanned the river. The bridge was one of my favorite landmarks in the city. Volunteers from the international Timber Framers Guild had built it about thirty years ago, basing it on a nineteenth-century design. Whenever I walked across it, with its dark wooden roof and heavy beams and latticed sides almost enclosing me, it felt like stepping back in time. I was about halfway across when I heard footsteps thud behind me, loud because of the hollow, echoing effect in the enclosed space. I glanced over my shoulder. A man in a dark brown ski jacket and black toque, his face in shadow.

I walked on, my thoughts swirling back to Hank. His lukewarm support for the issues I'd raised bothered me. Sure, he had to be mindful of his constituents with competing agendas. The farming community around here would not be happy if he spoke out against the ag-gag law. Hell, the farm lobby across the whole country might give him flack. They were all stakeholders. But so was I, damn it. The trouble was, I had none of their enormous lobbying power.

Still, I sensed Hank's heart was with us, with the work we did to protect the animals. So I told myself: *Don't push him; let him get there his own way.* Besides, he'd agreed to get me in to see the college dean, and I was so hoping that meeting might lead me to DuPre. Plus, he'd asked me out. A date. Amazing. Suddenly the gulf between his world and mine had shrunk, and I found myself smiling. New shoes, definitely.

I reached the far side of the bridge. The riverside path branched, one arm leading into woods, the other skirting the trees. Normally I would have enjoyed a stroll through the silent depths of the woods, but the footsteps kept on behind me, and something made me feel it was better to stay in the open and not dawdle. The path brought me to Argyle Street. The light was green, and as I crossed with a few other pedestrians, I glanced behind me again. The man kept his distance, but I hadn't imagined it.

He was following me.

Now I could see his face. A scar on his cheek, the raised flesh a livid purple in the cold. My heart skidded. The thug from the sail loft. The monkey trafficker.

I threaded through the people and hurried the last three blocks to my office, knowing he was still following. I quickly turned down Gordon Lane. When I reached the office door, I looked back to the mouth of the lane.

He was gone.

16

"It's Nat!"

"Tell her!"

I walked into the office to find a dozen excited volunteers gathered around the communal table. Lady Gaga's raunchy "Marry the Night" was turned up full blast, and Nathan and Ruth were dancing. Someone had opened a bottle of wine. They all looked pretty happy about something.

"What's up?" I asked, taking off my coat. I turned my back to hang it up. I needed a minute to get a grip after seeing the scar-faced guy. How long had he been following me? Just from The Boathouse? Or all the way from Hank's office?

"Fantastic news, Nat," Heather said, bringing me a paper cup of red wine. "A moratorium on the cormorant cull. It was on the noon news. We won!"

"Really?" If it was true, it *was* great news. "Annika, what did they say?" She'd been the point person on our campaign. The rich folks in cottage country didn't like the big birds shitting on their docks, so they'd banded with the fishermen's lobby, who complained to the Ontario government that the birds ate all the fish. That nonsense claim had been debunked by every credible biologist, but votes trump science to politicians, so the government initiated a cull. Hunters loved it: open season on cormorants. We had launched a campaign to halt the slaughter, and it had quickly gained a lot of support.

"Here, have a look," Annika said, swiveling her laptop on the table to show me the video she'd cued up.

I watched the news anchor's statement. It was very brief, less than a minute, but oh so welcome. Few of our initiatives resulted in this kind of unalloyed success.

The partying around me picked up again, and it did my heart good to see these volunteers celebrating. There had been a tense undercurrent between them and me for the last few days, since I'd taken each person aside to question them about the cash missing from Janice's desk. I didn't for a moment suspect any of them of the theft, but I had to try to get to the bottom of it. Janice still insisted Nabil Ahmadi was the culprit. He hadn't returned to finish the kitchen cabinet job. Maybe we would never know what happened to the 412 dollars. Whatever, I felt the whole unpleasant business was finally behind us, and this little party had got everyone back to a happy place.

"A toast!" I said, raising my paper cup of wine. "To all of you. To your insanely dedicated commitment. What a great team. I mean it, you guys. You're just the best. Cheers!"

They grinned and toasted one another and drank. Lady Gaga hit her high note. Amber shrieked a matching note and shook her booty, which brought laughter and hooting and applause. I gave Annika a small, private salute for her fine work and she returned the gesture, beaming. I would have to sit down with her later and get all the details. The moratorium might be just the government's stalling gambit, so we couldn't let down our guard, but that work could wait. Right now, the cheerfulness around me was balm.

Trevor came up to me. "Nat," he whispered in my ear, "could I talk to you for a sec?" He looked nervous. I so hoped it wasn't about the missing money.

"Sure," I said. We moved a little away from the others, though their chatter and the music hardly made it necessary. "What's up?"

"I'm afraid I . . . I may have got you in a bit of trouble. That cop who was here last week? He called about an hour ago, asked for me. Asked a bunch of questions. All about you. I tried to—"

He didn't finish. The whole room has suddenly quieted. Everyone was looking toward the front door. Detective Rourke had walked in.

"Just a few more questions, Ms. Sinclair. And, please, the whole truth this time."

What the hell did that mean? Rourke's tone was much more stern than the first time he'd questioned me. It made me wary. Constable Crocker had come with him again, her vigilant eye on me as she opened her notebook. The three of us stood in the kitchen nook. Silence around the corner in the office. No more partying.

"I'm following up on some troubling history," Rourke said. "Three years ago you were arrested near Toronto and charged with criminal mischief."

I let out a puff of disbelief. "Seriously? I gave water to a pig."

"You stopped a tractor trailer on a major route, endangering lives."

"The only lives in danger were the sixty pigs. And the road was more like a lane, the access road to a slaughterhouse."

"You make light of it. But the law was clear."

"I do not make light of it. I take torture very seriously. It was a scorching summer day, and the pigs were suffering extreme thirst. I let a couple of them suck from bottles of water." My four friends with me had done the same. The pigs had strained their snouts through the open metal slats, frantic to reach our bottles. It was pitiful. "It was an act of mercy."

"Inviting a penalty of up to ten years in prison."

"The trial took five minutes. The judge looked annoyed that it even came to his court. I was acquitted. Anyway, why are you dredging that up? It has nothing to do with Paul Leblanc."

"Your emotional attachment to animals might. When I spoke to you before, you said you had no problems with him."

What a weird segue. "I meant it. We got along fine."

He was keenly watching me, frowning. I suddenly felt cold. He didn't believe me. And he was looking for Paul's killer. "This is crazy. There was absolutely no animosity between me and Paul. Good God, I *liked* him."

"There's evidence that you felt otherwise."

"What? What evidence?"

"Regarding the loss of your horse in the fire." He had brought an iPad. He tapped it a couple times, then turned it to show me. On the screen was video: picture and sound. Mont-Joli, Paul's country house. The stable on fire. Billowing orange flames and people shouting above the roar of the fire. Then me. And Paul. I was screaming at him, "Your fault! *Your fault!*" I lunged at him, fists up, and beat his shoulders, pounding him over and over, screaming, "*Murderer!*" Someone yanked me off him. Paul staggered back. The picture veered off, wobbling, back to the fire. Rourke stopped the video.

"Leblanc's neighbor took the video on his phone. When I questioned him, he said that you were hysterical. That it took two men to stop your attack on Leblanc and pull you away."

My heart thudded painfully. My mouth felt as parched as the air at the fire.

Rourke handed the iPad to the constable, his eyes never leaving my face. "Your employee here, Mr. Wapoosh, told me he accompanied you ten days ago to a Toronto location where you witnessed some imported animals being moved. Monkeys. He said that you thought the importation was connected to a widespread trade in wild animals. He said the sight of the monkeys made you very upset."

It was hard to find my voice. "Volunteer."

"Pardon?"

"Trevor Wapoosh is not my employee. He helps us voluntarily."

Rourke ignored my correction. "He told me that you said—" He looked at the constable. She looked at her notebook and read aloud: "People who hurt animals deserve a special place in hell."

Rourke went on. "That very evening, your horse died in Paul Leblanc's stable fire. Later that night, Leblanc was killed."

Silence. He watched me. I felt a dizzying slippage of control, as though the floor beneath me had turned to sand.

"Ms. Sinclair, were you so enraged by the death of your horse, and your belief that Paul Leblanc was involved in a trade you abhor, that you went to his house that night and killed him?"

I snatched hope from a surge of logic, of reason. "I was the one who *found* him."

He said quietly, steadily, "It wouldn't be the first time a killer returned to the scene of the crime."

I swallowed hard. This could not be happening.

He let out a troubled sigh. "Look, as I told you before, I only want to eliminate you from our inquiry, but you've got to help me do that. You've got to tell me the whole truth. So, let's go through it again. I want to go back to your late-night visit to Leblanc. You told me you asked him if he had a connection to a company called ERV Financial

Services, and that it was because you suspected a connection to the animal trade you had witnessed. Is that correct?"

"I only wanted . . . yes, I asked him that one question. And he said he'd never heard of them. Period. End of conversation."

"Was it? Seems odd that you would abandon a topic that concerned you so deeply. You didn't press him for more information? If so, did he *give* you more information?"

ERV. The name zinged in my head like a ricocheting bullet. Should I tell him my suspicion about Paul's brother? "There is something . . ."

"Yes? What is it?"

What could I say? That I found Logan Leblanc repulsive, plus he had the same initials as his brother? Hardly incriminating. No, I had nothing. And yet the bullet ricocheted again. ERV . . . the sail loft . . . the scar-faced guy. "There's something I want to report. A man was following me, just now. Through Riverside Park. I'm sure it was one of the men at the location where we saw the monkeys. Superior Sails."

He looked slightly startled. "Did this man accost you?"

"No. But like I said, he was following me. All the way here."

"Do you know his name?"

"No."

"Can you describe him?"

I did, with as much detail as I could recall, and Constable Crocker wrote it down. But I could tell from Rourke's expression that he was barely interested. Or worse, he thought I was blowing smoke, since this had no connection to Paul's murder.

"Let us know if it happens again," he said. "You have my card." He thanked me for my time. The constable tucked away her notebook. As they started to go, Rourke stopped to say, "And Ms. Sinclair, please don't make any plans to leave Craigmuir."

I watched them go, a twist of fear in my chest. Were Hank and Dad right? Was I was going to need a lawyer?

17

"Still no answer." Janice slammed down the phone with disgust.

I was passing her desk on my way out and stopped. Everyone else had gone for the day, and before driving home I wanted a walk to calm my nerves after Rourke's questioning, but Janice's dramatic tone was meant to draw my attention. I took the bait. "What's the problem?"

"The Syrian. I've left a half dozen voicemail messages. Not a peep in return."

Nabil Ahmadi. The missing 412 dollars. She still believed he'd absconded with it. "Give it up, Janice," I said as I got my coat. "You did your best. He's obviously avoiding us."

"That's for sure."

"Or maybe he's sick. Didn't that occur to you?"

Nabil had never looked well to me. He was sad and skinny, with a long gray face, as though the terrors he had fled in Damascus had hollowed him out.

"No," she said, then added darkly, "but something else did."

Again, the melodrama. Again, I bit. "What do you mean?"

"I mean, we don't know anything about him."

"That's not quite true. He's a diligent worker." As a refugee with broken English, he'd had a terrible time finding work, one of the reasons I'd hired him. And he took pride in his craftsmanship, though the job here was beneath him. A master woodworker in his native country, he'd been reduced to installing kitchen cabinets in our little low-rent office.

"I'm not talking about his work. Something else. Maybe theft isn't his only crime."

Enough cat and mouse. "Janice, if you know something, tell me."

"Well, this wasn't his only job, was it? He was working at Mr. Leblanc's, too, on the reno of his house, remember?"

Sure I remembered. I'd recommended him to Paul, and Paul, good guy that he was, had asked the contractor to take him on. "Not a house reno," I corrected her, "just a new deck."

The deck. Saying the word sent a splinter of ice up my backbone. The frigid shadows beneath the overhang. Paul's body.

"All I'm saying is, he was there. And I imagine Mr. Leblanc's house is pretty fancy, right? Artwork. Silverware. His wife's jewelry. Maybe the Syrian tried to steal from him too. Maybe Mr. Leblanc caught him in the act and then . . . you know."

I stared at her. "You can't be serious."

"Why not? Killed him and took off. It all fits."

I almost laughed. "You've been watching too many movies."

I wasn't laughing, though, as I left the office. I'd meant to take a brisk walk downtown to clear my head, then loop back for my car, but my footsteps led me across town to Pine Street, an area of tattoo shops, potholed pavement, and boarded-up stores. If ever there had been a pine tree here, it had long ago become kindling. A bony gray cat padded down the chipped concrete steps of a shabby little house, eyed me, then darted across the street and down an alley. On the next block I stood in front of the Pinecrest Motel. I knew the address from the checks I'd signed and tucked into Nabil's pay envelope.

It was a sorry-looking place, an L-shaped string of rooms with scabbed wooden doors and scum-fogged windows. My skin itched just imagining the dirty carpeting and stained bathtubs. It also made me incredibly sad. This was no home. Poor Nabil. *We don't know anything about him*, Janice had said. Did he have a wife back in Syria? Children? Was he sending his meager pay to them while living in this seedy place? Could he be facing actual hunger? I thought of Jean Valjean, who'd stolen a loaf of bread and been condemned to the death-in-life of forced labor in prison.

Stop it, I told myself. This wasn't nineteenth-century France, and 412 dollars was no mere loaf of bread. Nabil certainly was avoiding us, and *someone* had killed Paul Leblanc. Was Janice's theory really so far-fetched? Working on our kitchen cabinets, Nabil had always kept to himself. The language barrier, of course, but was there more to it? Did he hate the world for blighting his life? Hate us all?

I reached the door with a plastic "203" nailed to the leprous pink paint.

I told myself I wanted to make sure he wasn't sick, wasn't lying in there with no one to take care of him, but that was only partly true. If there was a chance that Janice was right, it meant I'd be off Rourke's hook. I felt a worm of shame. Was I going to betray a man to save myself? But not ashamed enough to stop me from knocking on his door.

The door opened a crack. "Hey?" Dark eyes peered at me above the safety chain. "What you want?"

"I'm sorry to bother you. Is Nabil Ahmadi here?"

"Why?"

"He works for me. Is he alright? I just wanted to check."

The chain slid with a metallic scrape. The door opened. A young man, swarthy, bearded, blinked at me in the pale sunlight. Baggy sweater. Striped pajama bottoms. Bare feet. He had the same furtive look I'd seen on Nabil. The wary vigilance of the refugee. "Check?" he asked.

Oh, no, did he think I'd come with a paycheck?

"I was just afraid he might be sick." There were two single beds behind the guy, one unmade, messy. "Is he here?"

He shook his head. It took several efforts from us both for me to follow his halting English, but I finally understood him to say that Nabil had not paid his share for the room in over a week, and that he had not seen Nabil in all that time.

"When was the last time you did see him?"

He remembered the day because of the ice storm. "When he go work for Mr. Leblanc."

A shiver touched my scalp. It was the day Paul was killed.

18

"Try the *pakoras*," Hank said, leading me to the buffet, his hand on the small of my back. "I know the caterer. Masala Palace. The best."

"Mmm, I will." The crispy veggie appetizers looked delicious, though Hank's broad palm, warm through my dress, was tantalizing enough. The art gallery, brightly lit and cheerfully crowded, buzzed with chatter for the opening of the artist's exhibition. The din reminded me of a cormorant flock settling to roost, the same excited communal prattle. I was enjoying my own quiet excitement just being with Hank. "Here," he said, and tonged a *pakora* onto my plate.

The crowd around us was dressy, though not in the tuxedos and gowns of my naive fantasy, just business suits and cocktail dresses. There were also a fair number of saris, kurtas, and turbans. Hank had told me that the artist's father, a condo developer, was a powerhouse in the Sikh community and one of Hank's major supporters. At this spot by the buffet, Hank and I stood beside a chattering group of women in silk saris, and I loved the vivid colors: jade, saffron, ruby, turquoise. The colors of high summer on this drab end-of-winter night.

"I've never felt more WASP-y," I whispered to Hank.

"Speak for yourself," he said with a wry smile.

I laughed. The Jew and the Gentile darkly dressed beside this bright throng of Hindus and Sikhs. But Hank looked dashing in his charcoal suit, and I felt fine in my all-purpose little black dress. It wasn't trendy, but I knew I looked good in it, and if my mirror hadn't told me so, Hank's face had when he'd arrived at my door. His smile had sent butteries flitting inside me. The dress, his smile, the spice-scented air, the buffet's candlelight reflecting off the atrium glass above us, it all made me feel lighter. Floaty. Free from work headaches and private worries.

I hadn't told Hank about my latest interrogation by Detective Rourke. Hank believed that was all behind me, that I was no longer a suspect, and I wanted to believe it too. Fight or flight were two responses to a predator, which is what Rourke's verbal attack had felt like, but neither response had kicked in. I'd simply shut down the scared part of me, hoping that would somehow vaporize the threat. For tonight, at least, I would keep that worry bottled up, private.

Hank's work, though, was very public, and he was subtly working the room. When we'd arrived, I'd seen people cast curious glances our way, several whispering to one another, and I was pretty sure the topic was: Who's the MP's date? As we'd moved through the crowd, Hank gave friendly nods to faces we passed and cheery waves to others across the room, and by the time he introduced me to the host—a tubby, gray-bearded man in a purple turban and a kurta embroidered with peacocks—and the gentleman gave me a courtly little bow, I felt like minor royalty.

Mr. Singh introduced us to his son, Jagdeep, whose artworks on the walls were riotously colorful images of Punjabi city streets and temples. As Hank chatted with father and son, it looked to me like the grinning young artist was as high as a Taj Mahal minaret. The Sikh prohibition against alcohol was being observed, but I figured some good weed had Jagdeep happily in the clouds. I returned his grin. I was having a good time too.

Hank and I took our plates of appetizers up a curved staircase to the mezzanine, which was less crowded, and went to the railing that overlooked the ground floor. We munched the nibbles as we looked down at the milling throng.

"You know everybody, don't you?" I said.

"Quite a few. Goes with the territory."

"Do you like being in government?"

"I do. I like getting things done."

"I'm sure you got lots done when you were in business." The Dutch Garden Centre, his family's business, was a thriving network of outlets across southern Ontario. Hank had run it with his brother, Art, until he threw his hat into the political ring in the last election and became our rookie MP. It was all in his bio.

"Different skill set," he said. "I'd worked at the Centre for so long, it stuck. Weekends during high school, summers during university. My brother, too. Our parents kind of groomed us to take it over."

"Makes sense."

"For Arty it definitely did. And does. He has the real business brains. It's in his blood, going back to our grandparents. Back in the sixties they started with just one big vegetable garden stand out on Concession Road 7."

"Wow. And built a family empire."

He smiled. "Kind of." He set his empty plate on the cocktail table next to us. He looked at me. "How about your family? I know of your father, of course—I watched his TED talk—but I mean going back further. Were your people go-getters like you?"

"Well, my great-great-grandfather made a killing. Literally. He got rich bashing the life out of beavers and selling the pelts."

"You're kidding."

"Nope. Came from Scotland with barely two ha'pennies to rub together and eventually slaughtered enough beavers and muskrats to build a mansion. I guess I'm doing penance for his sins."

He laughed. I enjoyed how he enjoyed that.

"Anyway, karma caught up with him. He invested in the wrong railroad. It went bust, and he lost everything."

"You call it penance, but I can see you love it. Saving animals."

"I do," I said, then, echoing him, "I like getting things done too. That's thanks to people who actually do the saving."

He cocked his head, looking curious. "You don't do it?"

"I just make it possible. I take the donations our wonderful supporters give us and use the money to fund all kinds of good folks. Kathleen Dahl runs our Forever Homes project, finding homes for abandoned and abused cats and dogs. Daryl Macpherson saves horses from the kill pens so they can live out their days on his acreage. Emile and Raquel Pereira rehabilitate orphaned bear cubs at Bear With Us."

"The bear thing. I think I've heard of them."

"Good, they rescue a lot of starving cubs during the spring bear hunt. What I'd like to do lots more of is public advocacy, like to stop that damn hunt. The word is such a grotesque distortion of what these guys do. They don't *hunt*—they bait a spot in the woods then climb a ladder up a tree and get settled on a comfy platform, a blind, and wait, and when a bear ambles out for the bait, they shoot it. More often than not it's a female, leaving motherless cubs."

"I'm guessing you're not popular with hunters."

"You guess right. Although one actually became a convert. It was last spring. This guy was up in a blind alone. He'd parked his truck a half mile away and hiked in, waited all afternoon up in the blind, downed a few beers and dozed off. When he woke up, night had fallen, and he was too scared to climb down in the pitch dark. The only local number he could think to call for help was Bear With

Us—the Pereiras had put their card in the blind. They came, got him down, and walked him out to his truck. The next day he sent checks, one to them and one to us at All Creatures Great and Small, and since then he's become one of my monthly donors."

Hank chuckled, relishing it. "That's a great story." His expression softened. "So, it seems we both like getting things done."

I loved that. That he felt we had this in common.

He took my empty plate and set it atop his on the cocktail table. "Natalie, I know you're anxious to find your dog," he said. "I've set up the meeting you want with Garry Walker at the veterinary college. We'll go together. I have to be in Ottawa for the next couple of days, so I made it for Thursday afternoon, when I'm back. Is that alright?"

"Perfect. Oh, Hank, thank you."

He took my hand. His grip, gentle and warm, shot a spark from my heart down to my groin. "My pleasure," he said quietly, and his eyes, looking deeply into mine, caught my breath.

A flurry of movement in the crowd below caught our attention. Mr. Singh held a microphone, and guests had gathered around him as he launched into a speech, beaming with pride at his son. Hank and I pretended to pay attention, but he still held my hand. Such a simple thing, yet it felt so erotic. Mr. Singh talked on. I think. I didn't hear much. I hoped he'd talk forever.

"Hank," a man behind us said jovially as the speech below ended. Hank and I turned, slipping our hands free. "Joe. Muriel," Hank said, shaking hands with the man and his wife. He introduced us and we all made polite small talk, until I noticed a face across the room that startled me. Denise Leblanc. She was moving past the paintings at the far wall.

How could she? Out partying, when her husband had been murdered just over a week ago. I remembered she was an artist, so I guess it made sense to come to this event. And of course I wouldn't expect her to mourn at home for months like some Victorian widow. Still, the way she calmly sauntered as she examined the paintings, her chic white satin pantsuit and careful makeup—it all spoke of a hard-nosed composure that brought my suspicions snaking back.

"Excuse me for a minute," I said to Hank.

I made my way toward her. She had stopped to study one of the paintings.

"Denise," I said. She didn't hear me above the din of chatter. I touched her elbow.

She flinched and turned. She looked surprised to see me. Annoyed, too, like I was a mangy dog that had fouled the floor.

"Natalie," she said coldly.

"Listen, I want to apologize," I said. "At the funeral, when we spoke, I was rude." True enough. When she'd dropped her bombshell about Julia, I'd been so stunned I'd turned on my heel and marched away. "Look, I don't want to get into . . . any of that. I just want you to know that I understand how you must have felt. You'd lost Paul just a few days before. It must have been such a terrible shock that morning when the police told you." I vividly remembered how, as I'd stood beside the ambulance while officers cut Paul's body down, I'd watched two others go up the walkway to the front door and ring the bell. "I mean, you were there," I barreled on. "In the house. All night."

The charge was so nakedly inept, I might as well have shaken her and yelled, *Did you kill him?*

She got it. Her astonished look said so. But maybe she was a good actress. Anyway, I wasn't going to backtrack. I needed to know this.

"As it happens," she said with great control, "I was not."

"Not what?"

"In the house."

"You were. I saw you. When I was talking to him."

"And then you left," she said, as though explaining to a dull child. "And then I left."

"At that hour? With an ice storm brewing?" She had to be lying.

"I often take the late flight to Montreal to visit my daughter. We were delayed at Pearson for—what do they call it ... de-icing?—but not for long. We were only fifty minutes late arriving."

My breath caught in shame as I remembered seeing her go up the stairs and Paul's words: *She's packing.*

"I told the police about the flight," she added. "Naturally, they checked. So, you see, I wasn't there when . . . it happened." A shadow flickered deep in her eyes. Pain? Grief? Fury at me? She had lost her husband, and I had just accused her of murdering him.

What a fool I was. A blundering idiot. I mumbled an apology, a sincere one this time.

She held up a hand to stop me. "Don't bother. We are not friends. I told the police about Paul and your sister. I trust they're investigating *everyone*."

What did that mean? Before I could demand an answer, she walked away, moving through the throng.

"Was that Denise Leblanc you were talking to?" Hank asked, reaching me. He sounded as surprised to see her as I had been. Or maybe it was my face, pale from her cryptic comment. "Natalie? You okay?"

"It's just . . . seeing her brought it all back. About Paul."

"Of course, so horrible. And poor Denise, she's lost so much. Paul. Mont-Joli."

"The estate? You mean the fire?" I couldn't sympathize. Val's death was still a raw wound. Denise's loss of a country house hardly ranked. "She can rebuild. I'm sure she'll do well from the insurance payout."

"No. Mont-Joli isn't hers."

"What do you mean? She was Paul's wife."

"The country place was never his. His father left it to Paul's brother."

That twitched my interest. "Logan?"

He nodded. "He was the older son. Their father died about thirty years ago, when Paul was just a teenager and Logan was establishing himself in business. So the will gave the widow their grand home in South Carolina, gave Logan Mont-Joli, and gave Paul their place in Muskoka, upscale cottage country. But then things took a turn. Within a few years Logan was using the Muskoka place a lot to entertain his city friends, while Paul was engrossed in the family business here in Craigmuir, expanding the company, so eventually the two brothers kind of informally swapped homes. The way Paul told me, it was sort of by mutually agreed default. But I'm pretty sure the Mont-Joli title is still in Logan's name." Hank shrugged. "I don't mean to tell tales. It's just that this'll almost certainly become common knowledge. A murder makes so many things public."

This picture of Paul's brother gripped me: Logan in his twenties, ignoring work to party with his pals at his late father's lavish cottage. It fit with every feeling of contempt I had for him, including his treatment of his "girl" and my suspicion of his connection to animal smuggling. That stream of thought eddied around Denise's disturbing words, and the two currents swirled together in my mind like muddied water. Nothing was clear.

It wasn't until the gallery party was over and Hank was driving me home that one sharp thought pierced the murk. *I hope they're investigating everyone,* Denise had said.

"I'll be back from Ottawa on Wednesday," Hank said, pulling up at my door. "Want to have dinner that evening?"

"I'd like that." I meant it, but I couldn't wait to get inside. We said goodnight, and as soon as I stepped into my dark hallway, before I even switched on the light, I pulled out my phone and tapped the number.

"Dad? I'm sorry to call so late, but there's something I'd like to ask you."

"Oh? Alright."

I could hear his surprise and I felt awful springing this on him without even saying hello. "Hope everybody's okay. Mom?"

"Some days are better than others," he said quietly.

"And Liam? You know I'll take him if he's too much for you, right?"

"Sure, but I'm fine with him. Keeps me busy. What did you want to ask?"

"That's just it, it's Liam. It's a lot for you, taking care of him until Simon gets settled in Sacramento and can take him. I mean, how long has Liam been with you now?" That's what I was really fishing for, that's all I wanted to know. "When did Simon leave to start with the orchestra?"

"Oh, about ten days ago. But I'm—"

"*About* ten days?"

"Well, I guess nine days, actually. March eighth. I remember the date because he'd originally booked his ticket for the fifteenth but then suddenly changed it to go a week earlier. But really, Natty, I'm fine having the boy. Don't worry."

We chatted briefly, me assuring him again that I'd spell him off with Liam if it became too much. As we said goodbye, a coldness crept around my heart. Why had I not thought of my brother-in-law in Paul's case until now? Simon's house was about twenty minutes from Paul's house. And he had left town the very day after Paul was murdered.

19

The next day, everything changed.

It started with my suspicion about Simon leading me to the door of Paul's neighbor. It ended in my own dark bedroom, with fears for my own life.

The morning wind had the bluster of spring, though the temperature was far from springlike as I rang the cold doorbell of number 9 Riverview Ridge. I waited, watching a ragged V of geese sail overhead, returning. They trusted winter's departure more than I did. The bare boughs of a line of maple trees rattled in the wind, a natural fence between this three-story faux-Tudor house and the Leblancs' house.

The door opened. A woman with stiff hair the color of cement lifted the glasses on a chain around her neck and examined me. She wore a beige blouse tight at the throat and an apron wrapped around her tweed skirt. I didn't know anyone still wore aprons.

"Yes?" she asked, partly wary, partly curious. Two corgis raced up to her feet, barking protectively, their triangle ears perked up. "Shush, you two," she said, closing the door enough to keep the dogs from getting out, though they were more interested in me than escape.

"I'm sorry to bother you," I said. "I'm a friend of your neighbors, Paul and Denise Leblanc."

"Paul's dead." Her eyes narrowed in suspicion. "If you're a friend you'd know that."

"Yes, I know. It's why I've come."

"Are you with the police?"

"No, just a friend. My name's Natalie Sinclair. I wondered if I could ask you something about that night. The night it . . . happened."

"Someone killed him."

"Yes. I know. Terrible." I also now knew Denise didn't do it. She'd been on a plane to Montreal. Someone came after she left.

The dogs kept barking. The woman gently scooted the near one away with her sensibly-shoed foot. She seemed about to shoo me away as well. To halt her, I said, "Cute corgis. Pembroke Welsh?"

"Yes, they are," she said, thawing a little.

"And twins?"

"That's right." She looked impressed, as though I had some special gift, though I'd only taken a guess.

"It looks like you're in the middle of something," I said, gesturing to her apron, "so I won't keep you. I just want to ask—"

"Look, I really don't know anything about it."

"But you did talk to the police."

"How would you know that?"

"They came to me because I'd visited Paul earlier that evening. They said you reported seeing a woman leave the house."

"Not Denise. She's a lovely girl." She sounded horrified, as though I'd accused Denise of the murder. "She'd told me early that morning that she was taking a late flight to visit Adele, but by then I was in bed."

"No, this was before Denise left. The woman you saw was me."

"You? Oh!" She peered more closely. "Yes, I suppose it was. It was dark, you know."

"Yes, of course. The thing is, because you saw me, I wondered if you also saw anything else after that. Later. Saw any*one* else."

"Oh, well, I already told the police about that."

"About what?"

"The man."

My mouth was suddenly dry. "I'm sorry . . . the man?"

"Yes, as I told that detective, I couldn't sleep so I got out of bed for a glass of water. Our bathroom overlooks Denise's driveway, and I saw a car drive up and a man get out. I went back to bed, but I still couldn't sleep. About twenty minutes later I heard the car leave."

"Can you describe the man?"

"Not really. Just a shape, actually. As I said, it was dark. And our maples block much of the view. But he was tall, I could see that. And he walked like . . . well, like a man."

"What about the car?"

She shrugged. "I don't know anything about cars."

"And you told the police this, about the man?"

"Of course."

I thanked her and walked back to my car, shaken. Simon was tall. And if he'd known about Julia's affair, he had good reason to hate Paul. Enough to kill him? I remembered the awkward FaceTime chat we'd had; Simon so curt, almost hostile. I had come to this lady's house asking a question, but now I wished I hadn't heard the answer. What was the right thing to do? Tell Detective Rourke to check out my brother-in-law . . . or call Simon for some answers?

I did neither. I had to get back to the office for a scheduled Zoom meeting with my board. I wasn't sorry, since it forced me to clamp down my personal anxieties. Simon. Rourke. The scar-faced guy who'd followed me. My parents' misery. DuPre. The whole shitstorm of worries and fears left me feeling helpless, which I hated. It was a relief to tackle a big advocacy issue where I hoped I could make a difference: challenging a new law that was bad for animals.

The office was quiet, just Nicole stuffing envelopes with our newsletter to supporters, Janice clicking at her keyboard, and Trevor quietly talking on the phone. Sounded like he was calming down an anxious caller who'd picked up an injured squirrel. Trevor had a real knack for empathy. His soothing voice even helped calm me.

I logged into Zoom. "Hi, guys," I said to the three businesslike faces on my screen, the members of my board. Elizabeth Fraser was an anthropology professor at the University of Toronto. Giles Beauchamp in Montreal owned a chain of gyms. Karin Johansen, an entrepreneur with a line of beauty products that were animal cruelty-free, was joining in from a Vancouver hotel room. They were fine, caring people who had been with me from the very beginning, through the early struggle to create All Creatures Great and Small right up to our current work, and I felt real affection for them.

We'd set up this meeting to discuss my desire to mount a court challenge to Bill 156, the act that prevented anyone from videoing the agony animals suffered on farms and in slaughterhouses. The torture of calves confined in veal crates. The torment of downer cows. Beaten pigs. Horses crammed together in kill pens, taking a bullet between the eyes. Video of such atrocities always, rightfully, brought public outrage. That scared the agriculture lobby, who'd demanded action from politicians, who'd obliged with this ag-gag law.

I got right to the point with the board. I'd previously told them Hank had sent me the name of a top constitutional lawyer to fight the law, and I was fired up now as I reported, "I've heard back from the lawyer, Colin MacPherson. He's agreed."

They were nervous about the cost.

"His retainer alone, Nat," Karin said. "Twenty thousand. It's way steep."

"Because he's good," I assured her. "He's argued cases before the Supreme Court and he wins. He's worth the money."

"I don't doubt it," Giles said. "I get paying top dollar for the best. The question is, can we afford it?"

"Can we afford *not* to? If we don't fight this law, countless animals will suffer and die. They already—"

"Nat," Elizabeth cut in, "a case like this could drag on for months, for *years*, and the costs will keep rising. They always do with lawyers. That'll mean cutting back on our other work."

"Besides," Giles said, "we wouldn't have any partners on it. We'd be going out on a limb—a very expensive limb—all alone."

I bit back my frustration. He was right. The big, established animal protection groups were notoriously reluctant to take any political action. They stuck to nonconfrontational stuff.

"Then so be it," I said. "We'll go it alone. This fight is what our members expect. And deserve. It's our unspoken contract with them—that for their donations, we produce results. *Measurable* results. Less animal suffering. More animal lives saved."

Their frowns told me they weren't happy to be lectured. They cared about the commitment to our donors as much as I did.

"Look," I blurted, "I'll find the money."

"Where?" Giles asked.

"I believe there's a potential donor who would back this constitutional fight."

"Really?" Karin said. "Who?"

"They prefer to stay anonymous. But if I can swing it, would you agree to go forward?"

They agreed that if the costs could be covered outside of our current operating budget and not disrupt our existing projects, I had their blessing to hire the expert lawyer.

I signed off Zoom. My hands had been balled into fists of tension since I'd mentioned an anonymous donor. Logan Leblanc did that to me. He had promised me thirty-five thousand dollars for All Creatures. After I'd seen the sickening pictures of his trophy kills, and sure he was lying about ERV, I'd vowed to reject his dirty cash, return it. But now? I needed that money. He'd told his "girl," Annemarie, to start the process for depositing it, and although it hadn't yet arrived in All Creatures' bank account, I decided that when it did, I would keep it after all. Use the bastard's money to save animals. That felt good.

"Natalie?" It was Janice, approaching my desk. "There was a call when you were on Zoom. A Rhoda Saunders, deputy fire chief, returning your call."

Put through to Saunders's extension, I told her I'd called to ask about the best sprinkler systems for barns and stables. Could she advise me?

"Glad to, part of my job," she said, and launched into a breakdown. Sprinklers, she said, were activated by heat, not smoke. "When animals perish, the most common causes are smoke, particulates, and carbon monoxide, not the fire itself. Sprinklers, in putting out the fire, help contain those toxins and smoke." She explained the features of various systems and the issue of water supply. "A property that doesn't have town water will need another source. A nearby pond works fine as long as it doesn't freeze completely during the winter. If there are no water sources, you'll need a holding tank."

"All good to know," I said.

She offered to send me some links and have some pamphlets delivered.

"I'd appreciate that, thanks. I want to get this information out to as many horse owners as possible. I hope it'll save other animals from a horrible death like the tragedy here at the Leblanc estate."

"Well, I don't think they meant that fire to reach the stable. The flames were windblown from the house, but yes, a sprinkler system certainly could have saved the horses."

They? "I don't understand." No reply from her. "Ms. Saunders? What do you mean?"

I could hear in her silence that she realized she'd said too much. "We're still investigating, so I really can't say more. Thanks for your call, Ms. Sinclair. I'll send you those follow-up materials. Goodbye."

"Wait. Are you saying the Leblanc fire was somehow . . . deliberate?"

"As I said, that incident is being investigated. Now, I must go. Keep up the good work." She ended the call.

A shiver touched the back of my neck. Was she talking arson? Good God. Who would want to burn down Paul's house? Wait, wasn't arson often the work of the owner, an insurance con? But that made no sense. Paul didn't need money. Besides, why would he set fire to his own house and then help the firefighters put it out?

Then Hank's words from the art gallery rushed back. That country place, Mont-Joli, actually belonged to Paul's brother.

Logan Leblanc, in my sights again. My scrutiny seemed to crisscross the man's life like a searchlight sweeping dark country. But the terrain was mostly shadow. If it was absurd to think Paul would try to burn down the house, it made even less sense to think his rich brother would. Yet I knew so little about the man. It occurred to me there was someone who might, though. My brother. Working at a major retail brokerage, James's world was finance. I called him.

"Logan Leblanc?" he said in answer to my question. "Of Gold Zone?" He was walking, he said, on his way to a lunch appointment. I could hear the whoosh of the downtown Toronto traffic.

"You know him?" I asked.

"Not personally, no, just the stories."

"Stories? Is he some famous mining magnate?"

He laughed. "Famous in his own mind. Not so much with the suppliers he's bilked."

"What does that mean? He doesn't pay his bills?"

"He *can't* pay. The guy's a bankrupt. A few times over."

"What? No way. He's rich."

"Rich in debt."

"But—" I'd seen his opulent office suite. "I was at his office."

"In the RBC tower? He's just been kicked out of there. Defaulted on the rent."

The workmen carrying out furniture. The bare walls. He'd told me they were moving.

"What were you at his office for?"

"Long story."

"Make it short. I'm almost at the restaurant door."

"He promised my nonprofit a big donation."

"Oh, boy. You'll never see a penny from Logan Leblanc."

I was stunned. A bankrupt. A liar.

"Nat, I'm serious. He's bad news. He leverages start-ups, uses investors' cash to finance a new company, files bankruptcy on the first, gets a new loan, and starts again. The guy's a walking Ponzi scheme."

"Why isn't he in jail?"

"He should be. But they'd have to catch him at it first, and he's good. A world-class master at the shell game."

My head was swimming. "James, was his brother part of this? Paul Leblanc?"

"That guy who was killed?"

"Yes."

"I don't know. I don't think so. Look, Nat, I have to go, I'm already late for this lunch. I'll call you later. We should talk about Mom. I'm worried. Do you think she might need . . . you know, some help?"

There was a tightening around my heart. "I've been thinking the same thing."

"Yeah," he said sadly. "We better talk." Then, "Hey, you know what? One of the guys I'm having lunch with might know about Leblanc's brother. I'll get back to you, okay?"

I said goodbye and burrowed into my Mac, trying to concentrate on work, but James's words haunted me. *You'll never see a penny from Logan Leblanc.* I'd been a fool to think I would. But why, then, had he offered it? Had some vestige of decency spurred him to honor his dead brother's wish? Or was it, like I'd suspected, his move to pacify me? Except, according to James, the whole question was moot—Leblanc didn't *have* thirty-five thousand dollars.

So where did that leave me? Without that windfall, how could I hire the lawyer, the constitutional expert, to fight the ag-gag law? I'd be on the hook for that cost. I could see it wiping out my meager savings. I'd managed to keep my credit card balance zeroed over the last year, so at least I could draw on a line of credit. What had I said to my board about going out on a limb alone? *So be it.*

It was almost five o'clock. Nicole had gone home. Trevor had gone home. Janice was getting ready to lock up when my phone rang. I snatched it as soon as I saw the caller. James.

"Okay," he said, "Paul Leblanc, CEO of Leblanc Agrisciences. His name says it all: mister white, pure as the driven snow. Also, he sat on the board of directors of Logan's one solvent company, Gold Zone. But there was bad blood between the brothers. According to my source, Logan wanted to accept a takeover bid of Gold Zone but Paul was against it, and Paul was winning support for that position from the rest of the board, especially after someone leaked to the *Financial*

Post. Apparently, Logan was furious. I don't know the details, but it sounds like it was shaping up to be a nasty personal feud."

He went on about securities and proxies and circulars, but I didn't hear much of it. I was overwhelmed by his two big revelations. From his first call I'd learned that Logan needed quick cash, which the insurance payout on Mont-Joli would have provided if the fire had destroyed the house. And now I'd learned that the Leblanc bothers were feuding. Had the feud become violent? I imagined Logan arriving at Paul's house in that fancy yellow Porsche, likely another showy item he couldn't pay for. I imagined Paul's neighbor at her bathroom window, seeing him, a tall man, walk to the door. Then the two brothers on Paul's deck, arguing. And the argument getting ugly.

I couldn't let it lie. I fished out Detective Rourke's card and called him.

Voicemail. Damn. What could I say in a message? Keep it short, I told myself. "Detective, it's Natalie Sinclair. I may have a lead for your investigation. Check out Paul's Leblanc's own brother, Logan." Saying it aloud sounded stupidly melodramatic. Doubly so, since I didn't have a shred of evidence. Too late; I'd already recorded it. "Just . . . call me, please. I'll explain."

I had a quiet solo dinner of green curry at the under-patronized, underappreciated Thai Tiger. There wasn't much in my fridge except week-old take-out zucchini lasagna and the dregs of some lentil soup. I hadn't had much appetite for meals since DuPre had disappeared. I watched the teenage waitress roll up napkins of silverware for future diners. Her young face made me think of Hank's two preteen boys. I'd liked the feel of his house, alive with three kids and Monty the sheepdog, warm with the cinnamony scent of apple pie. A happy home. It was getting dark by the time I drove back to my place behind Mrs. Carson's mansion. The driveway curved around her house, and I noticed a car parked there. She must have a guest. I didn't see Mrs. Carson's Mercedes, though, so likely it was her daughter, with her own key. I drove on and parked under the coach house gable.

I tossed my keys in the hallway dish, hung up my coat, then started up the stairs, looking forward to a bath to relax after this trying day. At the top of the steps I caught a faint smell. Cigarette? Had Mrs. Carson let in a workman earlier in the day? I had told her about the water stain in my bedroom ceiling.

The bedroom lay in shadows. The cigarette smell was stronger as I stepped in. And another smell, the sharp, unmistakable bite of urine.

A man sat on the foot of my bed.

My heart banged at the shock. Even in the dim light I knew it was the man from the sail loft. Stocky. Bald. One earring, a crucifix. The monkey bite scar on his cheek. Ever since he'd followed me two days ago, I'd known, in a part of me that didn't want to face it, that something like this was going to happen.

"You work late," he said. The words were low and slow, as though he was tired. The menace in his voice terrified me.

He had trashed my room. Drawers open, clothes flung on the floor. Books tossed. Papers strewn. Bedside lamp knocked over.

"Get out of—" My words were choked by thick hands around my throat from behind. I jerked in terror, heart hammering. The hands dropped to my shoulders and spun me around. The bodybuilder from the sail loft. The Russian. His broad face loomed above me.

He smiled. Raised one big hand. The blow to the side of my head sent me staggering, stunned with pain. Stars careened through the sudden darkness of my vision. I gulped air. Felt liquid dribble into my mouth. Tasted the metallic bite of blood.

"What . . . do you *want* from me?" I yelled . . . no, *thought* I yelled, but the voice that came out was thin.

"We start this way," the Russian said, still smiling. His fist rammed my stomach. I reeled, bent double at the fire of pain, fell to my knees. He clamped my arm, hauled me up to my feet. He spun me around again like a rag doll so I was facing the scar-faced man on the bed, then gripped my shoulders and pulled me back, pinning me against his chest. I struggled. His leg from behind clamped around my knee. I thought my leg would break. "I hold her. See? Your turn."

They were going to kill me.

The scar-faced man got up from the bed. He waved away the Russian's invitation. He looked almost pained.

"No?" the Russian said. "Ha, you just big pussy, Mancuso." He roughly turned me again, facing him. "Okay. More for me." His smile told me I wouldn't survive this. I raised both hands to claw his face, but he was faster. He gripped my hair and snapped my head back. Pain seared my scalp.

"Enough." The one word came from behind me. The scar-faced man. It was an order.

The Russian grunted his displeasure, then suddenly let me go with a shrug. "Sure. I keep hands clean and pretty for Indian chief."

My legs went limp as I twisted away from him and collapsed to my knees.

"Your one and only warning," the scar-faced man said, looking down at me. "Keep your fucking nose out of other people's business."

"Monkey business," the Russian said, enjoying his own joke.

"You hear?" Scarface said. "Or next time he'll get his hands dirty by cracking open your skull."

He walked out. The Russian followed, kicking my shoulder on his way and knocking me to the floor.

I lay on my side, sucking sharp shallow breaths like sobs. My head roared with pain. My gut was on fire. I listened to them stamp down the stairs, out the door. Silence. Except for the two words that echoed in my ears. *Indian chief.* Trevor. He'd been with me at the sail loft.

I forced my muscles to raise myself onto hands and knees. Blood seeped between my teeth, dripped onto the floor. I crawled over my clothes, my papers. Crawled to the door. Crawled to the top of the stairs. I had to warn Trevor.

20

I dabbed my chin with a wet dishtowel, wiping away the last of the blood.

"No loose teeth?" Trevor asked, clattering with my broom and dustpan.

I shook my head. No.

"Well, that's something."

I was sitting at my kitchen table. He was sweeping up glass from the smashed window in the kitchen door. We were waiting for the police to arrive. I'd called Detective Rourke to report the attack.

"Why do they even *make* doors like this?" Trevor said in disgust as he swept. "Just break the glass, reach inside, and unlock the latch. It's a fucking invitation to bust in."

"It's way old. This was a coach house." Built in a trusting time when the idea was to enjoy the view outside, not barricade yourself in. I thought it but didn't say it; it hurt to move my jaw much. My stomach muscles ached too, like after you vomit. I hadn't thrown up, but the terror of the attack had left me feeling trembly, cold.

Trevor dumped the glass from the dustpan into the garbage. He came and took the towel from me, went to the sink and rinsed it, wrung it out, and brought it back. I waved it away. The bleeding between my teeth had stopped.

He shook his head sadly. "Jesus, Nat, look at you."

I looked down. My cotton shirt was splotched with blood that had dribbled from my mouth. One spot, still wet, stuck to the skin of my breastbone.

"You need to get out of that shirt. "

"Nothing to wear." I pointed up. My bedroom. "They tossed all my clothes and pissed on them."

"Seriously? Shit."

"No just piss. I hope."

We shared a bleak smile.

"How about your landlady over there in the big house? She'd have something."

"She's not home."

"Well, let me go see if there's something to salvage." He went upstairs.

I sat still, hating being alone for even a minute. When the two men had left me gasping on the floor of my bedroom, I'd staggered down the stairs and outside and seen their car reversing from Mrs. Carson's parking area. I saw the license plate. I hurried back inside, every step spiking more pain, and called Trevor. The moment he answered, I told him to get out, told him they were coming for him. "Get out *now.*" Then I'd hobbled across the flagstone path to Mrs. Carson's house and knocked on the door. No answer. I remembered that when I'd come home her car was gone.

Trevor came back downstairs with a clean T-shirt. "Found it in the back of a drawer."

He turned away while I unbuttoned the bloodied shirt and pulled it off. My bra edge was tacky with blood, so I took it off too. I pulled on the big T-shirt, my fingers trembling.

I hadn't told Trevor what bothered me most in the wreckage upstairs. They'd taken a photo out of its frame on my nightstand, my favorite picture of me and Julia. She was twelve, me ten. Her arm was slung around my shoulders, a sly grin on her face, and I was laughing my head off at something. One of the men had stubbed out his cigarette in my face. There was just my torso, next to Julia.

I got up and threw the dirty shirt and bra into the garbage. The burst of exertion made my legs feel weak as straw. Trevor took my arm. "It's shock," he said.

Tears burned behind my eyes. I looked away.

"It's natural," he gently assured me.

I wanted to scream: *Nothing about this is natural!*

He guided me back to the chair. I sank into it. He found a half-full bottle of Chardonnay in my fridge and poured me a glass. "Here."

I waved it away. My jaw still hurt too much.

"Go on. Alcohol's a disinfectant."

I sipped some wine. It stung.

"I'll make some tea, okay?"

"Trevor, you don't have to do all this."

"Are you kidding? You probably saved my life."

I had told him that the men who'd done this were the ones who'd beaten him up at the sail loft over the baby monkeys. I was pretty sure who they were working for. Ever since I'd started looking into ERV Financial Services, the only link I could see was Logan Leblanc. I remembered how, in his car, he'd questioned me. I'd thought then, like a fool, that he was interested in my work—a greedy fool, because I'd wanted his donation. I realized now that he'd been probing me for how much I knew about ERV. That had to be why he'd made the phony offer of a donation. Now he'd sent those men to attack me to stop *my* probing. My skin tingled at the thought that the attack might actually help me expose him, because now I had a name for one of the men, the scar-faced guy. The Russian had said it. Mancuso. Plus, I had a license plate.

Trevor was filling the kettle to make tea when Detective Rourke arrived. Again, he was accompanied by Constable Crocker. I explained what happened, the connection to the monkey operation, and told him the name I'd heard and the license plate I'd seen. He surveyed the broken kitchen door, and I showed him the damage upstairs. The constable took notes, and some photos. Coming back downstairs, Rourke asked me for a full description of the two men. After I filled him in he said, "Call me if you remember anything else. Anything." He motioned to the constable and started for the door. They were done. That's it? I thought. No fingerprints taken? No sample of my urine-stinking clothes to check for DNA? But maybe I'd seen too many TV cop shows. They had the license plate to track. That should be enough.

As they were leaving, Rourke stopped at the open door and gave me a serious look. "I'll be in touch, Ms. Sinclair. In the meantime, be careful."

When they'd gone, Trevor asked, "Think they'll catch those guys?"

"I don't know." But I was forming my own plan, and being careful wasn't part of it.

I waited a day, in case I heard back from Rourke. But when I heard nothing, I assumed he wasn't going to call. I figured detectives didn't share their investigative findings with the citizenry unless there was a strategic reason. It was time to check out Mancuso myself.

Early the next morning, driving twenty minutes out of town, I slowed behind a school bus. Its cheerful sunny color looked out of place on this drab, deserted rural dirt road, but obviously kids here went to school the same as town kids. The bus chugged on up the road. I didn't follow it. My eyes were on the emergency locator number on a post at the end of a short gravel lane. The address had been surprisingly easy to trace: Trevor's cousin worked at the Service Ontario office that handled vehicle registrations.

I took a deep breath, my jaw still tender from the Russian's fist, then turned onto the lane and drove up to the house. It fronted a spindly woods, and the house, like the school bus, looked vaguely out of place, a well-kept stucco bungalow with a satellite dish on the roof and a trampoline in the front yard, the kind of home you'd see in any suburban neighborhood, except here the nearest neighbor was a half mile away.

I parked, got out. I'd expected country silence, but instead I heard barking, loud, and from more than one dog, maybe three or four, excited by the sound of my car's arrival. The barking came from behind the house. A kennel, I figured.

I went to the front door, aware of the stiffness of the jeans I'd found lurking at the back of my closet, a bad purchase months ago, too big so never worn. After Rourke had left my house the other night, it had taken me and Trevor hours to bag my piss-fouled clothes and get my bedroom livable again. What a good guy. I felt very grateful for his friendship.

I knocked. The door flew open. A pudgy little boy who looked only a couple years older than my nephew, Liam, looked up at me. Loud rock music pulsed from down the hall.

"Hello there," I said.

"Daddy!" the boy yelled above the music.

The boy and I waited, looking at each other. No one came. "Can I come in?" Part of me knew this was a bad idea. But I'd come this far. I had to find out.

I passed the boy and followed the wailing guitar music. It brought me to the kitchen. Mancuso stood with his back to me, chopping something, jerking his head in time with the bass rhythm blasting from the speakers. Black T-shirt and baggy jeans. Red bandana tied pirate-style over his baldness. The room was warm from a big pot of water boiling on the stove next to a simmering pan of what smelled like spaghetti sauce. On the counter, beside him, a tall can of Molson Canadian sweated.

The boy shouted above the noise, "Daddy, there's—"

"Ten minutes, Buddy," Mancuso calmly yelled back, not looking up, still chopping.

"But there's a *lady!*"

Mancuso turned. He gaped at me, the knife rigid in his hand. "Holy Christ!" He looked behind me.

"I'm alone," I assured him. I had to yell too above the blaring music. "I came alone."

"What the fuck—?"

"I just want to talk to you."

He let out a stunned, incredulous laugh. Then shot a look at the little boy and raised his free hand as if to swat him. "Get outta here, you." The boy took off down the hall.

Mancuso hit a button on the stereo and the music stopped. He looked at me. "Man, you are one crazy bitch."

"So I've been told."

He raised the knife. "I could carve you up right here."

"I don't think so. I don't think that line of work appeals to you at all."

He scowled. "What the fuck are you talking about?"

He and the Russian had been sent to scare me, to hurt me, but Mancuso hadn't hurt me. I'd seen his reluctance, the opposite of the Russian's zeal. I'd seen that look before—in men watching Stampede chuckwagon races when galloping teams of horses collided in a hideous pileup of death. Men wanting to look away, repulsed, but unwilling to be called soft.

Mancuso stepped toward me, the knife between us. Fear spiked my chest. Had I called this insanely wrong? I stepped back. My heel touched the wall. Nowhere to go. "Look, I just want to talk. I'm glad I found you. I thought they might have arrested you."

"Yeah, you went to the cops, didn't you." Not a question. An accusation.

"They came here?"

His eyes narrowed. "After I told you to keep your nose out of other people's business."

"I'm not good at taking orders."

"You should learn."

"I'm curious. What did you tell the detective when he questioned you about attacking me?"

A sneer curled his mouth. "Was with my uncle at the lake when it happened. Just ask my uncle."

"So that's how it's done."

"We're done here, lady. Now get the fuck out of my house."

And yet, no knife in my flesh. I was alive. I could go. It gave me an unexpected sense of calm. "Don't worry, I'm not staying for dinner. I just want to know one thing. Who sent you? Who told you and the Russian to come and scare me?"

He snorted, a scoff. "Like I'd tell *you*."

"I'm pretty sure you didn't decide on your own. Who do you work for?"

"I said get out of—"

"Is it Logan Leblanc? Is he behind the animal trafficking? The baby monkeys?"

A flinch from Mancuso. A spark of jubilation shot through me. *So it's true.*

"I'll tell you one thing," he said, almost to himself. "I'm gonna regret not letting Dimitri finish you."

I heard the new note in his voice. Was *he* afraid? I snatched at the possibility. "*Why* will you regret it? Because of Leblanc? Are you really so afraid of him?"

"Me? Fuck off."

"Because, if so, I think I know how to stop him."

There was a flicker of interest deep in his eyes. A subtle shift. His voice, though, was flinty with skepticism. "How are you gonna do that?"

"I think he may have set the fire at his brother's house. Arson."

"They'll never catch him for that."

My breath snagged. Had he just told me I was right? You don't "catch" someone for an accident. "So that fire *was* deliberately set," I said eagerly. "And how would you know that unless you do work for him. My God, did *you* set the—?"

In a flash his hand was around my throat. He rammed me back against the wall. "You keep asking questions, lady, you're gonna die. You and me both." He was choking me. The knife glinted in his other hand. I tried to knee him in the groin, but he forced his body against mine so tightly I couldn't lift my leg.

"Dad!" A girl's voice, shrill, behind him. "Dad, stop!"

Mancuso let me go, twisting around in surprise. I coughed, rubbing my throat, sore from Mancuso's grip, my eyes on the girl who had saved me. She looked about fourteen, petite, pale faced. Short spiked hair dyed purple. A haunted look in her dark eyes, made darker by smudgy eye makeup. The little boy peeked around her, eager to watch.

"Who's she?" the girl asked nervously.

"Nobody," Mancuso said.

"What's she want?"

"Nothing. And she's leaving."

"Wait," I said. Maybe it was crazy, but despite everything I sensed Mancuso was an ally, someone who wished he could get out from under Leblanc's control but was too afraid to make a move. I couldn't let it go. "Report the arson," I said. "He'll go to jail."

"No way. He's got lawyers. He'd walk. *I'd* get jail."

"What if you agreed to testify if they gave you immunity?"

"Ha. So *you're* a lawyer now? You don't know squat." He looked at his two kids, both watching us. The boy looked excited by the drama. The girl looked anxious.

Mancuso raised the back of his hand with the knife and bellowed at them, "Get outta here, the both of you." The boy shot off down the hall again. The girl slunk away after him.

"This has scared your kids," I said. "I'm sorry."

"Yeah?" Mancuso slid the knife down on the counter in a slumping gesture that spoke of both disgust and defeat, as though the rage had been sucked out of him and he was just plain tired. He gave me a searching look, as if probing how much he could trust me. "You know what happens if I rat? He sends someone to shut me up for good. If I'm at the bottom of the river, who looks after those two?"

"Where's their mother?"

"Who knows."

I was unexpectedly moved that he'd shared so much with me. And yet I had never felt so furiously powerless. I couldn't promise him immunity, couldn't promise anything. But neither could I let Leblanc get away with his crimes. "Well, *I* could report him," I said. "Report everything."

"No you won't. Listen to me. The guy's connected. You think *he's* bad, you don't want to know about the Russian mob he's thick with. That's why he's doing these scams all over the place, like that fire to collect the insurance, other shit too. He needs cash to buy his way into the Russian mob, the Bratva. So if you don't want a bomb going off in your little clubhouse with your bunny-hugger pals, you'll keep your mouth shut. In other words. Stay. The. Fuck. Away. From everything to do with Leblanc." He picked up the knife again. "Got it?"

I got it.

As I walked to my car I snatched at the hope that Detective Rourke might track down Leblanc on his own. After all, before the attack on me, I'd left him that message about a possible lead in the murder investigation: "Check out Paul's own brother," I'd said. So maybe he was following up at this very moment. Then again, that message might have sounded like I was just desperate to deflect suspicion away from myself. I had no evidence. Leblanc was getting away with everything. Arson. Trafficking wild animals. Maybe even murdering Paul. But Mancuso would not testify to any of it. I had nothing.

I slid behind the wheel and started a three-point turn, ready to head down the lane, but as I backed up, about to shift into drive, a hand slapped my window. I almost jumped. It was Mancuso's daughter. I stopped, lowered the window.

She looked at me with skittish intensity. "My dad's boss," she said, her voice tight, urgent. "Can you really stop him?"

What was this about? "I don't know," I said. "I want to." She just stared at me. "Do you?" I asked.

She shot a furtive glance at the house, clearly not wanting her father to see her. But I could tell she wanted to talk. She was like a frightened puppy, trying to be fierce but just plain scared.

"What's your name, honey?"

"Gina."

"It's okay, Gina. I'm on your dad's side. I want to help him. But I can't do that unless I know more about the man he works for. About the things that man does. Have you heard something? Seen something?"

"Yeah." Again, the nervous look at the house.

"I understand, we can't talk here. Is there some place I can meet you?"

She bit her lower lip. "My school? Lunchtime?"

"John R. Blaine or Westside Secondary?"

"Westside."

"I'll be there," I said. "Tomorrow."

"Park across the street."

I watched her in my rearview mirror as she hurried back to the house.

21

I pulled up across from Gina Mancuso's school eight minutes before noon. Any earlier, someone might think I was lurking. But for the last hour I'd sat, jumpy with anticipation, at the Tim Hortons donut shop a block away, going through coffee refills, checking the time every few minutes, excited. Did this girl really have information about Leblanc's crimes? Maybe even Paul's murder?

The lunch bell sounded. A bunch of kids swarmed out the front doors.

Gina spotted my car and came over, slinging her backpack over her shoulder. Her jean jacket was too tight, as though she'd grown out of it. Her legs, bare below the faux-leather miniskirt, had to be cold. I lowered the window. She avoided eye contact, anxiously watching kids saunter off along the sidewalk toward the Tim's. "There's a park down the block," she said, jerking her head in the opposite direction the kids were going. "I'll meet you by the baseball diamond."

I pulled into the deserted parking area behind the baseball diamond fence. Three minutes later Gina opened the passenger door and climbed in, but she held her backpack tightly to her chest as though ready to bolt out again.

"Thank you, Gina. I know this can't be easy for you. But if you know something about the man your dad works for that—"

"You said he'd go to jail, right? His boss?"

"It depends."

"On what?"

"The evidence. I don't have enough. I'm hoping you might."

"I don't. It's just . . . "

"Just what? Gina, if you've seen something or heard—"

"It's not like that. Not, like what you said, evidence. It's just . . . I don't . . ." She looked down at her knees.

"Don't what?"

"Don't . . . know what to do."

A tremor shook her shoulders. She clutched the backpack tighter to her chest and squeezed her eyes shut. It was clear she was wrestling with something personal and painful. I felt a needle of dread.

"Honey, what's happened?"

It tumbled out of her in a rush. "It was at that hotel in Toronto. The Hilton. March break. Dad's boss said come for brunch, his treat, so Dad took me and Leo. It was packed, families eating, a guy making waffles, a big fountain. Leo stuck his hand in the fountain and I had to tug him away. So we all sit down at the table with my dad's boss and his secretary, that blonde lady, Annemarie. And there's a girl, old, about twenty, really pretty, in a dress like Taylor Swift wore at the Grammys, and Dad's boss says this is my niece Sandra from Nova Scotia, she's staying here, her folks went shopping. So we're all eating and Sandra's talking to me, she's really nice, you know? And then my dad's boss tells him to go get the Porsche washed and my dad leaves. The waiter comes and asks what we want for dessert. Leo says ice cream, and Sandra says to me, 'Want to come see the clothes I bought with my mom?' So we go up to her room. She pours us some Cokes, but in fancy glasses, which was pretty cool, and she gives me one. It tastes a little off, kind of bitter, but she's so nice I don't want to be rude. But after I finish it, I'm feeling really tired and kind of fuzzy. And Sandra says, 'maybe too much syrup on your waffle, it can give you a headache. Just lie down, it'll pass.' But it's not a headache, it's more like my legs have gone weird and I can't walk right. So I fall on the couch and I tell Sandra I'm feeling kind of funny, but there's no answer. She's gone. But I'm not alone. It's hard to see right 'cause I'm so dizzy, but I can see my dad's boss is there, right in front of me, and he's undoing his pants, and then—"

Tears ran down her cheeks.

"Oh, Gina . . ." Horrified, I reached for her hand.

She was choking back sobs. I felt gutted, watching her, holding her hand.

"Then I'm back downstairs . . . only now I'm in the lobby, where they have those big easy chairs , so I guess it's later . . . only I don't remember how . . . or what, exactly . . . just that the chair feels scratchy . . . and I hurt . . . and he's there too, sitting on the far couch, chatting up his secretary, and Leo's goofing around at the revolving door . . . and then my dad comes back and joins us, and his boss says, 'Hey, Frank, the car all bright and shiny?' And my dad says, 'Yup' . . . but I . . . I can't look at him. I just can't . . . I don't remember exactly what happened up in the room, but I know . . . and it hurts . . . and I can't look at my dad . . . you know?"

"I know," I said gently, and squeezed her cold, trembling hand. I felt such fury. They'd used some date rape drug on her. Some super-speedy new thing, maybe. I'd heard ketamine works fast and wears off fast, and victims often don't even remember the assault. I forced calmness into my voice so as not to scare her and asked if she had told anyone. "No way," she said with sudden vehemence. I asked if she'd had her period since it happened. "Yes," she whispered. *Thank heaven,* I thought.

But she wasn't finished. "My dad's boss . . ." she said, wiping her wet eyes, her runny nose, fighting to keep from crying any more. "When we were leaving for our car, he takes me aside, says there's going to be a party and I should come and I'll get a text to tell me when. Says to tell my dad I'm going to sleep over with a friend and he'll send a car to pick me up at school. He says my dad owes him money, and sometimes when people owe him money they get hurt, but that won't happen to my dad if I come to the party. So yesterday I get the text. The party's on Friday. So I don't . . . know what to do when—"

"Nothing. You're not going."

"But my dad—"

"No, Gina. Your dad can take care of himself. You forget all about it."

"Really?"

"Absolutely. You take the bus home from school that day like always. Okay?"

She nodded, looking relieved, but also still a little scared, lost. I felt out of my depth. This girl needed help that I couldn't give. I started the car. "Honey, I want to take you to see someone." Amber's sister was a social worker at the sexual assault support center known as Allison's Place. They took walk-ins.

"Who?"

"It's a place where they can help you understand what you've been through. What you're still going through. Tell them as much as you want or as little. No one else will know. Okay?"

She looked nervous, but after thinking for a bit she gave a determined little nod. Brave girl.

I drove her to the clinic. Amber's sister wasn't in, but a therapist who introduced herself as Lucy welcomed Gina, led her into her office, and closed the door. I sat in the waiting room, still stunned by the horror of what Logan Leblanc had done to this girl. The cold-blooded premeditation, the web he'd spun with his accomplice "niece." The revolting prospect of his partying. How many other young girls had they snared? When Gina came out, I was glad to see she wasn't crying. In fact, she looked calmer.

"Lucy was nice," she said quietly as we left. She looked at me and added, "Thanks."

I gave her an encouraging smile, filled with admiration for her. I couldn't imagine coping with what she'd been through when I was her age.

We reached my car, and as she got in I read her troubled face. She was wrestling with some new turmoil. "What is it, honey?"

"Lucy said . . . she said I could go to the police and report him if I wanted to."

"Do you?"

"Part of me does. I hate him. He should go to jail."

No shit. No prison sentence would be long enough.

"But, like, first, wouldn't I'd have to go to court or something? Then my dad would know. I couldn't stand that. I'd rather die."

I understood. It was hell of a decision for a traumatized kid to have to make. "Sleep on it, okay?" I told her. I started the car. "Come on, I'll drive you home."

"No, no way. My dad can't know where I've been. Just take me back to school. I can make the bus."

22

The next morning, after nightmares too troubled to untangle, I was up early. This was the day Hank had scheduled our meeting with the dean of the veterinary college. I jogged, showered, got dressed, going through the motions on autopilot, still sickened by Gina Mancuso's story, the terrible thing she had been through.

Hank picked me up, apologizing for getting home too late last night to make our dinner date. An immigration committee meeting had run late, keeping him in Ottawa into the evening. Truth was, I'd been relieved to get his text postponing the date. There was no way I could've carried on a carefree conversation over wine and pasta, not after everything I'd heard from Gina just hours earlier.

Hank drove to the university and parked, and we took the tree-lined path across the campus toward the vet college's main building. Hank was chatting about watching skaters on Ottawa's Rideau Canal.

"Looked like fun. Ever been?"

"To Ottawa? Not in winter. I've seen pictures, though." I was trying to be polite, match his breezy small talk. Tourists and Ottawa residents alike skated on the capital's famous frozen waterway that wound through the heart of the city just a few minutes from Hank's office on Parliament Hill, and I could imagine him lacing up his skates on a lunch break. But my thoughts twisted back to poor young Gina. To Logan Leblanc. To how powerless I was to stop this terrible man. I was sure Gina would not report him for the rape, and her father had made it clear he would not report him for the arson, and I had nothing concrete to tie him to the animal trafficking. Or, possibly, to murder. It made me sick. Leblanc's perfect storm of evil.

I forced all that to the back of my mind. For this visit to the veterinary college, I needed to focus on just one thing: finding DuPre. Garrison Walker, the dean, knew my reputation for animal advocacy—radicals, he'd once called my group—so he would never have agreed to see me alone, but he'd been happy to oblige the district MP's request for a meeting. When I'd originally asked Hank for this favor, all I'd had in mind was the hope that it would yield some news about DuPre.

Now, I had a plan.

"Natalie?" Hank said as we walked. "Did you hear me?"

"What?" I realized he'd been talking.

"Dinner tonight? Bistro Praha? If you're free."

I looked at him. Those warm eyes. That friendly, hopeful smile. Our postponed date. He didn't give up. I realized I loved that about him.

"You're a million miles away," he said.

No, it went beyond being pleased by his pursuit of me. Went deeper. I really, really liked this man.

His smile faded to a slightly puzzled look. "Something bothering you?"

Where would I start? Gina Mancuso. Leblanc's crimes. Paul's murder. But for the moment I let a small wave of happiness wash all that away. I stopped him on the path. We were just steps from the vet college door. "Hank, I'm so glad to be here with you. Doing this together. Thank you so much."

"Sure, no problem." He looked a little surprised at my earnestness. "Let's hope it helps you find your dog. Anyway, I know this issue means a lot to you. Animals used in research. I know how much you're against it."

"It's about what I'm *for*. I'm for life." I went up on my toes and kissed him. A quick, heartfelt kiss.

He frowned. "You didn't ask first."

"What?"

"Bit of a double standard, don't you think? Women are right; there has to be consent."

Whoa. *What?*

Then I caught the twinkle in his eye. "So, Ms. Sinclair, would you find it acceptable if I were to kiss you?"

I sputtered a laugh. And grinned. "Mr. Verhagen, nothing would please me more."

He took me in his arms, and the kiss was long and lovely, and I wanted it to never end. A couple of people passed us. I pulled back, and Hank and I smiled at each other in a wondering way. "Hold that thought," he said quietly. "For dinner tonight."

"Mr. Verhagen? Dean Walker will see you now." The assistant ushered us in.

Walker's office had pride of place on the ground floor of the building, with French doors that opened onto a broad terrace sheltered by tall old maple trees. I imagined he hosted fancy parties under fairy lights strung through the trees, though the boughs now were bare.

The two men greeted each other with hearty handshakes. "Hank, it's good to see you. The Discover grant funds have done wonders, especially the Accelerator Supplements. The recipients are over the moon. I'd love you to meet them. Really, my sincere thanks."

"Good to hear," Hank said. He introduced me, and Walker was instantly wary. The two of us shook hands like civilized people, but Walker eyed me like a nervous cat. As for me, I saw him as a predator. I knew his college still did terminal surgeries on dogs: After the students did the spay or neuter operations, the dogs were killed.

"Come on, Garry," Hank coaxed, giving him a fraternal squeeze of his shoulder, "you two have a lot in common. Vets take care of animals. So does Ms. Sinclair. Anyway, this visit is purely personal. She's lost her dog."

"I don't understand."

I quickly reassured Walker, saying exactly what I'd told Hank—that I feared DuPre might have been nabbed, and I just wanted to know if the college was in contact with any research institutions that might be using animals bought from bunchers.

Walker willfully misunderstood and immediately defended the college. "No, no, we rarely purchase random source animals, and in those rare instances when we do, it's always from licensed dealers." His assurances were all to convince Hank, not me. But I knew the truth. His lab still bought from bunchers.

Hank looked at me. "I assume random source means the stray pets you told me about?"

I nodded. "Some bunchers grab them off the street. Some get them from notices people put up about kittens or puppies. You know, 'free to a good home.'"

Hank looked dismayed. "What?"

"Sure, the guy comes to the door, lays on the charm, saying he has animal-loving friends, and takes away half a dozen kittens or pups. Then sells them to researchers."

Walker was quick to tell Hank, "We much prefer to use purpose bred animals. They're healthier coming from that controlled process, which makes for better training of our students. That produces better science. After all, science is how we find cures for animal diseases. That's our job. Occasionally, animals come to us from pounds, but they're always animals nobody wants, ones that could never be adopted out. Animals that would be euthanized anyway."

I wanted to yell: There's *always* a home somewhere. That's *my* job.

Hank saw my stormy face. "Garry," he said, stepping in as mediator, "Ms. Sinclair's only interested today in finding her dog. She just wondered if you know of other research institutions that buy strays."

Walker finally answered quicky and unequivocally. "I know of none." Then, just as quicky, he said, "Now, let me introduce you to a couple of the grant recipients. They're right here in the lab, and I know they'd be thrilled to thank you personally."

Hank waved away the thanks. "Not necessary."

"Oh, but you'll find their projects fascinating. Do come have a look. It's just across the walkway." He was already reaching for his phone, and I could see that Hank was too polite to refuse.

It gave me my opportunity. "I'd like that, Mr. Walker. Always eager to learn."

Hank looked pleased.

"While you arrange it," I went on, "could I use the washroom?"

"Certainly." Walker gestured to the outer office. "Doris will show you."

I passed Doris's desk without bothering her, but I noted her puzzled look as I bypassed the door to the lobby and instead took the side door to the stairs. Nicole, my volunteer who was a vet student here, had explained the building's layout. This stairway was the dean's private access to the basement.

Down I went, two flights, and reached a door marked "Authorized Access Only." I slid in the key card Nicole had given me; the lock was like on a hotel room door. It clicked open. I stepped into a corridor with fluorescent strip lighting and cinderblock walls, the air as cold as cement. This was the holding area.

I heard the animals before I saw them. Whimpering. Mewling. Feeble barking. Turning the corner, I reached a room where the smell made my stomach clench. The smell of fear. Of despair.

Rows with cages stacked three high. The animals who saw me shuffled backward in fear, those who could move at all. The ones further on, agitated as they sensed my presence, moaned and whined.

A brown-and-white beagle lay on his back, his abdomen hideously bloated.

A gray kitten, restrained by plastic bands, had electrodes implanted in her head.

A marmoset monkey, shaved of all his fur, his body scabbed all over, wandered in crazed circles.

A rabbit writhed, her head locked inside metal stocks. Her hind leg spasmed, incessantly trying to scratch.

I forced down my nausea. I was here to look for DuPre. I saw several healthy dogs awaiting their torture. A standard poodle, expertly groomed by a salon. A French bulldog still wearing his collar and tags. A Yorkshire terrier, looking up at me with hopeful trusting eyes.

I methodically searched up and down each row, peered into each miserable cage, met the eyes of each suffering creature. No cage held DuPre.

I stopped at the end of the last row. A heartbreaking dead end.

I swallowed my despair—and felt a new determination welling up in me. I hadn't found DuPre, but I could still do something for these tortured animals.

I pulled out my phone. Opened Facebook Live. My hands shook as I videoed the pitiful creatures. Row after row. I knew I didn't have long. Walker's assistant could have alerted him by now, and if so he'd have figured it out. But I carefully videoed each individual animal in each cage. I wanted the world to see their agony in this place.

"Hey!"

I whipped around. A security guard marched toward me. Another, on his heels, said, "She's the one."

"Stop!"

One grabbed my arm. The other snatched my phone. They hustled me up to the lobby. Walker was waiting, fuming. Hank was with him, looking shocked. I couldn't look at Hank.

"Here's her phone, sir." The guard handed it to Walker.

I heard sirens. Then everything moved very fast. I was led outside. Two police cruisers, lights strobing, pulled up at the curb. People on the treed path—students, staff—stopped to gawk. Some lifted their phones' cameras—I'm sure they recognized Hank. There was tense confusion as Walker, pointing at me, shot back answers to the officers' questions, the sirens muffling their voices. Two officers moved toward me.

I met Walker's eyes. He still held my phone. "Too late," I told him, loud enough to be heard. "I livestreamed everything. It's already out there."

An officer told me my rights as he led me to a cruiser, opened the rear door.

I heard the word "accomplice" as another officer went for Hank.

"No, he had nothing to do with—" I started to say, but hands shoved me onto the back seat and the door slammed shut.

23

Chandra took my elbow and led me to a corner of the police station lobby, away from the cluster of people surrounding Hank, his staffers and his lawyer, conferring with him in hushed voices. Outside, media types were milling at the glass doors, hungry for video and quotes, but kept at bay by a line of four constables inside.

"The statute is the Trespass to Property Act," Chandra told me.

"Which means what? A fine?"

"And more. In court, if a judge decided you trespassed for malicious purposes, the judgment could include punitive damages and an award for costs."

"Well, that would make for a good fundraising appeal."

"It's not funny, Nat."

"No, it's dead serious. Which was exactly the point. We'll fight this."

She shook her head. "Walker would love a fight, but the university not so much. They're not pressing charges. They don't want any more bad publicity."

The letdown felt weird. My body thrummed with adrenaline with nowhere to go. "So . . . that's it?"

"That's it. We're done here. Oh, and I got your phone back." She handed it over.

I quickly scrolled the messages. There were dozens in response to the video I'd live streamed on Facebook. I felt a spark of jubilation. The world had seen. Thank you, Mark Zuckerberg.

One of Hank's people was pointing to the elevator. It would take Hank down to the parking lot to evade the media outside. His handlers were clearly urging him to go, but he was looking at me, his face stiff with anger. He held up his hand to quiet his staffers. He walked over to me.

I made myself meet his accusing eyes.

Chandra glanced at Hank, then at me, sensing the storm. "I'll be over there finishing the paperwork," she said, starting toward the desk.

Hank's voice was low, tense. "You used me. For a stunt."

"No, for a good cause."

"So that's your idea of trust? Lying and using people?"

"Look, I'm sorry it got you into trouble. I didn't think they'd bring you in."

"You didn't think, period." He had raised his voice. His staffers winced. I didn't appreciate how they looked at me, like I was some kind of witch who'd put a spell on him.

"It's just a bit of bad press, Hank. You'll survive. Unlike Walker's animals."

"And my political career. So congratulations. You've got your kill."

"I never intended that."

"See, that's the messy thing about war. Collateral damage."

"Oh, enough self-pity. What do you think is the *point* of a political career? I helped you get elected so you'd do some good. But you don't stand up for anything, Hank. You told me you would put forward a bill to regulate animal research, but you were just stringing me along—you've done nothing. And when I asked you to make a simple public statement about the ag-gag law, you flat refused."

"Seems I misunderstood. I didn't realize our relationship was purely transactional. But, hell, Natalie, even in a business deal you don't stick in a knife."

"A deal? No, deals are what you do with people like Walker. You bring his college a juicy grant and, in return, he brings you votes. I thought you were above that. I thought my issues were your issues."

His look was withering. "Such a sordid place, the real world."

"Oh, I know all about the real world."

"But very little about me. You wanted me to *remake* the world for you. You even made me want to try. But no more. Not with a partner I can't trust."

He went back to his anxious people. They marched him to the elevator. He didn't look back at me. The elevator doors closed. Then he was gone.

Coldness crept over me. The hollow coldness of loss. No—I didn't want that, I wanted the hot satisfaction of triumph. I stalked out the front door to the waiting reporters.

"I'm Natalie Sinclair of All Creatures Great and Small," I announced. "Today we revealed the appalling cruelty that animals suffer at the university's veterinary college. I speak as an advocate for those voiceless animals, and I encourage you to look at the video I captured. It tells the whole story. It's up on our website."

A few tapped at their phones. Several yelled questions at once.

"Animal rights activists are on police terrorist lists. Do you consider yourself a terrorist?"

"A freedom fighter," I said.

"By breaking laws?"

"You want the real criminals? They wear white lab coats, and their business is torture. They're allowed to buy lost pets from unscrupulous dealers and from the city pound to carry out their experiments. The pound wants the animals gone to save money, and labs want them because pets are easy to handle; they trust people. And what does trust in people get them? Cruelty and death. *That's* criminal."

"So you think people should get away with breaking the law?"

"When it's necessary. Women had to break laws to win the right to vote. Marchers had to break laws to end segregation. Miners had to break laws to win the right to unionize. The fight to protect animals is no different. And every time, the fight is hard. Throughout history, people who fought for a better future for all were labeled terrorists. They were assaulted, jailed, tortured, and stoned. They were assassinated. They were even crucified."

There was a sudden silence. I was on a high. My face felt flushed. I'd created the heat.

Someone yelled, "Are you comparing yourself with Jesus Christ?"

"Hey," I said cockily, "if the halo fits."

A roar of voices hit me, a volley of questions.

Chandra was tugging my arm. "Nat, come," she said tightly in my ear. "We're done."

I thanked the Uber driver and got out in front of Mrs. Carson's mansion. The late-afternoon quiet felt like a void around me as I took the flagstone path around to the coach house. A few flakes of snow drifted past the mansion's oaks, melting on the ground, where the tips of purple crocus blooms dared to poke out of the soil. Winter was losing to spring. It should have made me smile. I had won today, won for the animals. But I thought of Hank's face, so furious and hurt. The cost of winning. The win had made me alone. Apart. I'd been alone for so many anxious days, ever since finding Paul's body. Blindly searching for DuPre. Isolated in tracking Logan Leblanc.

Silenced by Mancuso's warnings. It felt like I was stumbling down one dark tunnel after another.

"Here she is!"

I stopped on the path. A bunch of my volunteers stood at my front door—five, six, seven of them. Seeing me, they burst into applause.

I couldn't speak, my throat tight with the threat of tears. Happy tears. I'd never been so glad to see these crazy animal lovers.

"We've been calling you," Trevor said, throwing his arms wide in exasperation. "No answer."

"They had my phone."

"Well, welcome home, Nat," Annika said. "You're a hero!"

"Which calls for some celebrating," Amber said, holding up a sixpack of Creemore Premium Lager. "Woot!"

"Cheers, indeed," Victor said dryly, winking at me as he held up a bottle of Pinot Noir.

I unlocked the door. Everyone piled inside. I set out glasses on the kitchen table for the beer and wine, and Bahira set down a bowl of her famous tabbouleh. "There's hummus in the fridge," I said. The team of Nathan and Ellen found it, while Amber dug out plates and forks. I grabbed a bag of tortilla chips from the cupboard, plus a package of pita triangles. The kitchen space was dim since Trevor had nailed plywood to cover the broken window in the door, so Nicole threw open the door to let in the strengthening sunshine. Everyone dug into the food, chattering, pouring drinks. Instant party.

For me, instant happiness. The happiness of solidarity. They say no one understands war who hasn't fought, and these were my fellow soldiers. Veterans. I'd seen them endure the gamut of insults from mockery to hateful name-calling, all for harboring "too many" stray cats or spending their savings on vet bills or going to jail for giving water to a pig on its way to the slaughterhouse. To me, *they* were the heroes.

Keith and his wife arrived with more wine. Food was gobbled, drink flowed, the laughter got louder, the war stories more Gothic, and everyone cheered when Annika found a tub of coconut vegan ice cream in the back of my freezer.

Ellen was entertaining us with the story of the two grim-faced officers from CSIS, Canada's CIA, accosting her at a Tim Hortons years ago to interrogate her about her role in defying the Seal Protection Regulations—the law that said sealers could bash out the brains of baby seals but it was a crime for anyone else to get near enough to photograph the slaughter. "They sent two of their finest. Both were named Jennifer," Ellen said, delighting in the idiocy.

"Women in Black," Nathan chimed in.

Everyone chuckled.

"Hey, guys, come in here. Nat's on TV."

We all squeezed into my small living room. A picture of the vet college with its sign out front filled the screen, and my heartbeat quickened with excitement that the story had made prime time national news. As the anchor launched into the details, I felt proud to have these friends watching it with me. Amber did her signature "Woot!" Everyone grinned. Trevor gave me a delighted thumbs-up.

The room quieted as we watched.

"Hank Verhagen, Liberal Member of Parliament for Craigmuir, Ontario, was involved today in an incident of unauthorized trespass by an animal rights activist. The incident took place at the University of Southern Ontario's veterinary college." Silent video ran of Hank speaking to the police officers beside the cruisers, their siren lights flashing.

I felt a clutch of dismay. *Hank* was the focus of the story? Where were the pictures of the suffering animals in cages? We'd sent my entire minutes-long video with a press release to all the media outlets.

"The activist apprehended is Natalie Sinclair"—video of the officer guiding me into the cruiser's rear seat—"who gained access to a lab area restricted to all except veterinary surgeons and their students, for the safety of the animals. Ms. Sinclair has a record of participating in disruptive protests."

A still picture of me filled the screen. Me eight years ago, outside a slaughterhouse, my mouth agape in anger at the officer restraining me, my messed hair damp with sweat in the heat, a manic look in my eyes.

"Wow, good one, Nat. Wild woman," Amber murmured, trying to lighten the moment. But no one was smiling anymore.

"It's unclear what role Mister Verhagen played in helping the activist gain access. No charges have been laid, but sources say the incident could cut short Verhagen's promising political career. There was no comment from the PMO about whether the Prime Minister would consider disciplinary measures against the rookie MP, the party's youngest, in his first Parliamentary session."

I was stunned. The coverage was all about Hank. Hank's part in the event. Hank's jeopardized career. There was not a single second of my video.

"Show the animals, you fuckers," Nathan said to the TV.

"Mister Verhagen's office has denied any connection between him and Natalie Sinclair. However, photos taken a half hour before the event indicate otherwise."

The picture hit me like a slap. Hank kissing me on the university path. A student must have taken it with a phone. It brought a faint gasp from Nicole. Puzzled frowns from the others.

The TV coverage cut to me speaking to reporters outside the police station, a five-second clip:

"Are you comparing yourself to Jesus Christ?"

"Well, if the halo fits . . ."

I cringed. Why had I said such a stupid thing? I'd been on a high, so eager to erase Hank's anger from my mind, to claim victory instead. *Idiot.*

The coverage cut to Detective Rourke opening a door, clearly stopped in the act of entering his office. The caption read: "Homicide Detective Sergeant Alan Rourke, Craigmuir Police." He looked uncomfortable, close-mouthed as a reporter asked him about the Paul Leblanc investigation. "Is it true you interrogated the animal rights activist Natalie Sinclair in connection with the murder?"

"I cannot comment on an ongoing investigation."

"But can you confirm that you questioned her?"

He said briskly, as if to end the discussion, "I can confirm only that she is a person of interest. That is all."

It felt like ice shards in my heart. My friends were staring at me in silent, nervous wonder.

24

I emptied the plate of leftover tortilla chips into the trash along with the last shriveled triangles of pita. They were all stale after their night on the kitchen table. As stale as my mouth.

After Trevor and the others had left, I'd been so wound up by the damning news coverage, so furiously frustrated at the media ignoring the horror I had exposed of those tortured animals, I knew I would never sleep. So I'd finished what was left of Victor's Pinot Noir, almost half a bottle, hoping the wine would calm me, let me sleep. Instead, it had given me a stabbing headache.

Coffee helped. Fresh ground and strong, made in the French coffee press my mom had given me when I'd first left home for university. My friends' solidarity helped too. They had been wonderful last night. Annika had assured me that our dedicated supporters—people who truly loved animals and understood what we were fighting for—were the audience that mattered. She and the others gave me big hugs as they'd said goodbye. Alone, I'd surveyed the dirty dishes, the scraps of tabbouleh and hummus, the dregs of wine and beer. It was the evening I would have spent with Hank, our dinner date. Instead, what I'd done had made him hate me. A stunt, he'd called it. The word was so wrong. What I'd done was expose horrific abuse. But Hank saw only that I had used him. The police saw only that I was a troublemaker. The media saw only a spicy scandal. That toxic brew had turned Hank against me. Nothing could be the same between us ever again. It hurt.

I finished my coffee then washed the wineglasses in the sink, still cursing the media. If they had played just twenty seconds of those poor animals' agony, it would have made all the difference. But they only wanted to skewer Hank by insinuating he was my accomplice, and skewer me by insinuating I might have killed Paul Leblanc. Insane, all of it.

A wineglass slipped my grip and broke against the edge of the sink, sending sharp pieces into the soapy water. I felt for them as carefully as I could, but one cut the web of my right thumb. I dabbed the blood then hunted for a Band-Aid. Damn it. Not good for playing the violin. I had my duet with Dad tomorrow night at the memorial concert. The cut thumb could screw up my bow hold.

There was a knock at my door.

My heart did a hopeful skip. Hank? Should I apologize? Say how truly sorry I was?

I opened the door. Mrs. Carson. Despite the morning chill, her Chanel suit jacket was unbuttoned over her silk blouse. She looked tight-lipped, her face pale.

"Good morning," I said, unsure what could be bringing her to my door.

"It may be for some, Natalie."

She looked so serious, I had to ask, "Has something happened?" For one anxious moment, I thought of Mom. But Dad wouldn't call my landlady, he'd call me.

"It's about what happened yesterday," she said. "You, at the university."

"You saw the news report?"

"I did. It kept me awake most of the night."

Now I got it. She cared about the animals. Thank God. After all, she was a major donor to All Creatures. I gave her a grateful smile. "I couldn't sleep either," I said, "and you didn't even see the worst. Please, come in. Can I get you coffee?"

"No. This won't take long." She stiffly held out an envelope. "For you."

"What's this?" I asked, opening it.

"Notice. I'm giving you sixty days. That's the law."

I blinked at her. Then unfolded the papers: "Notice to Vacate Tenancy." I looked back at her. "But—why? Are you selling?"

"Selling? Goodness, no, I've lived here all my life." She crossed her arms, a shield against me. "But *you* must go."

"I don't understand." We'd always gotten along. I'd taken care of her cat, Yuly, when she was away. She'd occasionally had me in for tea. "Have I neglected the coach house in some way?"

It came out in a high-strung rush. "You have defamed a grand institution, our university. I won't have it. Not only have I lived here all my life, the university has *been* my life. My great-great-grandfather was one of the founders. My late husband was chancellor. And I myself taught there for decades, in the highly respected department of geology. Faculty members remain my dearest friends."

"I'm sorry, but that's hardly the point. My action was about saving animals."

"It's *my* point. When you strike at USO, you strike at me."

I couldn't believe it. How could she be such a generous benefactor of our work for animals and yet ignore their plight right in front of her? I reminded myself that she hadn't seen the stomach-turning video I'd taken. None of the general public had.

"Mrs. Carson, I'm afraid you may not be aware of how the animals at the veterinary college are treated. There is terrible abuse, and I was there to—"

"To drag an august institution through the mud. Police. Arrests. TV cameras. And, apparently, even the taint of a murder."

"That investigation has nothing to do with—"

"Enough." She raised her hand to preempt my explanation. "I'm not here to argue, Natalie. I'm here to ask you to leave. You will kindly obey that notice."

An awful thought struck. "Mrs. Carson, of course I'll go, if that's your wish. But please tell me this won't affect your relationship with All Creatures Great and Small. There is so much important work to be done, and we so need your continued support."

A taunting smile twitched her lips. "My money, you mean. Well, there are other groups whose work for animals is just as important. Groups who understand the requirements of science, and of civility. Our relationship is finished. I will be investigating my options."

I had scheduled a morning Zoom meeting with my board members, and I arrived at the office determined to give them the good news about the positive response to my video from many of our members before breaking the bad news about the loss of Mrs. Carson as a major donor. On my way I'd read dozens of emails and texts from people sharing their horror about the animal abuse and thanking me for exposing it. Contributions were coming in too. Janice had told me as soon as I arrived.

"Nat, another e-transfer," she said now, eyes on her screen. "Fifty dollars. That's four in just the last twenty minutes. Wow, here's another."

"Love it," I said as I booted up my Mac. "Victor, get that fancy fountain pen of yours ready. You've got some serious penmanship ahead." A personal handwritten thank-you note from us to every contributor was my policy, and I knew Victor enjoyed the task.

"My pleasure, Madam." He gave me his courtly little British bow and settled down at the communal table with his take-out coffee to get started.

If only the morning could have stayed that cheerful. Janice tabulating contributions. Victor writing thank-you cards. Nicole shaking cat treats into the dish of our resident tabby, Pico. Amber arriving, singing along with her earphones. Later, I would remember these moments as a lull, a calm, like an unruffled lagoon before the tsunami hits.

The first big ripple was an email from a supporter who was also a member of the congregation of my father's former church, St. Timothy's. My halo comment to reporters yesterday, replayed on the morning's national news and talk radio, had deeply offended her. "Your father would be ashamed of you," she wrote. I winced, regretting again my stupid words. She was canceling her All Creatures newsletter subscription and terminating her substantial monthly donations. Thousands of dollars, gone.

They say a tsunami is not a single wave but a series of waves, a wave train. And that's how it happened.

I took the phone call from the next major donor, the wife of the president of the Liberal Party association for the electoral district of Craigmuir. She told me I had done irreparable harm to our MP, Hank Verhagen, as well as to the party, and informed me that she could no longer support an organization led by someone so reckless and selfish. I took a deep breath and respectfully asked that she reconsider for the sake of the animals, but before I finished she cut the call short. Thousands more dollars, washed away.

The following waves—the unstoppable train—came in a dozen calls and messages from aggrieved Liberal Party members, angry university alumni, and upset Christians, each with their own version of my sins, each canceling contribution pledges that ranged from a hundred dollars a month to multi-thousand-dollar donations, plus one really big, promised bequest. All of it, swept into oblivion.

"Amazing work, Nat," Giles said happily as soon as he popped up on my Zoom screen, followed by Karin and Elizabeth. "The video is incredibly damning."

"And the outpouring of support from the membership is wonderful," Elizabeth chimed in. "I'm looking right now at the deposits coming in. Eighteen hundred dollars so far—"

"And it looks like we can expect more," Karin said.

Oh God. They didn't know.

"Listen, guys," I began, "it's great that so many good people support what we're doing." I meant it. Many of our members lived on tight budgets, watching every penny, but still found it in their hearts to help animals by sending us fifteen or twenty dollars a month. I had never admired those people more. "But . . . look, there's been some blowback, too. I have to tell you—"

"That's bound to happen," Karin said. "You can't please everyone."

"Oh, believe me, I haven't. I'm being told—"

"No, don't you dare apologize," Giles said. "Not to anyone. What you did is heroic."

"Epic," Karin said.

"Nat," Elizabeth said, "we're behind you 100 percent."

"Stop. Please. Listen to me. The response—" I had to stop, take a moment to steady my voice. This was so hard. "These small donations—"

"It's impressive," Giles said. "Eighteen hundred dollars."

"So far," Elizabeth reminded us all.

"But I'm afraid there are thousands of dollars—many thousands—that we've lost," I said. "That *I* lost."

"What do you mean?"

They were silent as I told them. Starting with Mrs. Carson and right through the dozen other major donors and that enormous bequest. By then their smiles had vanished.

"Jesus," Karin muttered. Elizabeth looked shocked.

"That's half our operating budget," Giles said quietly.

"Exactly," I said. "It's too big a hit. Listen, the positive support from so many members is wonderful; you're right, and you should hang onto that. You should build on that goodwill."

"*We* should? What are you saying?"

I looked at Pico sauntering across the floor to his water bowl. Looked at Victor writing a thank-you note. Looked up at the skylight, dirty with a residue of grimed snow. Anywhere but at the three earnest faces on my screen.

"Nat?"

I met their eyes. "I think I should resign."

Silence. Then, from Karin, "No way."

"That's nonsense," Elizabeth said. "Nat, you're the heart and brains and soul of this organization."

"I agree," said Giles, "so that makes it unanimous. We're behind you, Nat. You're not going anywhere."

The threat of tears pricked the back of my throat. I had never felt so grateful for the support of these fine people. I had to dig my nails into my fists to hold back the tears.

"It's not that simple," I said. "The loss of so much income jeopardizes all our projects. If we can't keep funding Bear With Us, orphan cubs will die. Without the Forever Homes program, abandoned dogs and cats will die. No more fighting the roadside zoos and the puppy mills, or saving horses from the kill pens. And we can't hire the lawyer to fight the ag-gag law. That's the awful outcome if I stay."

Elizabeth looked ashen. "But . . . I don't see how your leaving can possibly help."

Giles said soberly, "She means we could hire her replacement. A new executive director."

"Exactly," I managed. "That could coax the donors back. I think it would. And then you can carry on."

I didn't wait for a reply. I was finally getting my voice under control, and my breaking heart. "Please," I said, "let me do this. For the sake of the animals."

25

I tried to ignore a throbbing headache as the audience funneled past me into St. Timothy's for the memorial concert in honor of Julia. People flowed past our little family cluster standing inside the doors, offering sympathetic nods to my brother, James, and his wife, Gabriella, and me, but the stream bottlenecked as people respectfully stopped to shake hands with Dad. As a well-known inspirational speaker and author, he was a bigger draw than the musicians who would play tonight. They were accomplished professionals, colleagues of Julia's, but they were strangers to most of the people filing in for the concert, whereas Dad had been St. Timothy's rector for decades before his semiretirement, and to congregation members and concertgoers alike, he felt almost like family.

I was relieved that James and Gabriella, standing beside me, were doing such a gracious job as greeters. Unlike me. I had no chitchat in me. I was just trying to hold it together, to get to the end of this god-awful day. The board had dejectedly accepted my resignation.

All Creatures Great and Small, the little kick-ass group I had birthed and nurtured, was no longer mine. The full realization kept coming back to me in panicky ripples. It was hard to imagine what my future could be. The work of All Creatures had been my identity, my reason for getting up every morning, eager to fight the good fight. With that work stripped away, who was I?

"Natalie, what a fine turnout." A woman's voice in my ear.

I turned to see Susan Fraser, St. Timothy's current rector. Trim, about fifty, she wore a black pantsuit, her clerical collar the only indication of her position. I didn't know her well. Apart from Paul's funeral here two weeks ago, I hadn't been inside the church, or any church, for years. "Just wanted to say that your comments yesterday to the press made quite an impact."

I stiffened, ready for her reprimand about my halo crack.

"I, for one, was not aware of the plight of the animals at the U," she said. "Good work."

An animal lover, my goodness. I thanked her, and meant it. "Could I send you some links? There's no one better than you to spread the word."

"Yes, do," she said.

We fell into the awkward silence of people who have little more to say to each other, not from animosity but from living in different worlds. To fill it, our gazes drifted to the stage platform erected in front of the altar, where Julia's poster-size photo stood beside the piano: the famous cellist in a strapless red gown, her cheek caressing the neck of her cello, her big bold smile so at odds with the somber mood in the church as people started filling the pews. The concert was a benefit to raise awareness about mental health. Everyone here was aware that Julia's struggle with depression had led to her suicide.

"I never did hear her play," Reverend Fraser murmured.

I was about to recommend to her my favorite of Julia's recordings but stopped as I saw, over her shoulder, the latest arrivals. Coming in with the mayor and his wife was Hank Verhagen.

Hank saw me, too, and for a moment our eyes met. The anger in his wasn't the hot resentment of yesterday; it had subsided to a cool glare, but the way he quickly turned to shake the hand of a man who'd approached him told me how much he wanted to avoid me. I bristled. Why the hell had he come if he was so worried about toxic association with me? I supposed the worst thing a politician could do was hide. He had to be out and about, had to be seen, especially at an event for a "good cause." It was bitter to think that's all Julia really meant to him, to so many of the people here: an elite night out to enjoy fine music.

Whatever, I had bigger problems than Hank Verhagen's reproach. Like finding a new place to live. And a new job. That brought another ripple of panic. I had to find a whole new life.

I tried to ground myself in the here and now. Not much solace, since my upcoming duet with Dad was something else to worry about. I was afraid my cut thumb would screw up my bow hold. Our piece was a small part of the program, scheduled just before the intermission, but I knew it meant a lot to him and didn't want to let him down. Luckily, the piece showcased the cello part, not the violin; I only had to accompany Dad.

It was almost time for the concert to start. The church was full and the audience was settling down, ready to be entertained. "Time to take our places," I said to James. Our role as greeters at the door was done. He and Gabriella would sit in a front pew, and Dad had already moved off to join the musicians in the side aisle, where chairs had been added for them as they waited to perform. I would sit beside him.

"I'll join you in a sec, Hon," James said to Gabriella. "I want a minute with Nat."

She nodded, offering me a supportive smile. "Good luck with the duet," she told me, then started down the nave to take her seat.

James looked at me soberly. "I was hoping Mom would come."

"Not her thing." I was fairly sure the emotion of this evening would be too much for Mom, too distressing. "Besides, someone has to stay with Liam." I didn't mention the thought lurking at the back of my mind, that there was someone who *should* have come. Liam's father. Simon had not flown back for this event to honor his wife.

"Nat, I'm really worried about Mom. She called me this morning, asked me if I had any Percocet left over from my surgery."

"Painkillers?" He'd had an operation on his shoulder a few weeks ago. "Why?" I asked, alarmed. "Did she have an accident? A fall or something?"

"No, nothing like that. Opioids, that's what she wants." He shook his head, overwhelmed. "Like she hasn't had enough."

This was terrible. I remembered the vials of pills on her bedside table. Valium? Xanax? Remembered how she spent whole days in bed. "You didn't give her the Percocet, did you?"

"No, I'm not going to give her drugs. Nat, she sounded really out of it. Fuzzy, you know? Even whispered something about keeping it secret from Dad, almost like she was afraid of him."

My heart ached for her. For both of them. "Dad can't handle this alone anymore," I said. "It's time we look at getting Mom some help."

"That's what I think." He threw up his hands. "But I haven't got a clue how. I mean, are we talking the psych ward?"

"No, no. She needs to see a specialist. Her doctor should be able to refer her."

"Oh. Okay. That's Donovan. So, should we ask Dad to call him?"

"Let's not bother him with it until something's lined up." I was afraid Dad would resist. "He's so sure it's his responsibility to care for Mom himself."

James nodded grimly. Neither of us touched the menacing undercurrent: Dad's possible fear that depression, which had taken his daughter's life, could now threaten his wife's.

"So, can you call Doctor Donovan?" James said. "I'm up to my eyeballs at work."

And I had *no* work. Though I felt I'd kill to have my job back. "Sure. I'll call him first thing tomorrow."

The chatter of the audience started to quiet down. The first musicians were getting up with their instruments, ready to file onto the stage. James gave my arm a squeeze. "Break a leg," he whispered. He had to get to his seat beside Gabriella, and I had to take mine with the other waiting players.

"James, hold on," I said quietly. "About Liam. It's too much for Dad. Do you know when Simon's going to send for him?"

"Didn't you hear? He emailed Dad. Something about trouble finding a house. He's asked Dad to keep Liam for a few more weeks."

Another dark thought that had been lurking reared up like a demon. Simon had originally planned to fly to California this week to start his new gig, but something had made him decide to leave a week earlier, the very day after Paul Leblanc's death. Had he left early to avoid detection as Paul's killer?

Normally I would have loved the music. I sensed that Julia's friends played the Albinoni "Adagio" with exquisite tenderness and that their rendering of Arvo Pärt's "Cantus" was magnificent. The rapt audience testified to that. But I was barely listening. My mind was a storm of crosscurrent winds.

Was I crazy to imagine Simon as a murderer? It suddenly seemed more crazy to have convinced myself that the killer was Logan Leblanc.

I hated Leblanc for the crimes I knew he'd committed—from raping a teenager to trafficking wild animals—and hated him all the more because I could see no way to bring him to justice. But had my hatred made me think him guilty of crimes he *hadn't* committed? After all, was a personal tiff with a brother really enough to drive a man to murder? Simon's motive was surely stronger if he'd found out about Julia's affair. Had Simon hated Paul enough to kill him?

At least one thing was very clear: Liam could not stay with my parents for several more weeks. Grief had exhausted Dad and sent Mom into some pitiful, personal black hole. But here I was, suddenly available, with nothing but time on my hands. My little nephew could stay with me. I didn't know much about kids, but Liam was such a sweet boy, I figured I could handle it. Take him to the swings in the park. Read bedtime stories. It actually gave me a faint tickle of delight, the first happy thought all day.

Applause burst around me. The musicians were taking their bows. They filed down off the stage. Dad started up the steps. He was next on the program. The audience hushed.

He thanked everyone for coming, then cleared his throat of uncharacteristic hoarseness and ran an uneasy hand through his hair. He looked bone tired. I felt tense, watching him. I'd never seen him nervous in all the times I'd heard him speak, whether sermons or public talks. No, I realized, it wasn't nerves. He was tired, of course, but also wound up. His jumpiness reminded me of my college roommate at exam time. She would take uppers to study, then downers to sleep, repeating the daily cycle. She aced the exams, then had a breakdown.

Dad's lifetime of experience kicked in, though, and he launched into his speech. He was eloquent, charismatic as ever, and no one listening could have been unmoved by his heartfelt appeal for everyone to be patient and vigilant in helping family and friends who were struggling with mental health issues. But his words did not calm me. Just the opposite. His entreaty was so achingly personal, so wrenching, that to me it was almost unbearable. He had loved Julia so much. My throat clenched with tears. For him. For Julia. And also, I was ashamed to admit, for myself. He had loved my sister more than me.

And now I had to join him on stage. The audience hushed as Dad and I took our seats, him behind his cello, me with my violin. How I managed to play with tears clouding my eyes, I hardly know. Amazingly, Dad played better than I'd ever heard him. It was like he was on a manic high, spaced out from love and grief and exhaustion. For me, emotionally, it was excruciating.

Then, mercifully, it was over. We bowed to a wave of applause. We hugged. Dad was so wound up, he was sweating. Covered by the applause, he whispered in my ear, "I think Julia heard. And forgives." It threw me, the raw intensity of his emotion. Our obviously charged moment together made the audience clap even more fervently, and I took his hand and squeezed, both to reassure him and to dam up my own tears. He managed a wobbly smile to me, and to the audience, and we left the stage. Intermission.

Chatter rose throughout the church, and loud shuffling as people got up, readying to take the break. I swiped away the last of my tears and joined the musicians on the move. As we merged with the audience, all of us heading downstairs to the church hall, I saw Hank behind several people, watching me. His frown had relaxed a little, maybe an unexpected moment of sympathy if he'd seen me wiping tears. Self-conscious, I quickened my steps to get far ahead of him.

The church hall was a din of voices. Audience and musicians mingled, helping themselves to coffee and tea, catered cupcakes and tarts. Church ladies manned the refreshment table just as previous ladies had at events here when I was a kid. The convivial mood was the same too, like the socializing after a baptism or the church's annual fundraising golf tournament. It was a mood I couldn't share. I stood with James and Gabriella, the two of them balancing dessert plates and coffee cups as they chatted with well-wishers. I couldn't eat a bite.

I didn't see how James could. Julia had been his sister, too. And didn't he find Dad's hyper-emotional state tonight disturbing? I glimpsed Dad across the crowd, surrounded by admirers. His exhaustion was plain to me, yet so was his unerring public cordiality. The mask of a lifetime.

Stop judging, I told myself. Who was I to call him out for letting his emotions carry him too far? I'd done worse, holding forth to those reporters yesterday. Besides, I needed to pull myself together to get through hearing the second half of the program, a violinist and pianist to play Vaughan-Williams's "The Lark Ascending" and then the big name, star cellist Amanda Forsyth, who would close the show with the Bach *G Major Suite* and Faure's "Elegy." Beautiful, soulful music. The emotional toll was going to be rough.

I excused myself to my brother to use the washroom, glad to get away from his chummy talk with a man about real estate. Gabriella, busy complimenting a woman on her shoes, didn't even hear me. I was making my way through the crowd when I saw a face that surprised me.

Trevor Wapoosh. He was pushing past people, making his way toward me. I felt a rush of warmth, glad to see a friend.

"Trevor," I said, smiling as we reached each other, "it's so good of you to come."

"Had a hell of a time finding out where you were."

That startled me. So did his serious expression. And he seemed a little out of breath. Something had happened. "What's up?" I suddenly dreaded hearing there had been more fallout at the office, more defections. Please, I thought, don't tell me that even the volunteers are bailing.

"I found DuPre," he said.

I stared at him. My mind was so clogged with other worries, it took a moment for the name to penetrate.

"DuPre," Trevor said more loudly, as if the din in the hall had kept me from hearing.

But I had heard, and the image of DuPre's trusting face burst through like sunlight through storm clouds. "How? Where?" Then suddenly the light was snuffed out. "She's dead, isn't she." That's why he was here. To break the horrible news.

"No, she's alive. At least, I'm pretty sure it's her. I couldn't get close enough to be absolutely sure."

Thank God. "Where?" I asked again.

"You know that strip mall across from the bowling alley on Woodson? I pulled into the Esso for gas, and in the parking lot right across from me, in front of the Seven-Eleven, there was a van. A guy was opening the rear door and inside I saw a bunch of cages. Dogs, cats. One of the dogs, the nearest one, looked exactly like DuPre. That black star in the white above her nose. The guy shut the door—he didn't see me looking. Then he got behind the wheel and drove off."

My breath caught. "A buncher."

"That's what I figured, too. So I hopped behind the wheel and followed him. Right out of town on County Road 12. Had to gun it to keep up with him. Past the water tower, past the fairgrounds, right out into potato farm country. Finally, just after that big billboard for some car dealer, he slowed down and turned onto a farm lane."

"He's a farmer?" Unlikely, I thought.

"I don't know. I pulled over onto the side of the road, didn't want him to see me following. I could see the farmhouse, though. Looked pretty crummy. Run down, you know? And an old barn behind it. And a lot of vehicles. Must have been about twenty—cars, pickup trucks, big hog motorcycles. A party, I figured. That's when I decided to give it up. Sorry, Nat, but I wasn't going to knock on the front door. With guys like that partying, I'd probably get someone telling me to go back where I came from. Then I'd tell him, 'Good idea, I'll pitch my tepee in your front yard.' Things don't tend to go well after that."

"No, don't apologize. It's just so great that you found her."

"Tomorrow you can follow up. I can't go; I've got classes. But take a volunteer from the office. That place didn't look exactly friendly."

He didn't know it wasn't my office anymore, my volunteers. "Absolutely. I can't thank you enough." I hugged him. A new energy coursed through me. I couldn't wait to see DuPre. There was no way I could go home, go to bed, wait for morning. By then the buncher might be driving her off to some research lab. And I didn't need help. Bunchers wanted only one thing, money, and I could deliver that as well as any lab.

"You said the farm's right after the Chrysler billboard?"

"Yeah. Just before the intersection with County Road 7. If you cross that, you've gone too far."

"Great. You've done so much, Trevor. Now get a bite. There are cupcakes. And coffee." I gave him a gentle push toward the food table. "Excuse me, I've got to see some people over there."

I wove through the throng toward my father. But I could see that his circle of admirers still held him captive. Impossible to get a private word with him. Worse, Hank stood not far from him, talking to one of the violinists. Hank was the last person I wanted to hear me say I was leaving to get my dog. I veered and crossed the room to my brother.

"James, I have to go. Please, will you tell Dad? He's holding court and I can't get through."

"Go? Why? What about the after-party?"

"You and Gabriella and Dad can manage that. No one will miss me."

"Nat, what's wrong? What's happened?"

"Nothing's wrong. Just the opposite." I was itching to go. To do this one thing I *could* do, a chance to make something turn out right. I felt Julia would understand. Six weeks ago I hadn't been able to save her, had ignored the warning signs, too wrapped up in my own life to see that hers was in danger. But tonight, right now, I had a shot at saving DuPre.

26

I made just one stop, the ATM at the Scotiabank branch around the corner from the church. The daily limit my account allowed was a thousand dollars. That had to be more than a lab would give a buncher for DuPre. If not, I would promise him I'd get more.

I stuffed the wad of cash in my pocket, ran back to my car, and in ten minutes I was driving under the massive shadow of the town's water tower hulking against the risen moon. Five minutes later, I sped past the fairgrounds.

Farmer's fields stretched out on either side of me, dark and silent, barren except for scattered pockmarks of snow. I switched on the radio for company. Miles Davis's trumpet was spinning his haunting rendition of "Summertime." Right now, summer seemed a long way off. I'd be satisfied with spring.

Ten minutes later, the huge Chrysler billboard loomed ahead on the right. Why some sales genius considered this lonely landscape the perfect spot to plug a dealership eluded me, but I was no marketing expert. Maybe the flashy car image spoke to farm wives who dreamed of leaving cranky husbands, or to tired truckers who dreamed of retiring to Florida. I was just glad it was lit up, creating a landmark I couldn't miss.

I slowed a little as I passed the billboard. In the distance ahead, to my right, a car beetling along the county road crossed the intersection, its headlights as antennae. I slowed, remembering Trevor's directions. If I reached that dark crossroads, I'd gone too far.

So the farm ahead to my left had to be the one. Here on the road there was no mailbox post to identify the place, not even an emergency locator number, but at the far end of its long lane I could see a house, and behind it the roof of a barn, plus a scatter of vehicles just like Trevor had described. Inside the house the party was likely just getting into high gear. I turned onto the lane. It was straight as a rifle, and the hard rutted dirt was so bone-jarring, I bumped along it slowly. In the darkness, my headlights were feeling the way.

I neared the house, passing under a halogen light atop a high pole that cast a wash of dead-white light over the ramshackle old place and its ragged yard. There were more vehicles than I'd expected. They spread across the front yard, where last year's overgrown grass was trampled, and they snaked around in the direction of the barn. I found a spot to park near the run-down porch, pulling in between a black pickup truck elevated on monster tires and a Harley-Davidson motorcycle.

The house was surprisingly dark. So, no festivities here. But a faint glow arose beyond its roof, coming from the barn at back. Clearly, that's where the party was happening.

I turned off the car, and Miles Davis's trumpet died. When I got out I heard voices coming from the direction of the barn, excited shouting, muffled inside the building. Sounded like a crowds' yells when you hear a football game on TV in the next room. There was barking, too, from several dogs.

I started walking around the edge of the house toward the barn, weaving past the cars and pickup trucks parked helter-skelter. Once around the corner, I saw light shining out from the barn's narrow entrance. Its two tall doors of scaly barnboard had been pulled together, leaving an opening just the width of a man. The shouting, as I got closer, came in waves with high-pitched peaks, more feverish than for football, more like at a boxing match or wrestling. I imagined an all-male audience. For the first time, I wished I had someone with me, one of my guy volunteers. Trevor's instincts were suddenly my instincts. The jeers he got as an aboriginal weren't that different from the taunts women got. I felt for my phone, more for the comfort of a talisman than any logical expectation of help. It would take anyone at least half an hour to get here.

That realization made me cautious. I decided not to march up to the entrance. First, I needed to check out what was happening inside. At the side of the barn, up a slight slope, a shaft of light shone through a crack between the boards. I clambered up the slope, my concert heels slipping on the damp dead grass. Worth the effort, because from this rise I'd be able to see down into the barn's whole interior, not just into some cow stall.

I brought my eye to the crack between the barn boards. My breath snagged at the scene. Maybe thirty people, almost all men, a few women, surrounded a ring of waist-high wood partitions like around a hockey rink. They stood yelling at two dogs inside the ring, a pit bull chained to a post, straining to lunge, barking wildly, and across from the pit bull a German shepherd cowering against the boards, whimpering.

I felt cold to my core, like I'd stepped into an abattoir freezer.

I had stumbled upon a dogfight.

The pit bull lunged to the length of its chain. The other dog cringed. A man made his way around the crowd, taking bets. Another man reached down to unchain the pit bull. The people's yelling rose to a fever pitch as the pit bull, let loose, charged its prey and tore into it. The yelps of the attacked dog were sickening.

I couldn't watch. I twisted away.

I dug into my pocket for my phone to call the police. Dog fighting was illegal. Unlike smuggled monkeys, the police cared about this because of the gambling. When the 911 dispatcher answered, I spoke quietly, though it wasn't necessary with all the shouting inside the barn. "I want to report a crime." She put me through to the police and I answered the questions as calmly as I could. Location. Number of people. I was told to leave the location, so I ended the call and was about to hurry down the slope to my car and get the hell away from this terrible place, but first I took a second to scan the parked vehicles, the cars and trucks and motorcycles, afraid one or more of the men might have come out. I had to get to my car without any of them seeing me.

That's when I saw something that yanked my heart up into my throat. A yellow car. Expensive. A car I had been in. A canary yellow Porsche.

In a stupefied flash, it all clicked together. Monkey trafficking. Trophy hunting. Dog killing. Logan Leblanc. He was here, just steps away from me.

I fumbled in my pocket for Detective Rourke's card. Thank God I hadn't changed my jacket for the concert; the card was there. *I've got you now, Leblanc, you bastard.* My hands were trembling as I tapped the number, so keyed up I almost dropped the phone. *Please, not voicemail.*

He answered. "Detective Sergeant Alan Rourke."

"Detective, it's Natalie Sinclair. I'm at a dogfight . . . I mean, I'm outside . . . it's happening inside a barn. On County Road 12." I tried to keep the amazement and excitement out of my voice as I connected the dots for him. "Did you get my message the other day? My suspicion about Logan Leblanc? After that I found out a lot more about him. Serious crimes. So it's not a stretch to think he murdered Paul. I've got—"

"Did you say . . . a dogfight?"

"Yes. That's where I am. Where *he* is. It's awful. There's a whole gang inside this barn and I can see—"

"That sounds very dangerous, Ms. Sinclair. Are you in a safe place?"

"Yes, I'm okay, I'm fine—"

"Where, exactly?"

"At the side of this barn. And *inside* Logan Leblanc is—"

"Stay where you are. Do not proceed inside. I'll handle this." He ended the call.

Wait—he hadn't asked the location. Of course he could trace it from my phone. But to make sure, I was tapping the number again to tell him—he *had* to catch Leblanc—when I heard barking inside the barn and I stopped. The sound was different than the other dogs, a different timbre. I listened, tense. I was sure I recognized that bark.

I turned back to look inside. A man stood over the two bloodied dogs that had fought. The German shepherd was dead. The pit bull lay gasping. "Loser," a man said to the pit bull. He lifted a gun and shot it. I flinched at the horror. Two teenagers dragged both dead dogs out of the pit through a narrow door. A man led in a fresh pit bull and chained it to the post. Another man announced, "Training match," and said the bets were for how many minutes it would last. Another man was pulling a new dog into the ring, a new victim. A black-and-white border collie. I felt so sick I was dizzy.

It was DuPre.

She was let off the leash and stood looking around in fear and confusion. The chained pit bull quivered with excitement, barking madly. The pit door closed again.

Save her! But how? I gulped breaths to keep from throwing up. Stop the fight . . . *somehow*. I scrambled down the slope.

I tore around to the entrance and bolted inside. "Stop this!" I yelled. Then stopped, my legs spongy, my breaths quick, painful. Thirty or more faces had turned to me, surprise etched on their features by the bright lightbulb hanging above the pit. I couldn't see past them to DuPre, but I knew, in the electric buzz of adrenaline, that I had stopped the fight, had saved her.

"Stop *everything*," I yelled again "The police are coming." I held up my phone to show them as proof.

"Holy shit," one of them said, and there was a wave of furious murmurs. It felt so good to scare them that I wanted to yell, *And you'll all be under arrest*. But I was alone so far, no police. I looked for Leblanc. Couldn't see him.

Behind me there was a loud *thud* of the big barn door slamming closed. I turned to see who had done it and was stunned to see Detective Rourke.

How . . . ? It was just minutes since I'd called him.

He walked toward me. "I told you to stay in a safe place, Ms. Sinclair."

Something was wrong. Why was he alone? Where was his backup?

"But you never listen, do you? Ever since those fucking monkeys." He grabbed my phone. Thumbed the readout. "Jesus, you did call them." He hurled the phone. His fist came up, and the punch to my stomach sent me stumbling. I doubled over in pain. My mind staggered.

"Everybody out," he shouted. "It's true, she called the cops. Everybody out *now*." There was a roar of voices as people sprang into action.

Rourke grabbed my elbow and dragged me toward the pit. People and dogs were moving all around us, men yelling and running, dogs barking.

I tried to straighten up, my stomach still cramping. I gaped at Rourke. "You . . . Leblanc . . ."

He shoved me into the pit ring, pushing so hard I stumbled. "You were warned, you stupid cunt. *Warned*."

I staggered past Dupre. She followed me, whimpering and cringing, coming to me as if for safety. Across the ring the pit bull barked at us wildly, lunging to the length of its chain.

A hand snatched my hair, yanked me around. The Russian. He pulled me down to my knees. With a shove, he let go of me. I swiped for his leg. He kicked me in the ribs. I toppled in pain. I heard Rourke say something to him, indistinct above the tortured breaths that sawed my throat.

Gasping, I tried to get up, managed to make it onto my knees. I flung my arm around DuPre's neck and pulled her close in a blind need to comfort her and steady my own terror. Someone was unchaining the pit bull from the post. Leashed, the dog was dragged out of the pit. My body and DuPre's sagged together in a rush of relief. They'd just wanted to terrify me, I realized. But now the pit bull was gone. It was over.

Except it wasn't. The part of my brain still logically functioning told me they just wanted to get the fighting dog out before the police came and confiscated it. A trained pit bull had value. I didn't.

The Russian snatched my hair again. I yelped in pain, grabbing his wrist to ease the fire in my scalp as he dragged me on my ass over to the post. He yanked my arms behind me, behind the post. I felt rope bite into my wrists. Tied tight, sitting there, I couldn't move my arms. Terror swamped me.

Rourke and the Russian walked out of the pit through its narrow door. Above its low walls I could see the faces of men hustling past. The hanging lightbulb swayed in the commotion. I called to the men, my voice thin with fear, "Help me . . . please . . ."

One man stopped. He stood at the open door holding a jumpy Doberman on a leash. His bald head gleamed under the light. His crucifix earring glinted. Mancuso. He scowled at me, looking torn. As Rourke passed him, Mancuso stopped him and pointed at me. Rourke shook his head. An argument? Hope shot through me. Mancuso wanted to set me loose? Rourke raised his hand and walloped the side of Mancuso's head. Mancuso reeled, still holding the Doberman. My hope plunged as he gave me a final morose glance then hurried away, joining the men fleeing the place.

They were all leaving. All I could see from the dirt floor of the pit was the swaying lightbulb, the cobwebbed rafters above it, and a thin veil of dust rising from the trample of feet across straw and dirt. Then, above the barking of dogs being moved out came the muffled roar of engines, cars and trucks starting, and the growl of motorcycles. I imagined them tearing down the lane. Following the yellow Porsche.

Then, silence. I was alone with DuPre. She nosed me, whimpering, as if to urge me to get up. "Sorry, sweetie, can't move," I said. It felt good to hear my own voice, shaky though it was. A kind of proof of life. "It'll be okay," I told her. "The police will be here soon. We'll be fine."

It was like she understood. She settled down, belly on the ground beside me, squeezing as close to me as she could. My ribs ached, my stomach muscles too, but the warmth of DuPre's shaggy body against mine eased the sharp edge of pain. Nothing, though, could ease the chaos in my mind. Rourke. The classic dirty cop. I thought of the times he'd questioned me, how he'd been keen to know what I'd discovered about ERV Financial Services. He hadn't done that to track Paul's murderer. He'd been probing me to protect Leblanc.

I strained to listen for police sirens. Nothing. No sign of them. I couldn't bear the wait. I bent my legs and dug my heels into the dirt and pushed against the post, backward and upward, trying to shimmy the rope up. The post was shoulder high, so if I could get the rope that high I might loop it off, get free. Sweat from the effort heated me and slicked my wrists. I managed to lift my ass a little off the ground, but the struggle was futile, the rope was tied too tightly. For all my pushing and grunting, I couldn't squeeze the knot any higher than an inch before the effort made me drop back down, catching my breath. And just catching my breath hurt because of the dust. It clogged my throat. Stung my eyes too. It seemed thicker. It *was* thicker. And yet, with all the people gone, how could that be?

DuPre hopped to her feet. Her nostrils flared as she sniffed. She whined—a warning.

I smelled it now too. It wasn't dust. It was smoke. I shot a frantic look over the top of the pit boards. Light flickered in a far corner. Flames. Fear scorched my skin. Rourke had set the barn on fire.

DuPre barked, coughed, wove in hectic circles. Smoke made my throat raw. The light of the flames grew brighter. A barnboard crackled. Hot air parched my nostrils.

DuPre ran to the pit's narrow door. It was still open. My heart jumped. She could get out. And the big barn door, too, would still be open. Instead, she stopped, looked back at me, barked at me to get up.

"No, don't stop, DuPre. Go! Run!"

She slunk back to me, whining.

"Go, damn it!" I kicked at her foot. I had come to save her. I *had* to save her. "Run!" It was hard to speak, the air so hot. "Please . . . run."

She nosed my arm, a kind of caress. She hunkered down on her belly again, pushing close to me. She wasn't going to leave me.

Tears at her loyalty stung my eyes, more painful even than the smoke and the heat.

My head thudded back against the post. I had no fight left.

I thought of my father in the church, his cello bow keening the doleful notes, keening his grief for Julia. I thought of Julia tying that nylon rope around her own throat. I thought of Paul Leblanc tumbling off his icy deck. I thought of Val, his hoof kicking at flames. And I, too, knew how dying felt.

27

Rough hands shaking my shoulders. A man yelling in my face.

They're back. Rourke. The Russian. Back to torture me. To finish me.

Fury erupted in me. *No more!* I kicked his leg. I lunged to bite his hand. I swung my fist.

"Natalie!"

My fist . . . ? My hand was free? Yes! My arms were free. The man was pulling me to my feet.

"Natalie, can you hear me? Can you walk?" He tossed the rope he'd loosed from my wrists.

Not the Russian . . . someone good, trying to help me. I blinked at him, half blind in the smoke, the searing heat. All around, the crackle of flames, the sizzle of wood.

"Can you walk?" he yelled again.

A firefighter? With his help I staggered to my feet, swaying, coughing. Legs like straw. Skin dry as paper. Lips too seared to speak.

"Who . . . ?" I coughed. I gaped at him. Hank? No . . . it couldn't be. I was hallucinating.

He swung my arm around his neck and looped his arm around my waist and dragged me across the pit. Both of us were coughing. Stumbling beside him, hacking, I thought my lungs would burst. He hauled me past blazing straw bales, past a swinging, fiery timber, and another on the ground, flames chewing the wood.

I glimpsed a rectangle patch of blackness ahead. The open barn door, the black night sky. Seeing it gave me a surge of strength. We hurried toward it, lurched through the open door together. Out. Safe!

I gulped down the pure cold air. The wave of relief, the joy at being alive was so powerful it swamped the last of my strength. My arm slid off his shoulder. My legs gave way. He caught me, held me. I looked at his face. Soot-smudged chin. Blue eyes tense with worry.

No hallucination. It was Hank.

"How . . . ?" I coughed.

He swiped a sooty hand across his face, catching his breath. "Are you okay?"

I heard myself laugh. Insane, but it bubbled out of me like a fresh spring, unstoppable. I was alive. Hank was here. Nothing could be more okay.

Then a thought struck, killing the joy. DuPre. I twisted around, looking for her. Had she followed us out? "Where is she?"

"Who?" He looked in horror back at the barn. "Was someone with you?"

"DuPre. My dog. Did she make it out?"

He looked around. "I didn't see a dog."

"She was with me. Right beside me." I turned, looking at the open door. The burning building. She was in there. She would die in there. I started forward.

Hank caught my arm. "Natalie, no. Help is on the way. Police, firefighters. Wait for them."

I tried to push him away. Help would come too late.

He held me firmly. "Stop it. Don't do this."

"You don't understand. She wouldn't leave me. I can't leave her!"

I broke free and ran. I plunged into the heat. My legs weakened as I lurched in a zigzag path around tongues of flame. The smoke forced coughs that tore my chest. My eyes were slits, the heat parching my eyeballs. I shut down my mind, my fear, my pain, and let my need take over.

I reached the pit. Half of its surrounding wooden ring was in flames. To protect my face, I backed into it, the heat beating my shoulders and the backs of my legs. I reached DuPre. She still lay beside the post that Hank had freed me from. She wasn't moving. *Please, not dead.* I gathered her limp body up in my arms. A section of wooden ring collapsed by my feet. I stepped clumsily around it, staggering as I held onto DuPre.

Again, I saw the patch of pure night sky ahead. Again, it pumped a final spurt of strength. As I reached the door, Hank was already starting in. He took DuPre from me and pushed me out.

Outside, I fell to my knees on the grass, coughing, gasping.

Sirens wailed. I looked up to see vehicles racing up the lane toward us. Fire trucks. Police. Ambulance.

Paramedics surrounded me. The last thing I saw as they loaded me into the ambulance and the door began to close was a glimpse of Hank beyond all the people, kneeling over the still form of DuPre, then him looking up to watch me leave.

28

I stood naked at my bedroom window, savoring the early-morning sunshine.

My stomach felt bruised from so much coughing last night, and my chest felt like someone had crushed a glass inside my lungs, but I was glad to be alive. But was DuPre? I remembered her body limp in my arms as I'd carried her out of that inferno. Had she made it? Or had the toxic smoke been too deadly? I ached to find out. But Rourke had taken my phone in the barn and hurled it, and here I had no landline. I didn't even know where she was.

I'd spent the night hacking up black mucous at the hospital ER. They had clamped an oxygen mask on me, probed my vein to do blood tests, and wheeled me in for chest X-rays, and I was still weak and shaky as I'd answered questions from a solemn police constable. I'd told him the shocking truth about Rourke, the dogfight crowd, and about seeing Logan Leblanc's car. I asked if they'd caught any of those men, but he replied, stone-faced, that he had no updated information. The nurses were skillful and kind, but I was trembling from sheer exhaustion and sick with worry about DuPre, since no one had heard anything about her. When another constable finally drove me home, I stripped off my smoke-fouled clothes and fell into bed naked and then into a bottomless sleep. A sleep like the dead—my mother's phrase.

No, like someone very thankfully alive, I thought now, standing in the sunshine. Because of Hank Verhagen. I still could hardly believe it. That he had saved my life seemed both thrilling and confusing, more like a dream than reality. But DuPre?

I quickly got dressed. I would ask Mrs. Carson if I could use her phone. Surely she wouldn't begrudge me that small mercy. I was pulling on a sweatshirt over my track pants, hating the smell of smoke still in my hair and on my skin but needing to get to a phone, when I heard a car crunch over the gravel at my front door. I went to the window and looked down at the roof of a dark blue car I didn't recognize. There was a knock at the door. The roof overhang obscured whoever was standing there. Another knock, more insistent. I felt a spike of fear. Rourke? The Russian?

Calm down. They've gone to ground. They wouldn't come to my house. And they certainly wouldn't knock.

I opened the door, startled to see Hank.

"Are you all right?" he said.

"I'm fine. But you—" His arm was in a sling, his hand wrapped in gauze.

"It's not broken, just burned."

"*Just?* My God, Hank, what you did . . . how can I ever thank you? Come in. Please, come in."

"Hold on." He turned to the car and waved at someone to come forward, calling to them, "It's okay, she's home."

The passenger door opened and his assistant, Esther, got out. Hopping out behind her was DuPre.

"Oh, sweetie!" I cried.

DuPre trotted to me and I crouched down to hug her. I looked up at Hank, happy tears clouding my vision. "Hank, I've never been so glad to see anyone." That went for both of them. I caressed DuPre's shaggy ear. She was looking around anxiously, even as I hugged her. I realized she was trembling.

"She's still a bit shellshocked," Hank said. "But Esther took her to the vet and he gave her a clean bill of health." He offered a wry smile. "The dog, that is. Esther's always in top form."

I had to laugh. "Thank you, Esther."

"My pleasure, Ms. Sinclair." She stayed beside the car.

I gave DuPre a reassuring squeeze, overcome with gratitude at having her back, and safe. I stood up. "Please, won't you both come in?"

"Thanks, but no, we're on our way to the airport," Hank said. "I just wanted to make sure you're okay."

"But, last night, how in the world did you find me?"

"Your pal, Wapoosh. I saw you talking to him at the intermission, saw you were upset, and then you bolted out. So I asked what happened. He told me about spotting the dog and said you were going to follow up in the morning. But I know how much this dog means to you and how you . . . well, you don't *ever* wait."

His smile had faded. Had he saved my life just because he was a good man, but one no longer interested in a radical like me? Would he never forgive me for using him?

"So Trevor told you where I'd gone."

"That old Henderson place has been abandoned for years, ever since old George died. I'd heard there've been squatters. Not a place I'd want you to be."

DuPre was sniffing the doorway as though she wanted to come in, come home, but wasn't quite sure it was safe. It hurt to see that, but I understood. Trauma from the hell she'd experienced in that pit. "Hank," I said, "do you know about Detective Rourke? The dogfight?"

"I do now. That's the other thing I came to tell you. I've spoken to the chief of police, Dev Thibodeaux. He was filled in about your eyewitness account. He was truly shocked to hear his detective might be dirty."

"*Might?*"

"You know how it is. Due process. They have just your word."

"But you believe me, don't you?"

"Of course. So does Thibodeaux. What's more, he suspects the gang you saw may be connected to an organized dogfighting ring with tentacles throughout Ontario and Quebec. The money in it is huge. Twenty thousand dollars can change hands in one fight. Anyway, Rourke's on suspension."

"They've caught him?"

"Not yet. But they'll soon track him down." He looked at me soberly. "Is he the one who tied you up and left you to die?"

"Yeah." I didn't mention the Russian. Didn't mention Mancuso. Rourke had been the one giving orders.

Maybe he took my hesitation as doubt about *due process.*

"Natalie, I swear to you, Rourke will not escape justice. Look, whatever the . . . problem between you and me . . . our different . . . worldviews, let's say. . . that has nothing to do with this crime. There will be an investigation, and I'll make sure it's very thorough and very public."

Coming from a member of Parliament, that had to mean something. I was glad, of course, but his other words snagged in my heart. Our *problem.*

"I have to go," he said, glancing at Esther waiting patiently by the car.

"You're off to Ottawa?"

He nodded. "Back next week." He gave me a last earnest look. "Take care, Natalie."

No dinner date invitation this time. Just goodbye. "You too. And thank you again, so much . . . for everything." I wanted to say more.

But he was already getting into the car.

I closed the door and turned to DuPre. She was anxiously sniffing everything in her path to the kitchen. I followed her. She looked over her shoulder at me, almost cowering, then slunk under the kitchen table. Hiding? It broke my heart.

I knelt down and murmured, "Everything's going to be alright, sweetie." She lay on her belly, still trembling. Her fur was clumped, thin in patches. Her nose was scabbed. Where had she been these past two weeks? What had they done to her? What abuse had she suffered since I'd lost her? Whatever it was, it had culminated in those men bringing her to the dogfight, where she would have been torn apart by the pit bull. I knew about so-called fighting dogs. Pit bulls weren't naturally vicious, they had to be trained to kill, trained by using little dogs as bait. Nauseating. So, in a twisted way, DuPre had been lucky to escape that fate long enough to make it all the way to the pit. Except that's where she would have died, in a final "training match." I looked at her now, watching me with anxious eyes, her head resting uneasily on her paws. It struck me that her greatest anxiety might be that she had failed *me*, failed to protect me as her herding instinct told her to. I pitied her so much, I could have cried. Healing was going to take time.

For both of us, I thought. I felt violated by Rourke, and not just physically. In his investigation into Paul's murder, he had deliberately made me feel I was his prime suspect, and now I saw why. He was in league with Leblanc, and Leblanc knew I was on his trail. So Rourke's interrogations were all about scaring me, distracting me, weakening me. Well, the police had my statement. I hoped I'd soon hear they had arrested both Rourke and Leblanc.

I put out food and water for DuPre, finally had a shower, and then left to go and get a phone. I drove to the mall—the police had brought my car back last night. I bought an iPhone and came right home. I didn't want to leave DuPre alone for long. My first call was to Trevor, to thank him, telling him his tip had brought DuPre back to me. He said he was glad to hear it. "But I heard there was a fire there later, and I was worried about you. Been trying to call you."

"Yeah, sorry about that. I lost my phone."

"Also heard a rumor that you're leaving All Creatures. Nat, what's up?"

"Just a leave of absence," I lied. I couldn't bear to go into it. "Keep in touch, Trevor." I gave him the new number and quickly said goodbye.

Next I called Dad to explain about leaving the concert and to apologize. No answer. I left a message for him to call me.

DuPre was still hiding under the kitchen table, but I was glad to see she had fallen asleep. The best medicine. Last night had taken its toll on both of us, and I felt I could use some of that medicine myself and was about to go back to bed when there was another knock on my door.

I opened it to find a woman in police uniform. Tall, at least six feet. About my age. Stern face. Hair in a tight military bun. I felt sure I knew her somehow.

"Natalie Sinclair?" she asked officiously.

"Yes. Is it . . . Gwen?"

She relaxed her military bearing just enough to allow a slight smile. "You remember."

I did now. Gwen Whitcombe, one year ahead of me in high school. She had beat me out of a coveted place on the track team. Deserved it, too; she'd been almost fanatical in her dedication. She looked like she still worked out. "My God. Gwen."

"How are you, Natalie? Sorry to hear you had a rough night."

"Come in." She did, and I closed the door behind her. We quickly caught up. While I'd studied political science at university, she had joined the Craigmuir police. Married the football quarterback and had three kids, all while moving up the ranks. "Wow," I said. "That's impressive."

"The career or the kids?" she said with a laugh.

"All of it. And now you're . . . ?"

"Detective Sergeant. I'm taking over for Detective Rourke." She clamped her soldierly bearing back in place as if lowering a steel visor. The switch was jarring, yet it filled me with hope.

"Has he been arrested?"

"No. But I'm taking his cases."

"Oh." I felt a prickle of caution. "The Paul Leblanc murder investigation?"

"Yes. I have the file. Constable Crocker's notes are thorough."

Crocker was the junior officer who had always come with Rourke. "Gwen, I swear I had nothing to do with that. Rourke was hounding me for—"

"I know," she said, holding up her hand to reassure me. "We know."

I relaxed a little. This was probably the closest thing to calling Rourke corrupt that she was allowed to say.

"I've come to ask about the event that happened earlier the evening Paul Leblanc died. The fire in the stable at his country estate, Mont-Joli."

The arson, I thought. Ordered by Paul's own brother. But I said none of that. It would mean telling her about Mancuso, and that would put Mancuso's life in danger from Leblanc.

"You were there, I understand," she said. "At the fire. Is that correct?"

"Yes."

"Did you see anyone enter the stable?"

"Enter it? You mean firefighters?"

"No. A civilian."

"No way. It was an inferno, impossible to even get near. Why do you ask?"

She didn't answer. She pulled a card from her pocket. "Please, get in touch if you remember seeing anyone go into the stable."

"Sure. But I can tell you right now, there was no one."

"Good to see you again, Natalie." She opened the door to go. "If something comes to you, call that number anytime."

"Wait," I said. "It seems you know everything I reported last night. About Rourke, the dogfight ring, Logan Leblanc. Have you found Leblanc, at least?"

"An officer was sent to question Mr. Leblanc at his Toronto home. He denied being at the barn. Said he never left home all evening."

"He's lying."

"Your statement indicates that you didn't actually *see* him, though. Correct?"

"I saw his car."

"Well, someone's car."

"He was there, Gwen. I know it."

Her eyes narrowed slightly. Maybe I'd offended her by not calling her Detective Whitcombe. "His fiancée, Annemarie Pascal, corroborates his claim that he was home all evening."

The receptionist at his Gold Zone office. She was lying for him. Probably so she wouldn't get beaten up. It sickened me.

"Thanks for your time," Gwen said. "And do try to remember if you saw anyone go into the stable."

"Why is it so damn important to you?"

She looked a little taken aback by my tone. I didn't care. I now had zero confidence that her whole bunch of cops would ever catch Leblanc.

"It's important because Alan Rourke buried the fire marshal's report. Now we've seen it and the conclusion was that the fire was an act of arson." I held back from snapping at her, *Yeah, I knew that.* She went on, "And bones were found in the ashes. Not just the horses'. Human bones."

She left. I went back to bed. Nightmares about Hank burning in the barn and DuPre finding his bones. I woke up late in the afternoon, stiff, groggy, with a pasty mouth and a headache. Someone had died in Paul Leblanc's stable. Died with the horses. Horrible. But I had no idea who.

I scrounged a supper of week-old pasta primavera and some limp raw carrots. I'd have to get groceries tomorrow. DuPre, at last, had ventured out from under the table to eat some kibble, and I was glad to see her curl up on her old spot under the living room window for more sleep. I sat on the couch and opened my laptop. It was depressing to scroll through work emails and realize I would have to reply to them all to say I was no longer employed at All Creatures Great and Small. Tomorrow. I would deal with all of this tomorrow.

I was about to close the laptop when it chimed an incoming FaceTime call. Simon, in California. I tensed as I clicked on it. After our chilly conversation last week, my suspicion about him had grown. What could he be calling about now?

"Hey, Simon," I said warily.

His bearded face betrayed no emotion. "Natalie. How are you?"

"Tired. The concert last night was . . . emotional."

"Sorry I couldn't make it. Had to work on the Stravinsky. Hellishly challenging, you know, and we play it in just two days."

"Sure."

"Were the Sony people there?"

Sony Classical, Julia's recording label. So that's what he cared about. The creep. "I don't know," I said. "I wasn't checking IDs." I forced down my anger as another concern reared up. "Are you calling about Liam?" I now had grave doubts that the best place for the boy was with this man. Still, a father had rights. "Have you finally found a house?"

"Soon. Maybe. We'll see. No, I wanted to ask you something."

"About Liam?"

"About Julia's things. You were the one who cleaned out her music studio, weren't you?"

"Yeah. Me and Mom."

"Before you did, I took a few things. Scores. Books. Mementos. I've been through them, but there's one I can't find, and I wondered if you might have come across it."

"What is it?"

"Her journal. She started a new one every year. It's this year's I can't locate."

"What does it look like?"

"Leather cover. Maroon color."

It flashed in my mind, that day Mom and I packed up the studio. The slim book, reddish-brown, that I'd seen her snap shut and jam into her purse. The color draining from her face. And the days after, when I sensed that had been the moment when something inside her had broken.

"I just hope it didn't go into one of the boxes sent to Goodwill," Simon went on. "I wouldn't want anyone to read it. Personal stuff, you know? Private. Not good for that sort of thing to get out, become public. I'm sure you agree it's important that we—all of us—protect Julia's legacy."

Now I got it. Legacy to him meant the royalties from sales of Julia's recordings, payouts that were now coming to him. But his avarice wasn't what gripped me. I suddenly wanted to see what was in that journal. Was he afraid Julia had written about her affair with Paul Leblanc? Was that the scandal Simon didn't want to become public, tarnishing her reputation and hurting sales? Or was he afraid there might be something even worse? That she'd written about his fury at the affair. Fury that, after her death, had driven him to kill Paul.

"Haven't seen it," I lied. "Gotta run, Simon. Talk later."

I needed to find that journal.

The question was, did my mother still have it?

29

I drove with a glorious sunset behind me, a luminous sweep of rose and gold filling my rearview mirror. Beautiful evening. And me coming to look for a killer.

If that's what Simon was. Did my sister's journal hold the answer?

"Just a friendly little visit to my folks, sweetie," I told DuPre.

I wasn't fooling her; naturally she'd picked up on my edginess. She sat beside me, her anxious eyes on me. I hated to add to her stress when she was still so traumatized by what she'd been through.

I slowed as I reached my parents' neighborhood. I'd called to say I was coming but got voicemail, and these days I doubted whether either of them regularly checked messages. I turned onto their street, a wide court lined with chestnut trees, the sunset's rose-gold rays slanting across the bare boughs. The street was quiet, all the neighbors inside enjoying dinner or settling down to watch the hockey game. Dad would likely be watching the game too.

I pulled into the driveway and parked behind their Lexus. In the wide space between their house and the neighbors', I glimpsed the tops of trees that lined the river down in the ravine. A stately V of Canada geese sailed across the treetops, honking, part of the waterfowl migration returning now that the ice was breaking up. The riverside path would be a nice place to take DuPre for a walk. Later. First I had to find out if Mom still had the journal.

I used my front door key, and as I let DuPre into the foyer I heard Dad's cello. He was upstairs playing. Bach's *Cello Suite Number 1 in G Major.* Julia's signature piece.

Mom wasn't in the kitchen or in the living room. I went upstairs, DuPre trotting behind me. I tapped on Mom's bedroom door. Across the hall, in Dad's bedroom, his playing went on behind his closed door.

No answer from Mom. I went in and found her sitting on the edge of the bed in her nightgown, her feet bare on the pinewood floor. It made my heart heavy. She wasn't getting ready for bed; she'd never even gotten dressed. She was fiddling with something on her lap. I came closer. "Hi, Mom."

She glanced up at me with a vague, faraway look, then looked back down at her lap.

"It fell," she murmured. "Broke."

She held two pieces of curved crystal, and I realized it was the bell I had brought her last week. Next to her, on the bedside table, lay a tube of glue. Beside it, several plastic vials of pills.

"It's okay," I said, sitting down beside her. "We'll fix it."

I noticed Liam across the room. He sat on the floor stacking wooden blocks. "Hello, sweet boy."

"Hi," he answered, though he was concentrating so intently on building his tower he didn't even look at me. DuPre padded over and sat beside him, eyes fixed on him. Her herding instinct, I knew. She felt she had to guard him, like a straying lamb.

Dad's cello keened on. Even across the hall and through his door, I heard the passionate grief in his playing. It gave me a sad shiver.

"Mom, I need to ask you something."

"You girls," she muttered, trying to fit the two crystal pieces together. "Always running around, always so busy."

"Did you . . ." I took a breath. "That day we cleaned out Julia's music studio. That book you found. Her journal. Do you still have it?"

She looked up at me, her eyes haggard. "My fault . . . all my fault."

What did that mean? Had she destroyed it? "Mom, it's important. If you have it—"

"Don't."

"Don't have it anymore?"

She shook her head with an odd vehemence, like a guilty child in denial. Her gaze slid across the room to the rosewood bureau, a dead giveaway. I got up, went to the bureau. I felt her anxious eyes on me.

"In here?" I opened the top drawer. Nothing but underclothes, a lavender sachet tucked among them. In the second drawer, sweaters, neatly folded. In the bottom drawer, a jumble of scarves, a couple of old family photo albums, a flashlight. And there, beneath a green silk scarf, an edge of maroon leather.

"Don't," she whispered.

A voice inside me said, *Listen to her. This can only be bad.* But I had to know. I pulled out the journal. "It's okay, Mom."

"No . . . nothing is okay. Nothing will ever be. I should never have showed him."

"Showed who? Simon?"

"Secrets. Too many secrets."

My hands were clammy as I opened the journal. Julia's bold handwriting covered the first few dozen pages. Then the writing became shakier. The pages were dated at the top by the manufacturer, and the last entry Julia had written was on February 6, the day before she committed suicide. After that, blank pages.

Paul says it's over. Not true. Cannot be true. Love can't be OVER. He says duty. He says wife. He says daughter. My heart screams SON. He doesn't know. Never told him. My secret. Secret love. Lovely Liam. I was crying so much today when Simon came in I told him. Told everything. Shouldn't have. He was so angry. Shouting. Now it's over. Everything is over. Me. I'm over. If love is over I cannot breathe. I will not breathe. I do not breathe.

"Secrets," my mother said again. "I kept them. Too long."

I sank down on the foot of the bed, still gripping the journal, stunned by its revelations. The first one made terrible, tragic sense—that Paul had broken off the affair and Julia had spiraled into depression and killed herself. What my brain could not make sense of, could not grapple with, was the second one. In shock, I looked over at Liam.

He was Paul's son.

"You read this," I said to my mother. "That day in Julia's room. You knew."

She nodded, her whole body so tense I could almost feel her muscles quiver. "Knew . . . and kept quiet. Told no one. That Liam . . ." She glanced at the boy. Playing with his blocks, he was oblivious. "Little Liam . . . he loves the ducks, you know? Takes after Julia that way." She shook her head. Took a deep breath. "It ate at me. I took . . . medication. But it ate at me even in sleep. Days and days. Too much to keep inside. So finally I went to him. Told myself that he should know . . . but really I just couldn't hold it in any longer."

She went to Simon about it? But why, when he already knew? Julia wrote that she'd told him everything the day before she killed herself. *He was so angry*, she wrote. Had he bottled up his anger until two weeks ago, when it finally burst and he went to Paul's house? "What did he do after you spoke to him?"

Silence.

"Mom, you don't need to protect him anymore. Tell me. What happened?"

She looked at me, anguish in her eyes. "I showed him that." She pointed a trembling finger at the journal. "I might as well have stabbed a knife. He looked like . . ." She closed her eyes as though in pain. "I saw a bullfight once. In Spain. The bull speared, gored. Maddened. He was like that. He shouted, 'Leblanc as good as killed her!' Then he left." She shivered. "It was dark, raining, cold . . ."

"The night of the ice storm?"

She nodded.

It still didn't quite make sense. Simon had known about Paul and Liam for more than a month. Still, his motive could not be clearer. I set the journal down on the bed. It suddenly seemed toxic. What should I do? Expose him as the killer? Ruin Liam's life?

That's when I noticed that the cello music had stopped.

"That's enough, Nora." Dad's voice.

I turned. He stood in the doorway. His face was pale. How much had he heard?

"Grandpa, look," Liam chirped. "My tower."

Mom looked at Dad, and tears welled in her eyes. "He left the house. Natalie, I couldn't stop him. It was dark, raining, cold, but he was so distraught he left his coat. Came home so late I was worried and stayed up reading here in bed."

Dad's mouth trembled. "Nora, I said that's enough."

"I ironed his shirt that morning. White shirt, Brooks Brothers. When he came in there were red speckles on the front. Blood. Smudged pink from the rain. I thought, *The cleaners will have to tackle that.* 'Did you hurt yourself?' I asked. He sat down. Right there, Natalie, where you're sitting. I'd never seen him cry before. Not like that. Not in thirty years. He sat there . . . crying."

Later, I would remember the terrible moment like a stopping of everything. Time. Breath. Thought. An endless free fall . . . falling forever. Nothing to hold onto.

Then, my father's stricken look at me broke the fall. I crashed to earth.

His arm flew up with a jerk, covering his face in a pitiful attempt to shield himself from my gaze. And right then, even in my state of blinding shock, I saw that the father I'd known and loved was gone forever.

Mom was sobbing. Loud, raw sobs that wracked her body. "We both kept it inside . . . too much . . . too long. I told him, Rafe, you've got to tell the police. You didn't mean to kill him . . . it was an accident. You've got to tell them," she wailed, "or it's going to kill *you*."

"No more!" he cried.

"Dad . . ." I lurched to my feet, went to him.

"No . . . no . . . no." He backed up, unable to look me in the eye. He turned and bolted.

"My fault!" my mother wailed. "All my fault!"

I heard a crash of glass and spun around. She had jumped up, knocking the crystal pieces to the floor. She groped for the vials of pills on the bedside table. She snatched one, twisted off the cap, dumped a mound of pills into her hand. They were almost at her mouth when I dashed back to her and knocked her arm so hard the pills went skittering across the floor.

She dropped down onto her hands and knees and groped for them.

"Mom, stop." I sank to my knees, took her by the shoulders. "Please . . . stop."

She trembled in my grip, then the fight drained out of her and she gave me an anguished look of surrender. She sank against me. I threw my arms around her and held her tight.

DuPre was suddenly beside us, whining in sympathy, licking Mom's cheek to comfort her.

Over Mom's shoulder I saw the tower of blocks across the room. Alarm jabbed me. "Where's Liam?"

Mom sank back on her heels. She shook her head, eyes vacant, lost in another world, a hell of her own.

I scooped up the pills, got up, grabbed the rest of the vials and jammed them in my pockets. "DuPre, stay here. Stay with her."

Liam wasn't in any of the bedrooms. I called his name as I hurried downstairs. No answer. I knew he loved being with Dad. That's where I would find him. But there was no sign of Dad. No one in the living room, the kitchen. I crossed the foyer and stepped out the front door. The Lexus was still in the driveway. They couldn't have gone far.

A graveled community walkway ran between the neighbors' houses and then sloped down to the river. *Liam likes the ducks*, Mom had said. I headed down to the ravine. Thickly treed, and lying so much lower than the houses, it lay in twilight shadows, untouched by the golden sunset. The riverside path ran alongside the wide expanse of ice where a windblown branch lay on the pale white surface. On the other side, trees and brush covered the far slope. I looked to my left. The path that way widened and wound back up among the houses. I saw no one. I looked to my right. There the path narrowed and curved and disappeared into thick woods. I walked toward the woods. It was noisy with starlings settling down for the night. A cloud of them lifted, disturbed by my presence, then darted away.

Among the trees ahead I could make out a small patch of red on the ground. I walked closer, my pulse thrumming in my ears. I broke through the trees. Liam squatted, holding a stick, drawing lines in the earth loamy with dead leaves. His red jacket was the only bit of color all around us. He was singing to himself, a soft, high, sweet sound.

Twinkle, twinkle, little star
How I wonder what you are.
Up above the world so high,
Like a diamond in the sky . . .

"Liam." I spoke gently as if I'd come upon a fawn and must not frighten it.

He looked up. "Aunt Natty."

"Where's Grandpa?"

He looked to his right further along the path and pointed with his stick. "There."

I saw no one, just trees. I couldn't leave Liam alone. "Let's go have a look," I said, holding out my hand.

We carried on along the path hand in hand. It was dark among these thicker trees. But then we came to a clearing with a full view of the river. I stopped. Dad was on the river, walking on the ice. He wore no coat, no jacket, his white shirt luminous in the twilight. He moved not in a straight line across the river but on a diagonal, heading out to the middle. He walked with single-minded purpose, like someone with a clear destination. I saw what that destination was. Beyond the pale white ice he walked on lay a darker swathe of river. Open black water.

"Dad!" I shouted.

He flinched, hearing me. He halted but didn't turn. He started again, striding on toward the open water.

I turned to Liam, trying to keep my voice calm. "Stay right here, okay?"

"Kay."

I stepped out onto the ice. Etched with grainy snow, it smelled of cold. I went out a few feet. "Dad," I yelled, "come back. It's not safe!"

He kept on walking. I went out a little farther, a little faster. The ice was granite-hard beneath my boots. I heard a shuffling behind me. I turned. Liam was scuffling out onto the ice.

"Ducks? Grandpa found the ducks?"

"Stop, Liam," I snapped. "Go back."

But his bright eyes were fixed on Dad, and he scuffled on toward him, giggling at the fun of this new game.

I twisted around to look at Dad. He was just a few strides from the dark water.

Liam started running toward him, slip-sliding and laughing as he gained momentum. He dropped to his knees and swept past me, sledding toward my father.

"Liam, no!"

I started to run toward him, but my boots skidded, slewing me awkwardly. *Get down. Low, like the boy*. I went onto my knees, then onto my stomach in one ongoing forward motion and slid almost to Liam. I heard a loud *crack!* The ice breaking near Dad. I reached out and snatched the hoodie of Liam's red jacket. It jerked him backward. He laughed at being caught. "I'm it!"

Ice crackled beyond us.

I pulled Liam to me, hugging him tight, my hand on the back of his head to bury his face in my shoulder so he could not see as I watched my father step out into the black abyss.

30

Police. A diver in a black wet suit. Ambulance siren. Paramedics. A stretcher . . . on it, my father's dripping body, unconscious. I was a pillar of ice as they lifted him into the ambulance.

Oh, God, did he move his arm? I was about to scramble into the ambulance beside him, talk to him, will him to live, but I lurched to a stop. Liam. Alone, looking scared. I couldn't leave him here.

I gave them my cell number. Then sirens again . . . and the ambulance's red taillights as they took Dad away.

I took Liam's hand. Mine was trembling. We walked away from the river, back through the trees. Like sleepwalking. *Follow Dad to the hospital,* that was my only thought. *Be there when he regains consciousness.* We'd almost reached my car when the call came.

They could not revive him. The icy water had stopped his heart.

That was last night. A night of frigid blank disbelief. Early this morning, reporters started phoning. My brother took the calls. My sister-in-law, Gabriella, made coffee. None of us had slept.

I had lain beside Mom in her bed all night, sleepless with shock while she slumbered in drugged oblivion. Giving her the zopiclone had seemed only merciful. Sleep of the dead—her old phrase. At dawn, my eyes gritty, muscles stiff, I was still watching her immobile face, envying her peaceful breathing. It did not seem possible that I would ever feel peace again.

Mechanically, I made another pot of coffee. It was ten o'clock. James, unshaven, red-eyed, was now on the phone with the family lawyer, pacing as he talked. I wanted to shut out his words. I loudly hummed a Bach minuet just to have noise in my head, avoid listening. Avoid trying to make sense of what my father had done. Avoid feeling.

DuPre lay on her belly under the kitchen table, head on her paws, keeping wary eyes on us. Gabriella had taken Liam to the playground. I was grateful. This house of sorrow was no place for a child.

I was standing at the kitchen window watching a blue jay peck at the bird feeder on the terrace when Detective Gwen Whitcombe arrived. I had called her as soon as I'd left Mom's bedroom. James led Gwen into the kitchen. With her was a young constable. I went upstairs to wake my mother. This had to be done.

We settled Mom onto the kitchen window seat. Pale-faced, she looked small, shrunken, wrapped in her rose velour dressing gown. I handed her a mug of coffee. She held it tightly with both hands as though desperate for its warmth.

"Mrs. Sinclair," Gwen said gently, "I'm very sorry for your loss." Coolly professional, she nodded at the constable. He opened his notebook. They took Mom's statement.

She began, her voice thin but steady. As she spoke, I could see it. Paul's house after midnight, dark in the rain. Dad banging at the door. Paul opening it, bleary from too much scotch. Dad storming in, making grief-crazed accusations. Paul telling him to leave, threatening to call the police. Dad, in impotent rage, stomping back out toward his car. Paul stepping out to the deck for cold air to clear his mind, sidestepping the workmen's debris and wiring. Rain battering the overhang that sheltered him, but the icy wind dampening his clothes. Then, Dad storming back through the house, out to the deck. Grabbing the two-by-four, swinging it at Paul's head. Paul toppling over the edge. Dad panicking, fleeing . . .

"My fault," Mom said, her voice so feeble now I could barely hear. "If I hadn't told him . . ." Her words trailed off, dying from guilt.

Gwen quietly thanked her, took our brief statements too, then she and the constable left.

But the pain of this day had not finished with me yet. There was a wrong I had to try to set right. I texted Denise Leblanc, said I had something important to tell her, asked her to meet me at noon. I couldn't leave Mom, so I chose a location nearby.

I was peeling an orange for Mom, hoping to get her to eat something before I left, when my phone chimed an incoming email. I frowned at the name of the sender: Little Bo Peep. Spam, obviously. No message in the body of the email, but a photo that made me freeze. Rourke's face. Bloodied. Mouth wet with gore. Eyes so swollen they were slits. Beneath the horrible image was a link. I knew I shouldn't touch it, but I could not stop my finger from tapping it. It opened a breaking news story from CTV:

"Detective Alan Rourke, a veteran officer of the Craigmuir Police Department in southern Ontario, was found dead today outside an apartment building in Toronto's Thorncliffe Park. He had fallen from a fourteenth-story balcony. Rourke was wanted for questioning regarding a fire set two weeks ago at an abandoned barn near

Craigmuir. A resident of the apartment building has come forward to suggest that foul play may be involved in Rourke's death. An investigation is pending."

I backtracked to the email. The image of Rourke's face beaten bloody. Below it was one line of text: "Keep quiet or you are next."

Fear leapt inside me. My thoughts thrashed. Call Gwen back? Have her trace Little Bo Peep? It could only be Leblanc. But she might take days gathering the evidence, and if Leblanc learned I'd gone to the police, he could get to me before Gwen got to him. He would send the Russian to silence me.

Keep quiet. It was the only sane option. And, my mind still numb about Dad, it was the only decision I could muster.

The civic art gallery near my parents' house was quiet at noon, just a half dozen people shuffling past the paintings on their lunch hour. Denise Leblanc, absorbing my halting recital of the awful facts, stood looking at a sculpture, a stainless-steel oak tree. I stood beside her, tensely aware of her utter stillness as we both stared at the sculpture, though barely seeing it. I was sure she was holding her emotions in check. To break down in this hushed space would draw attention, intolerable to a woman so proud. It was exactly why I'd chosen a public place: to shield myself from an outburst.

"It's good of you," she said quietly. "You could have waited for the police to tell me." She looked at me, clear-eyed. "Thank you."

Of all the responses I had expected, this was never one. Rage, perhaps. Weeping, maybe. A barrage of confused questions. But thanks? I feared I was going to be the one to cry. I balled my hands into fists and squeezed to keep the tears in.

I stammered, "I feel I should . . . somehow . . . have known."

"To love someone is not always to know them."

Paul, I'm sure she meant. Dad, that was the meaning that knifed my heart.

"Blind," I said. "I was blind."

She nodded, a bitter look on her face, maybe because those words were so often used by someone discovering a spouse's love affair. Her husband and my sister. What a pitiful bond Denise and I shared.

"Don't blame yourself," she said in that unemotional way of hers. "No one had any idea it was your father."

True. Yet the reality still felt crushingly unreal. Dad, a killer. And now, his own death. I still couldn't take it in—that he was gone. Unable to grapple with that, I swung back to Paul's death, ashamed to recall my half-baked theories. "I actually suspected you, at first," I said.

"As I suspected you."

We shared a bleak smile.

"I saw suspects everywhere," I went on. "My brother-in-law, Simon. Paul's brother. Even, insanely, a Syrian carpenter, a poor refugee doing some work for me."

"Nabil Ahmadi?" she said absently. "He's been doing work for us too."

I remembered Janice's nasty-minded scenario of Nabil stealing from Paul and killing him. "Right, I forgot. At your house."

"Both places. The house deck. The Mont-Joli stable."

A shiver touched my scalp. "The stable?"

"Repairing the loft." She looked at me as if unsure why I was picking up on such a small thing when tragedy surrounded us. But I was horribly, electrifyingly sure. I remembered what Nabil's roommate had told me at that seedy motel, that Nabil had gone to work for Leblanc the day of the ice storm and hadn't come back. I had assumed he meant that Nabil had gone to Paul's house in town. But he meant Mont-Joli.

The jumbled bits flew together in my mind like metal filings racing to a magnet. The conclusion overwhelmed me. *Human bones*, Gwen Whitcombe had told me yesterday. *Nabil*, I realized now. He was working in the stable that evening of the fire and the ice storm. After, the police hadn't mentioned finding a car there, but I knew Nabil's cousin had driven him to work at All Creatures, so maybe he'd also gotten a lift to Mont-Joli. Maybe, finishing his work late, he'd decided to wait until morning to call his cousin to pick him up and settled down to sleep. Was he asleep by the time the fire started?

I hoped with all my heart that he was.

Then, another realization gripped me. I was the only person who knew all the pieces of the puzzle about that fire, including the piece named Logan Leblanc. A new energy shot through me. After being so devastatingly wrong about my father, I craved to right *this* injustice. I wasn't wrong about Leblanc's crimes. One, he had ordered the arson, though only Mancuso could corroborate that, and he refused. Two, he had raped a fourteen-year-old, though only Gina could corroborate that, and she would not. Three, I was sure he trafficked wild animals, though I had no evidence of that. Now, though, everything had shifted. The arson he'd ordered had killed Nabil Ahmadi.

Could this, finally, be the way to bring Leblanc to justice?

Was it enough?

31

Three days later I walked into the Craigmuir police station. Three days of hell.

I was spattered with mud. I was soaked wet with rain. I was shaking. In the last hour I had seen nightmare things. Now, lives lay in my hands.

Detective Gwen Whitcombe looked up, startled, as I reached her desk. "God, Natalie, what happened to you?"

It took my last ounce of determination to slap my phone down on the desk. "Here."

"What's this?" she asked.

"The end. Of everything."

I had cued up the recording. My legs felt suddenly weak. I braced myself stiff-armed on the desk edge. "Listen to this," I said, nodding at the phone. "Then tell me, is it enough?"

It began the day after I'd broken the news to Denise Leblanc. Beyond the anguish I felt about Dad's death and pity for Mom, I was living in fear of Leblanc, holed up at my mother's house like a fugitive. James and Gabriella had to go back to work, so I was alone with Mom, and whenever I went to buy groceries for her, or took DuPre for a walk, or took Liam to the swings in the park, I was forever looking over my shoulder for the Russian sent to kill me. Again and again, I picked up the phone to call Gwen, tell her what I had pieced together about Leblanc, but a chaos of indecision always kept me from making the call. I had no evidence, and it would mean turning in Mancuso, endangering his life. Plus, Leblanc could slip through the net again like he did after the dogfight. I'd reported seeing his car then, and the police had questioned him, but Annmarie had lied for him, vouching that he'd been at home with her. If he evaded them this time, and learned they'd come because of me, I had no doubt he would track me down.

But I couldn't go on living like this, in fear. Fear kills. Fear of being unmasked to the world had driven my father out onto the ice. Before that, fear for him had plunged my mother into drugged silence. I could not let *my* fear overpower me.

That was the decision that finally sent me back to Mancuso.

The country road was deserted. The scrubland around his house lay quiet. When I pulled up and got out, all I heard was his dogs. I couldn't see the kennel behind his house, but I heard them barking, alerted by the sound of my car.

Once again, his little boy answered the door. Once again, I found Mancuso in the kitchen, this time stirring a big soup pot on the stove while rock guitar wailed from speakers.

"Smells good," I said. "Minestrone?"

He twisted around with a jerk of surprise. "Jesus."

"No. Just me."

Feeble joke, and he didn't smile. He switched off the music then looked at me, shaking his head in wonderment. "Well, *somebody* up there sure is looking out for you. Last time I saw you, Dimitri was tying you up in the pit. I heard you'd got out. I was glad."

"Me too." I remembered seeing him argue with Rourke about leaving me there, and Rourke hitting him in response. "No thanks to Detective Rourke, may he never rest in peace. You know he's dead, right?"

"Yeah, I heard," he said guardedly.

"He never did question you after what you did at my house, did he, because that whole time he was working for Logan Leblanc."

Mancuso shrugged as though to say the issue was ancient history. "What are you doing here? What do you want?"

"We need to talk."

"No, we don't. You are trouble, lady. The kind I like to stay out of."

"But you're *not* out of it. Rourke was working for Leblanc, like you are. Now Rourke's dead, and I think Leblanc had him killed because he failed to finish me off. Doesn't that scare you? The police are already trying to track down anyone who was at that dogfight. Before they find you, Leblanc might think it's best to kill you too."

He glared at me in silence. I knew I'd touched a nerve, but was it enough to budge him? Outside, a dog barked. I glanced at the kitchen window. "The kennel out there," I said. "You breed pit bulls for the dogfights, don't you." It wasn't a question. I'd realized it when I'd seen him at the fight.

"What the fuck do you want?"

"Facts. About the fire at his brother's place, the fire that burned down the stable. Leblanc was behind that, right? So who did he get to do it?"

Mancuso's face tightened. No answer.

I plowed on, "Was it Dimitri?"

He crossed his arms over his chest in defiance.

"It's important," I said. "Really important. I've learned that a man died in that fire. A poor refugee who was working there. No one knew he was in the stable, but he was, and he died. So if Leblanc ordered the fire, he's guilty of manslaughter. If he's convicted, he'll go to prison."

Mancuso's eyes widened in surprise. A whole new look came over his face, like a light had switched on inside him. "Seriously?"

"Seriously. I knew the man, the refugee. I know he was in there. I'm the only one who does."

"Holy shit." He ran a hand over his bald head, taking in the news, clearly enthused by it. "That's great. That's perfect. So what are you waiting for? Go tell the cops. Jesus, if they put Leblanc away, he's off both our backs."

"I can't go to the police because I have no *evidence* that he ordered the fire. The closest I have to evidence is you, and last time I was here you made it clear you're keeping quiet no matter what."

"Fucking right. He'd finish me for sure."

"Not if we do this carefully. We can get him. If we work together."

His enthusiasm had vanished. In its place was a deeply skeptical frown. "How?"

"Could you get him to come here?"

"Maybe. Why?"

"Maybe's not good enough. Could you or not?"

"Sure. The dogs. He owns them. I know he's looking to unload them for cash. If I say I have a buyer here, that'd get him to come. But why? What good would that do?"

"I'll get him to admit he ordered the arson."

His eyes widened again, this time in disbelief. "How could you possibly get him to do that?"

It felt like the floor beneath me was turning to sand, sliding way. "I don't know. Yet. I'll just have to try. I know he's a man who likes to brag."

"Jesus. You don't know squat."

"We'll think of something."

"We?"

"Look, you want him in prison. I want him in prison. We know he's guilty. We just have to get him to *say* it."

He shook his head in disgust. "You're so full of shit. Get outta here, and don't come back. I'm done with you."

"No! Wait." Gina's voice. It made us both turn.

She stood in the doorway to the hall. Her face was white. "Dad, listen to her."

Mancuso looked irritated. "How long you been standing there? I thought you were feeding the dogs."

"Please, listen to what she's saying."

"She's nuts. And this is none of your business."

"No, she's smart. She's okay. She was nice to me."

Mancuso frowned in surprise. "What? When?"

Gina bit her lip, clearly afraid she'd said too much.

Mancuso glared at me. "You been bothering my kid behind my back?" He came at me with a menacing look. "Never do that again. Not if you want to keep breathing." His raised his hand spread wide and held it an inch from my throat just to show he could. I flinched and backed up.

"Dad, stop it! You've got to listen to her. She says you can get him sent to jail. So *do* it."

He twisted around to her, looking bewildered. "What do *you* know about it?" He shot accusing looks at both of us. "What the fuck is going on?"

I wanted to plead with her: *Gina, help me out here.* But it wasn't my secret to tell.

"Please . . . *please*," she said to her father, her voice breaking. "Do what she says. It's the only way." Her shoulders suddenly caved. "He's terrible. I *hate* him. He . . . at the hotel . . . he . . ." She burst into tears. Then turned and fled down the hall.

Mancuso looked dumbfounded.

"Go after her," I said. "Hear her out."

The next day went by. And another. I'd heard nothing from Mancuso and doubted I ever would. The desperate half-baked idea I'd taken to him had been ludicrous. For all I knew, Leblanc might already have sent the Russian to silence him forever. Would I be next?

Whatever, I was on my own. I did my best to care for my devastated, silent mother. I shut the door to Dad's bedroom, too heartbroken to even look at his things—his books, his cello, his music still on the stand. I nodded numbly on the phone to James's words about arrangements for Dad's funeral. I fed DuPre. Played with Liam. But I kept them with me inside the house. I was afraid, and not just for myself anymore. I feared I was putting Liam in danger too. I was just going through the motions of living. Jumpy with tension, I startled at the sound of every car braking, every shout on the street.

On the third day, I couldn't stand it anymore. The only rational course was to go to the police, tell them about the arson and hope they would arrest Leblanc, though without Mancuso to verify my claim, I doubted they'd act on it. If they did nothing and Leblanc heard I'd told them and came for me, so be it. I could not live like this any longer. It was four o'clock in the afternoon and I was about to call Detective Gwen Whitcombe when my phone rang. It was Mancuso.

"Get over here," he said. "Now."

I turned onto Mancuso's lane and almost jumped out of my skin. Parked in front of his house was the yellow Porsche. Leblanc. He was here.

Was Mancuso lying dead inside? Should I turn around and run?

No. No more running. I parked beside the Porsche.

I found Mancuso in the kitchen, but this time he wasn't cooking. He looked set to leave, wearing a scarred leather jacket, a suitcase on the floor at his feet, and he was all business, stuffing a stack of messy sandwiches into a plastic grocery bag. What was going on?

"Where is he?" I said. "What's happening?"

"He's outside."

I heard quick footsteps. The two kids hurried past, heading down the hall toward the front door, the little boy dragging a duffle bag, Gina hefting a suitcase.

"Outside?" I parroted back to Mancuso, utterly confused.

He was grabbing Coke cans from the fridge, filling the bag. He gestured to the window. "Have a look."

I went to the window. It overlooked the backyard and the kennel. The kennel was a wooden shelter big enough for maybe ten animals, with a dog run attached—a long, roofless rectangle of cement enclosed by high chain-link fencing. No dogs in sight; they must be in the kennel. Then my heart banged in horror at what I saw inside the dog run. A single form lay unmoving. Leblanc.

Dead?

Mancuso guessed my thought. "He's alive. And, the shape he's in, I think you'll have no problem getting what you need. If not, deal with it however you want. Leave him to rot or call the cops. Either way, I'm out of here."

I whirled around to him, stunned. "How long has he been in there?"

"Three days."

I gaped at him. He jammed a bag of potato chips into the larger bag then stopped and looked at me. "Gina told me. Everything. Once I got him here I would have cut his throat, or shot him in the gut and let him bleed out, real slow. But then they'd lock me up. Your way's better. Got your phone? Go have a chat. Record him."

Revulsion thrashed in my mind. "Three . . . *days*?"

"Then there'll be a trial, right? They'll need a witness who's—what do they call it?—credible. That's not me. That's you. You can say you had no part in holding him here, that I did it. All you did was arrive and find him. Okay?"

"But you—"

"Me, I'll be long gone. Me and my kids." He picked up the suitcase, the bag of food in his other hand. He nodded toward the kitchen door that led to the backyard. "Go on now. Do what you came to do."

The first cold drops of rain hit me as I came out the kitchen door. I walked slowly toward the dog run, dreading what I would see up close. Through the chain-link fence I could see Leblanc lying on his side, curled up as if desperate for warmth, his back to me. The gate at the far end, to my right, was closed. So was the door to the dogs' shelter to the left. Between them, he was in a virtual cage. No roof. Nothing in it with him but a metal bowl of water. Had Mancuso not even fed him?

His head jerked up. He'd heard me coming. He struggled to haul himself up onto hands and knees. I stopped an arm's length from the fence, couldn't bear to go closer. It was even worse than I'd expected. His black suit, damp and rumpled as a rag, was splotched with cement dust as if from bird droppings. His hair was a nest of filth. His shoes were gone, his socks tattered. One pant cuff was smeared with mud, or feces. Sickness shot up my throat. I choked it back.

Leblanc staggered to his feet. He gaped at me, disoriented, swaying on the spot.

"You?" His voice was parched.

In spite of my hatred of him, I couldn't let this go on. Couldn't let him suffer the way he'd made those caged baby monkeys suffer. I went around to the dog run gate and tried to open it. Locked. There was a keypad, but I had no idea what the code was. The other end, the door to the dogs' shelter, was probably locked too, bolted on the inside. How else could a man be kept captive for three days?

We stood staring at each other. Rain spattered us both.

I pulled out my phone to call 911. As I was about to press the first number, Leblanc hurled himself toward me, crashing against the gate. I lurched back in shock. His face was scratched with spidery red welts. His eyes were bloodshot, his lips cracked. His grimy fingers were claws around the metal links.

"Get me out!" he roared.

An order. It seeded the old anger inside me. *Do what you came to do*, Mancuso had said. So why not try? Help could wait a few minutes more. I swallowed hard, moved my finger on my phone to "record," and tapped.

"Logan Leblanc. Is that your name?"

"Fuck you. Let me out!"

"Sure, just a few questions first. Won't take long. Unless you refuse to answer, and then it might take another day or so. Up to you."

He gaped at me in confused fury. "What the fuck do you want?"

"The truth."

He glared, but I could see the feverish energy drain from him. His body slumped, and he hung onto the fence, holding himself up like a man grappling a lifeline. "Questions? Like what?"

"What is your full name?"

"Leblanc."

"Full name."

"Logan Leblanc. Now open the—"

"Are you the CEO of Gold Zone Mining?"

His legs were trembling. The tremor through his whole body shimmied the fence links under his fingers.

"Are you the CEO—"

"Yes, alright . . . CEO . . . Gold Zone. Yes."

The rest, amazingly, didn't take long. As the rain soaked us, I asked my questions and he answered. Date of the fire? March 7th. Name of Paul's estate? Mont-Joli. Name of the man he had sent to burn the house? Dimitri Kuznetsov. I asked what materials were used, and what fee he had paid Kuznetsov. He answered it all.

"Done?" His word was a sneer. He blinked, looking at my phone, then at me with a new light in his bloodshot eyes, as though he'd got a second wind. "You recorded this, didn't you? Well, it's worth fuck all, you bitch. My lawyers will bury you. You and your Wop pal who put me here. He's dead meat."

"We'll see."

"Fucking fire. Christ, who cares?"

"I care. It killed my horse and two others." And Nabil Ahmadi. Leblanc didn't know that yet. But his lawyers soon would. "My horse's name was Val. He died in the fire you ordered."

"You're insane," he said.

I ended the recording. Then tapped 911. "I'm calling for help." He scowled at me as though he didn't trust that he would soon be free. I answered the dispatcher's questions and asked for an ambulance. "They're on their way," I told Leblanc, pocketing my phone.

I turned to go. I was shaking from the tension, from the cold rain, and from the high of getting his confession. The ground was slippery, last year's dead grass already muddy, and I lost my footing, slipped and fell, though I caught myself and landed on one mucky knee. I heard Leblanc laugh, a hoarse, manic laugh. I got to my feet, not looking back.

I had almost reached the house when I heard a noise behind me like a door slamming open. Then frantic barking.

I turned. Gina had come out of the dogs' shelter into the dog run. She held a snarling pit bull straining on a leash. She unsnapped the dog from the leash. It lunged for Leblanc. He screamed. The dog leaped for his throat.

"No!" Mancuso yelled, catching up to his daughter. He called the dog back. The dog took its time.

Detective Sergeant Gwen Whitcombe had listened to the recording. She sat back in her office chair, digesting it.

"How did you get this?"

I told it just like Mancuso said, that I had found Leblanc captive, called 911, and asked him some questions. "Then the ambulance took him. The paramedics told me he'd live." By the time they'd arrived, Mancuso and his kids were gone.

"Gwen," I said, "there's more. Those bones they found in the Mont-Joli stable? Have them checked out. I believe you'll find they're the remains of a man called Nabil Ahmadi."

"You knew this person?"

"I did. A hardworking refugee. A fine man." I pointed to the phone. "Tell me, is it enough? To put Leblanc behind bars?"

She nodded slowly. "It's enough."

32

Five Weeks Later

The party was impromptu, as so many joyous things are.

There was food: tasty wonders brought by Heather and her Lebanese husband. There was wine: Saint-Émilion Bordeaux thanks to Victor, and a kick-ass home-brewed cider thanks to Annika. There was music: Stéphane Grappelli's jazz violin swinging "Sweet Georgia Brown" from my stereo, which Keith had hooked up. There was dancing: Nathan and Ellen gleefully showing off while Amber did her own wild swing and pulled shy Raoul to his feet to join her. All afternoon my friends had been helping me move into my new home, and everyone was happily relaxing now that the grunt work was over.

Joyous, yes. All the more so because on that terrible evening when I'd watched my father sink to his death, I thought I would never feel joy again. It did my heart good to watch my friends' fun, hear their laughter.

"Nope, these are people treats, not for you," Nicole chided Anya, her young Siberian husky, who was sniffing at the food-laden table where we stood. She gave me a wink then shepherded the little pack—her pup, and Heather's spaniel, Ollie, and the trio's alpha female, DuPre—away from the table.

There was plenty of room for the dogs to romp in the spacious living room. My huddle of furniture looked a bit lonely and forlorn, but it would soon have company. My mother couldn't bear staying in the Oakdale house with its tragic memories of Dad, so James had quickly sold it for her. She'd bought this handsome Victorian home in Craigmuir, and now it would be my home too. The moving van would be bringing all her furniture tomorrow, and James would bring Mom and Liam.

So much had happened in the five weeks since I'd seen Logan Leblanc trapped in Mancuso's kennel. He had recovered from the pit bull attack, bruised and a little bloodied, and the police had arrested him, charging him with manslaughter for the death of Nabil Ahmadi in the Mont-Joli fire. For that crime, I hoped he would spend many years in prison. His crime of raping a teenager would go unpunished, unknown, but that had always been Gina's call, and she and her father and brother were long gone. I hoped the psychological wounds Leblanc had inflicted on her would heal with time and her father's support. Mancuso, I had no doubt, would land on his feet somewhere.

As for Leblanc's crimes of animal abuse, during their interrogation the police had learned that he ran the dogfighting ring, with several locations throughout Ontario and Quebec. He had been using it to raise money, big money, to buy his way into an international operation in trafficking wild animals run by a Russian mafia outfit known as the Bratva. Smuggling the baby monkeys had been his first modest foray into that illicit but hugely profitable trade. Sadly, removing one player like Leblanc from its sprawling network made little impact. The suffering and death it caused to untold creatures worldwide would continue.

Suffering, I thought, as I stood watching the dogs trot past the dancers. Impossible to save every animal. Or every person, however much you love them. For a while I had tried to fool myself into believing that Dad's death was a tragic accident. He'd taken Liam to the river and walked out on the ice to look for the ducks the boy loved. That was the fiction I'd struggled to hold onto. But I'd seen him step out into the water, and deep down I knew. He did it to escape. I'd known it at that moment in Mom's bedroom when the truth of what he'd done to Paul crashed over me. He'd flung up his arm to hide his face from me, and that pitiful gesture haunted me. Rather than be unmasked to the whole world—his family, his friends, his public, who'd embraced his uplifting religious precepts—he had chosen to die.

I was glad to be out of my parents' house with all its reminders of Dad. James and I had packed up his clothes to go to Goodwill, his books to go to the library. But I held onto his cello. It was the purest manifestation of the father I had loved, and who had loved me. A man of passionate affection. His love for Julia had destroyed him.

"Good evening, Natalie," Heather's husband, Omar, said gently as he reached me at the food table.

"Omar," I said, snapping out of my sad thoughts. I picked up one of his pumpkin kibbeh squares. "So," I asked, "what's the secret of these delicious little devils?" As I bit into the savory treat, I glimpsed the front door opening, a new guest arriving.

"No secret," he said with his scholarly precision. "Just the essentials: za'atar and pomegranate molasses."

"Now where in this town would one find pomegranate molasses?" I asked.

"Annapurna Foods on Duncan Street," Chandra said, joining us. "They have everything. It's the only place my grandmother can get the bhut jolokia chilies she needs for her Kolhapuri masala."

"Ah, now those chilies," Omar said, "are the very ones I use for—"

"Hold that thought, guys," I said, going to greet the newcomer. Except it turned out not to be a newcomer but Trevor, returning. "Glad you're back," I said. "I was afraid we'd worked you too hard." He had been the first to arrive to help unload my furniture, and he and Heather's teenage son had hefted all the heavy stuff upstairs, but then Trevor had left early.

"Just went to get this before they closed." He handed me a bouquet. "Happy housewarming."

"Oh, my goodness. Thank you." It was a lovely mix of yellow zinnias, blue cornflowers, pink cosmos, and mauve sweet peas.

"I asked for all spring flowers," he said proudly.

"It's beautiful." I sniffed the sweet peas' scent. "I'll get a vase. If I can find one."

"On the kitchen counter," Nicole said, passing us as she headed to the food table. "First box to the left of the sink." She had helped me pack up the kitchen things.

Trevor followed me to the kitchen. "This is so nice of you," I told him. "Especially after all you've done today."

"Nothing compared to what you've done for me. Being with All Creatures—with you—is the best thing I've ever done."

"Gets into your blood, doesn't it?" I said, pulling a vase from the box. His enthusiasm warmed me. Trevor had been with me at the very start of the whole Logan Leblanc affair, when we'd found the poor baby monkeys. It was a bond we shared.

"Nat," he said quietly, "I just want you to know that any time you want my help again catching bad guys, I'm your man."

He was blushing. It was sweet, really. "Well, it's not quite as adventurous, but there are still three pit bulls to find homes for. I know Kathleen would love your help." Kathleen Dahl and her Forever Homes program funded by All Creatures had already placed five of Mancuso's dogs in good hands. I still felt a glow inside at being back in the thick of our programs and plans. After a *Globe and Mail* journalist did a major interview with me about exposing the international animal trafficking operation, donations had poured into All Creatures. My five minutes of fame was no big deal, but I was very grateful that the story had gotten me my job back.

"Come on," I said, taking the bouquet in its vase to the living room. I set it down in the center amid the food platters. "Hey, everyone, look what Trevor brought."

There were oohs and ahs, and Trevor blushed again. "Just a little housewarming gift," he mumbled and moved off to get some cider.

Chandra came to my side. "Nice house," she said, raising her wineglass in a toast.

"Yeah. Mom has good taste."

"Gorgeous big yard for DuPre."

"And for Liam." The boy was always in my thoughts these days. I had already bought cans of robin's egg blue to paint the bedroom that overlooked the backyard. It would be Liam's room. Poor little kid. He didn't outwardly show any sign of suffering, but I worried about the trauma that must lie buried inside a child who had lost his mother, then the grandfather he'd adored, and had been virtually abandoned by the man he believed to be his father. Maybe, at least psychologically, that's exactly what Simon had done: cut himself off from the boy on the day Julia told him Liam was not his. He hadn't replied to any of my phone messages and emails. Part of me hoped he never would. This child was going to need a lot of love.

"It's so good you're back at work, Nat," Chandra went on. "It's cheered the place up."

I nodded happily. "I'm still a little surprised, actually."

"How so?"

"Well, I called the *Globe* journalist after the interview made such a splash, just to thank him, since it got me my job back, and he said Hank Verhagen was the one who'd suggested the story. Weird, right? I mean, you were there at the police station the day of my disaster at the vet college. You saw how furious Hank was at me." It was confusing, frustrating. "Anyway, good to know he's on the right side of the issue. I guess."

"You guess? You haven't heard from him?"

I shook my head. "I read he's been in Spain. Climate change conference in Madrid."

"And your email doesn't work? You couldn't be the one to reach out?"

"Chandra, I did a bad thing. I used him. You know that. He's not likely to forgive me."

"Wait, this is the man who ran into a burning barn to save you, right?"

"Well, because he's such a decent guy."

"The same man who pulled strings to get you your job back, right?"

"I doubt that was his intention. He probably just wanted to keep the *Globe* guy sweet with a good story. That's what politicians do, cultivate good press."

"Hmm, if you say so. Is he still in Spain?"

"No, I read that he's back."

"So call him. Invite him to come over."

"What, now?"

"Why not? It's a party. Good neutral ground for having a chat."

"You think?" I suddenly so wanted to.

"Sure. Clear the air."

Crazy, maybe, but it was like being given permission and I jumped at the chance. I pulled out my phone and texted him. A brief invitation: simple, short, straightforward. "Done."

Again, she toasted me. "Let me know how it goes."

We split up to mingle. I went back to the kitchen to refill the bowls of chips and peanuts, but I kept looking at my phone for a reply. I was putting the empty bag of chips in the trash when Hank's text came: *Sorry, not possible.*

Simple, short, straightforward. An effective brush-off. It hurt more than I thought it would.

I heard Amber's laugh. She seemed to be having a good time with Raoul. He was grinning, then he turned to talk to Victor. I tucked my phone away and joined Amber.

"How's life at O'Dowd's Pub these days?" I asked.

"Quiet. Ugh." She made a funny, conspiratorial face. "Like they say in the horror movies, *too quiet.*"

I laughed. "You like action."

"I like to be busy. And I sure need the tips."

"How would you like to come work at All Creatures as my office manager?"

She looked startled. "What? Wow. Seriously?"

"Absolutely. Janice resigned, and the temp's heart isn't in it." That wasn't strictly true about Janice. She had been so shocked to hear that Nabil Ahmadi had died in the stable fire, she admitted to me that she had taken the 412 dollars herself. Said she needed it to cover her shopping debts. Good God, she had blamed Nabil for the theft and accused him of murdering Paul Leblanc. I fired her on the spot.

"Nat, I'm so honored you'd even think of me," Amber said, "but I don't have any experience like that."

"Got to start somewhere. I've watched you, Amber. There's no one more conscientious and dedicated."

She all but glowed.

"So, would you like to?"

"Are you kidding? I'd love to."

"Good. We'll talk later, work out the details."

The party wound down. I thanked everyone as they left. It was just before midnight when I took DuPre for a walk. The lamplit street—my new street—was lined with big old chestnut trees, whose plump buds were about to burst into greenery. What was that line from Shakespeare? *The darling buds of May*. DuPre trotted contentedly beside me, her ordeal forgotten. I wasn't sure I would ever forget the terrible things I'd seen. Finding my dead sister. Watching my father step into that black water. Life had defeated them. But right here, right now, with the chestnut boughs filtering the streetlights' glow to dapple me and DuPre with gold, I could only think, *Be thankful for what you have. Life is good.*

The next morning, Saturday, I was making coffee, congratulating myself at having found all the makings in the third box I'd rummaged through, when DuPre began barking. She dashed to the front door. Seconds later the doorbell rang.

Hank stood there. His little girl, Lily, held his hand.

"Natalie. Hope it's not too early."

"No," I stammered, thinking why the hell had I put on the rattiest track pants I owned? "No, it's fine, hi. Hello, Lily."

"Hello," the little girl said shyly.

"Sorry about last night," Hank said. "I got your text just as I was about to give a speech at the Italian-Canadian Association. Hard to text back. Then the banquet went on and on, so . . . "

"Oh, no worries. I understand."

"Anyway, just wanted to let you know I would have liked to come to your party. As it was, I ate too much chicken cacciatore, which wouldn't have been a problem here with the vegan fare."

I had to laugh.

"Daddy, can I pet the dog?"

Hank looked at me for an answer.

"Yes, of course," I said. Dupre sat quietly beside me. "She's very friendly," I told Lily. "Her name's DuPre." I looked at Hank as the little girl stroked DuPre's shaggy head. "Would you like to come in? I'm making coffee."

"Thanks, but no. We're on our way to the dog park." He gestured to his car, where the big old sheepdog, Monty, sat watching us from the back seat.

"Monty will enjoy that, Lily," I said. "Dogs are much more relaxed when they're off-leash."

She looked up at me. "Won't he run away?"

"From you? No way. He loves being with you."

"And if he does," Hank said, "this is the lady who'd find him."

I smiled at him. If this was forgiveness, I was gratefully taking it.

It made me suddenly bold. "Hank, what do you know about adoption? I mean, what if a child had been abandoned and a relative wanted to adopt him? Is that a legal option?"

He looked at me curiously. "Asking for a friend?"

"Just asking."

"Sounds like something your MP might be able to help with. Luckily, my office is just across town. Always happy to listen."

It was hard to hide the smile in my heart. "That *is* lucky. Or, how about DuPre and I come with you guys to the dog park? We can talk there."

He looked genuinely pleased. "That would be nice."

I was getting my jacket and keys and about to close the door with DuPre when the rumbling sound of a truck made us all turn. It was the moving van, loudly pulling into the driveway, and, right behind it, James's car with Mom and Liam.

"Looks like you've got company," Hank said.

James parked, got out and waved at me, then opened the rear door to let Liam out of his car seat. I had to hold DuPre back from bounding out to greet the little boy and knocking him down in her excitement.

The moment Liam was out, he ran toward me. "Aunt Natty!"

I crouched down and opened my arms to him.

Hank and I exchanged a look, mine colored by a mix of gladness and regret.

"Another time," Hank said.

I smiled at him. "Another time."

His car pulled away with Lily and Monty. I took Liam's hand, squeezing gently, accepting a calm joy for myself and peace for Julia and Dad, and went to greet my mother in her new home.

Acknowledgments

My thanks and admiration go to the exceptional people who daily dedicate themselves to protecting animals. Their work inspired this book.

Chief among those fine folk are my husband, Stephen Best, and his colleague Liz White of Animal Alliance of Canada, an outstanding organization whose motto is "fighting cruelty wherever we find it." I have long admired Stephen's commitment to the cause, and many of his experiences in fighting the good fight fueled my writing of this story. Liz read an early draft and I am grateful for her help in clarifying for me many specifics of her work for the animals, in which she is such an expert. Any errors that may have crept in are mine alone.

Annemarie Belford was an early reader as well, in fact the very first one when the book was a work-in-progress. Her enthusiasm for the story and its characters cheered me greatly to carry on.

Special thanks go to Alec Shane, my agent at Writers House. With finely tuned storytelling instincts, he offered me masterful suggestions that improved the book tremendously. Laura Katz was a great help, too, and has my sincere thanks.

It's been a pleasure to work with the team at Woodhall Press, in particular CEO David LeGere and editor Miranda Heyman, who so keenly understood the soul of this story. Paulette Baker did a perceptive and meticulous job of copy-editing the manuscript, making it all the better.

This book is the first in a projected series of mysteries featuring animal protection activist Nat Sinclair and her spirited band of volunteers. I'd love to hear any thoughts you might have about Nat's possible future. Feel free to get in touch with me through my website https://www.barbarakyle.com/.

If you would like to help the animals, please reach out to Animal Alliance of Canada. Their dedicated campaigners will transform your compassionate support into life-saving results for countless of our fellow creatures. Contact AAC through their website: https://www.animalalliance.ca/

About the Author

Barbara Kyle is the author of the acclaimed *Thornleigh Saga* historical novels (*"Riveting Tudor drama"* – USA Today) and thrillers including *The Experiment* (*"Haunting...Kyle keeps the cinematic action scenes and nail-biting suspense rolling throughout."* – Publishers Weekly). Over half a million copies of her books have been sold in seven countries. A screenwriter as well, Barbara co-wrote the screenplay for the feature film *Saving Dinah*, available on Amazon Prime and Tubi. Before becoming an author, Barbara enjoyed a twenty-year acting career, playing characters that ranged from Shakespearean heroines on stage to starring roles in daytime TV dramas and characters in Disney made-for-TV movies. Barbara and her husband live in Ontario. Visit Barbara at www.BarbaraKyle.com and follow her on Twitter @BKyleAuthor.